CHRISTMAS PRESENTS

A Saint, a Sinner, and a Town of Spirits.

Three Romantic Novellas

MARILYN CAMPBELL

Cover and Book design by eBook Prep.
www.ebookprep.com
December, 2015
ISBN: 978-1-61417-803-3
ePublishing Works!
www.epublishingworks.com

CHRISTMAS PRESENTS

TABLE OF CONTENTS

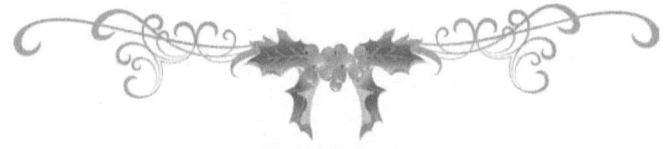

ANGELS

AND

SHAMROCKS

Christmas Presents Series

Novella One

MARILYN CAMPBELL

CHAPTER 1

BAM!

The crashing sound reverberated through the guardrail next to Angel Cheswick, warning her to look up in the nick of time. Barreling down the sidewalk directly toward her was a tire the size of a Smart Car. She dove onto the grass and rolled away with a second to spare then watched in horror as the wheel careened into her bicycle. The collision caused the bike and the wheel to ricochet into the air. With a sickening crunch of metal the bike landed again, only to receive another powerful body slam before the mindless attacker continued on its way along the sidewalk.

Her chest clenching with residual panic, Angel's stunned gaze flew from the scene of destruction to the wheel, now wobbling to a stop on the grass, then back to the direction it had come from. Over a quarter mile away, on the opposite side of the street, she could see a man setting up orange hazard cones around a truck with a lopsided forklift on its flatbed. Apparently the wheel had come off the forklift, negotiated three lanes of moderate traffic and a considerable length of sidewalk, without coming into contact with a single thing except the guardrail and her poor old bike. Some cars slowed as they passed but no one stopped. Had they not witnessed the impossible happening or didn't anyone care?

The realization that *she* could be the mangled remains on the sidewalk instead of her bike had her body trembling as she forced herself upright. It never occurred to her that being a crossing guard could be life threatening.

As she brushed dirt and dried leaves off her dark blue polyester uniform, her temper ignited. *Someone* was responsible for almost killing her! A few minutes earlier, a pack of children with bikes had been jammed together in that spot. There was no way they could all have escaped the danger as she had. Determined to vent her fury on the responsible someone, she marched to the truck as soon as she was certain no more children were coming to cross the intersection.

The driver, a slightly built, older man, looked more frightened than she had been. The name *Garcia* was embroidered on his gray work shirt, above the words, *SHAMROCK CONSTRUCTION.*

"You…okay, officer, ma'am?" he asked with several head bobs and a hopeful expression.

"No, I am not okay. Did you see what happened to my bike? You totaled it! That could have been me!" He was beginning to look ill but Angel was beyond caring for his welfare. "Now I'm going to have to walk home. That's over a mile away! And it's nearly a hundred degrees out here. Do you realize how hot this uniform is? I may die yet today…from heatstroke!"

The man's mouth moved from side to side. Finally he shrugged and murmured, "*Lo siento, senora.* No speaky *ingles* so good."

"Arrgh!" Angel threw up her arms, stomped around to the rear of the truck and made a mental note of the tag number. Somebody at Shamrock Construction was going to be very sorry they crossed her path today.

For most people, the accident would be a zillion to one shot, but not for Angel. Improbable things like this happened to her all too often. Ever since she first heard her mother refer to her as an accident, the word hovered around her life. But this time, she positively could not be held responsible. Her mishaps usually occurred because she was so high-strung. The more nervous or excited she got, the more likely an accident would occur. It wasn't so bad once she learned to expect the impossible and deal with it efficiently when it happened.

It was the eighth of December but in Coral City, Florida, it felt more like the Fourth of July. Only the big red bows on the street lamp posts and the silver-and-gold garland wrapped around the royal palm tree trunks gave evidence that Christmas would soon be here.

Thirteen years in the tropics had accustomed Angel to the year-round heat but the long walk home in the polyester uniform under the blistering sun had her head pounding like a steel drum. At least she could be grateful that her Italian heritage, which cursed her with a body too short to carry her full figure, also blessed her with skin that tanned instead of burning as her redheaded friend Becky's did. She stopped under a live oak to take advantage of the little shade to be had along the sidewalk and redid the ponytail that now had as many hairs out of the elastic band as were held by it. The only reason she kept her unruly hair long was that a ponytail was faster than maintaining a specially-cut style. About once a month she trimmed the thick row of bangs that usually kept her from dealing with stray hairs coming loose and hanging in her eyes. As long as she wasn't attacked by a runaway tire, her hair was one thing she didn't have to think about. For Angel, grooming was all about saving valuable time.

"Shamus O'Grady. I saw that."

With a sheepish expression, Shamus looked up into the stern face of his boss. "Ah, now, Your Holiness, ya know I've tried all the regular tricks ta get me boy Sean and that little spitfire together, but nary a thing has done it."

"I know," Archangel Gabriel said with a sympathetic nod. "But endangering lives and destroying property are hardly angelic behavior. We have discussed your less than pious streak before, Shamus, and I warned you—"

"Aye, but ya know how much it means ta me ta see me grandson happy and tis already the second week o' December..." Shamus knew he had the old one on that point. No angel's wish could be flatly refused during the month before Christmas.

"*Hmmph.* All right. You may proceed. But I'll be keeping a close watch, so no more dangerous stunts. Angelina is a particular favorite of mine and she has enough trouble getting through her days as it is."

Shamus crossed his heart. "Ya got me solemn word, Your Holiness. I'll be playing it by the book from here on." Me own book, that is, he added to himself, knowing his boss would be too busy in the coming weeks to look over his shoulder the whole time.

For the last ten months, since Angelina Cheswick had caught his eye, he'd done all the little things an angel was permitted to do to assist an earthbound soul. He was absolutely certain she and his grandson should be together, but no matter how he meddled, they failed to notice each other. They were both so busy, they'd passed one another a dozen times without a glance.

Since he had no doubt the two of them would be blissfully happy together, he felt justified in doing whatever was necessary, even if it meant bending a few heavenly rules.

* * *

Two hours after reporting the accident to the police, hauling her twisted bike home in her car and taking a shower, Angel's body had cooled down, but her temper still roiled. Becky had come next door for a cup of coffee and some gossip, but got an earful of Angel's exasperation as a side dish.

Angel's orange, white and blue kitchen complemented her vibrant personality. It was a big, bright room that encouraged friends to stay and visit...when she wasn't on a tirade over an injustice.

When Rolf, the chocolate Labrador retriever that was more child than dog, began whining with his tail tucked between his legs, Angel softened her voice and stroked his head. "I called the police and they took a report—in between fits of laughter—but they said it wasn't technically a crime, so they couldn't actually arrest anybody. In fact, they said it was barely a traffic accident." The peal of the doorbell interrupted her rant.

Remaining in the kitchen, Becky added her two cents as Angel walked through the dining room toward the front door. "At the very least you should sue the construction company to get your bike replaced."

"Oh, the bike was a relic anyway. What I'd really like," she called over her shoulder as she opened the door, "is to see the owner of that forklift flogged in front of City Hall!" She turned her head back to greet her visitor and found her eyes leveled at a man's chest—a firmly toned one, packaged very nicely in an aqua knit shirt.

Tipping her head back to get the full picture, she took in his sun-streaked dark blond hair and gray eyes. This was the clean-cut boy next door grown to a mature man. With one eyebrow lifted, his mouth twisted in a way that suggested he had heard her wish and wasn't certain whether to laugh or run for cover. He conducted a brief, but very definitely masculine, scan of her person that made her bare toes curl under in response.

"Mrs. Cheswick? I was told you had a bicycle accident." His voice stroked her with rich, velvety tones, like that of an announcer on an easy-listening music station.

"Yes, that's right, but how..." She stopped as she realized he looked familiar. A television anchorman? No, that's not it. He was explaining something about the police giving him her address but she was distracted by his features. A newspaper or magazine picture? Possibly.

"...and my driver said—"

"What did you say?" Her brain raced to catch up with her ears.

"My driver—"

"No. Before that. Something about you owning the truck and the forklift."

"Yes, I'm—"

"The man responsible for demolishing my bicycle and endangering thousands of innocent lives!"

"*Whoa.* You want to slide that by me again?"

The horrified expression on his face forced her to reword her accusations. "All right, so no one was critically injured but only because I've got great reflexes. However, I am suffering from an extreme case of traumatic shock. And you should see my poor bike!"

"That's one of the reasons I'm here," he replied with forced politeness.

"Fine. Follow me. I don't know why I bothered to put it in the garage. It belongs in a recycling bin now." As they entered the kitchen, Rolf rose, wagging his long tail and panting anxiously for an introduction. He had never learned he was supposed to protect her from bad guys. Becky, on the other hand, just panted. Angel frowned at the overly friendly smile her friend bestowed on the villain behind her. "This," she said with a jerk of her thumb, "is the man who owns the truck that was hauling the forklift that lost the wheel that wrecked my bike."

"Who lives in the house that Jack built," he added in a sing-song voice. "Sorry. That just sounded so much like the old nursery rhyme, I couldn't help myself."

"Try harder," Angel muttered. She glared at him but her extended sentence echoed in her head. The man was struggling so hard to look contrite that her mouth rebelled against her bad mood. Her reluctant grin allowed him to smile in return. "I may have let my temper get the best of me."

"Not at all. You have every right to be upset, but maybe we could start over. The police told me how to find you and said no one was hurt, but I wanted to make sure. Naturally, we want to make amends, and I really am sorry about your traumatic shock. As soon as I get back to the job site, I plan to investigate how that wheel came off. If it was due to someone's negligence, I promise I will have the individual responsible publicly flogged as you requested."

Her eyes widened in surprise, then sparkled with humor. "I'd prefer to wield the cat-o'-nine-tails myself, if you don't mind."

"Such a wholesome-looking lady to be into deviant behavior," he shot back with a distinct twinkle in his eye.

"Excuse me," Becky interjected, glancing from one to the other. "This conversation is taking a decidedly intimate turn and I haven't even been introduced yet. I'm Becky Hays, Angel's next door neighbor."

"Angel?" The disbelieving look he gave Becky suggested he was thinking of a character from the other end of the spectrum.

"It's short for Angelina," Angel quickly explained, bringing his attention back to her. "Sorry, I'm afraid I was too busy attacking to catch your name."

He smiled again and held out his hand to her. "How

do you do. I'm Sean O'Grady, owner of Shamrock Construction."

Her hand was already enveloped by his when the name registered. She withdrew her hand and took a step back. Now she knew why he looked so familiar. "*Mayor* Sean O'Grady?"

He nodded, taking in her crossed arms and stern face. "Now what? Was my last opponent a friend of yours?"

She considered holding her tongue for about two seconds. "No. As a matter of fact, I voted for you. I was too busy with my children and their school and my jobs and everything else that goes on in my life to personally check out your record, so I made my choice based on all the positive things being said about you by my acquaintances. I won't make that mistake again."

He clutched his chest. "Wow. Direct hit. Before they bury the body, do you mind expounding a little?"

"Not at all," she said, raising her chin a notch. "This was a nice, small town before you took office five years ago. I don't approve of the direction it's gone since then." As his smile disappeared completely, she knew she had personally insulted him and actually felt a little proud for doing that. He was a politician *and* owner of one of the construction companies making money on the overdevelopment of Coral City. It was about time someone called him out on it.

The mayor glanced from Angel to Becky and back, taking their full measure before he spoke. "Let me ask you this, Mrs. Cheswick. You said you voted without researching the candidates. Have you ever attended the monthly city council meetings? I'm sure I would have recognized you, and you, me, if you had."

She straightened her posture. "No. I'm the den mother of a cub scout troop that meets on that night."

"Don't you think you owe it to yourself to get involved in the city government before you criticize it?"

Becky laughed out loud, breaking the growing

tension. "If this woman got involved in one more thing, God would have to add a few hours to every day."

Angel turned away from him and walked to the garage door off the kitchen. "You said you wanted to see the bike."

When he got a look at the wreck, he was clearly shocked. "Thank heavens you weren't on it when the tire hit."

"Yeah, I'm lucky like that."

Returning to the kitchen, he said, "Look, there's no question about my buying you a new bike but I'd like you to pick it out yourself, to make sure it's one you'll be happy with. If you have time now, we can go right over to the bicycle shop on Baldwin Drive."

Angel shook her head. "Can't. My son, Christopher, has soccer practice in a half hour. It's my turn for the car pool."

"After practice?"

"Uh-uh. Parent-Teachers' Association meeting. I'm the chairperson for the upcoming Book Fair."

"Tomorrow afternoon then."

Another negative head shake. "Josh and Jeff—my twins—have dental appointments."

"Tomorrow night?"

"Cub Scouts."

His expression revealed his bewilderment. "I have a Wednesday night commitment, but how about Thursday?"

"My church's carnival committee heads are meeting here."

"Good grief, woman. I thought I was busy."

Becky couldn't resist enlightening him further. "Yep, she's Coral City's very own Sicilian cyclone. Besides all that, she volunteers in her children's classes every Monday, and has her own business besides. You should have come around last football season when she filled in for the Optimists' cheerleading coach."

"You have a daughter also?" He was now visibly dumbfounded.

"No, but no one else was willing to make a fool of themselves, and without a coach, there would have been a lot of very disappointed little girls."

Sean was at a momentary loss for words. "And what does your husband do when he wants to see you? Make an appointment?"

Angel swallowed once before answering. "My husband died two years ago."

His regretful expression looked genuine. "I'm sorry. I didn't mean to be flippant. Let me try one more time to get you a new bike. How about Friday evening?"

Angel opened her mouth but nothing came out. She walked over to her wall calendar and stared at the clean white square for the day in question. How could this be? She had nothing scheduled, not a single excuse to refuse to accompany him.

"Bzzt," Becky sounded, mimicking a game show buzzer. "Round one goes to the persistent man in the blue shirt. I was planning to take my boys out for pizza and a movie then anyway. I'll take your three also."

Angel sent her best friend a lethal glare to get her to stop being so helpful but Becky ignored the silent threat.

Sean grinned victoriously. "Great. I'll pick you up at six, we'll go to the bike shop then get something to eat."

"No," Angel blurted out quickly. "I mean, I appreciate your replacing my bike but dinner's not necessary."

"Consider it my payback for the traumatic shock."

"An apology is more than sufficient."

"Not in my mind," he countered. "Consider this. If you let me treat you to dinner, I promise to discuss every one of your complaints."

Darn him. She really would like to hear him try to defend what was happening to Coral City. "Well..."

"Bzzt," Becky sounded again. "Time's up, kiddo.

Round two goes to the smooth-talking politician."

Angel rolled her eyes at her friend's foolishness and the mayor let out a husky laugh.

"You know, Becky," he said with pretended concern, "maybe you should hire a sitter Friday and come along as our mediator."

"What? And give up a chance to referee five boys on sugar highs? Not a chance."

He confirmed the arrangements and left before Angel could think of a single valid reason to get out of them. No matter what he was calling it, she had the sickening feeling that she had just agreed to go out on a date with the enemy.

CHAPTER 2

Becky let out a whistle the instant the mayor was out the door. "Can you just imagine cuddling up to that every night?"

Angel clucked her tongue. "What would Larry say if he heard the mother of his children thinking of such a thing?"

"I wasn't referring to myself. You're the one with the vacancy in your bed."

"And it's going to stay that way, so just give it up." Angel took a sip of lukewarm coffee and shuddered with distaste.

"How can you be in the same room with a man like Sean O'Grady and not think about sex? He is prime beef…and *single*."

"There's no time in my life to think about sex, let alone indulge in it."

Becky leaned forward in her chair, always ready to pass on a little gossip. "A woman sitting next to me in the salon was telling her stylist about a friend whose sister—"

"Becky, *please*. I only have ten more minutes."

"Okay. The point I was going to make is that she

called him a saint, in a good way, not the holier than thou way. She said he's definitely a bachelor and she's pretty sure he's straight, but no one's ever heard of him dating anyone. The rumor is, he was engaged to be married—before he moved to Coral City—when his fiancée was killed in a car accident. Apparently, he never got over it. What if you turned out to be the first woman he was attracted to in years?"

"I'm not listening." She took both their coffee mugs over to the sink and began noisily emptying the dishwasher.

But Becky simply raised her voice. "It's been two years since Warren passed away. Nobody expects you to live like a grieving widow anymore. You're always blaming bad luck for all your little mishaps but I don't buy that. The problem is that you need to get lucky...in the good old fashioned, doin' the nasty, dirty dancing way. You say you don't have time for sex. I say you desperately need to make time for it. And I'm betting Mayor O'Grady might be just what you need to change your luck."

"You just don't understand, Becky. Just because you believe sex is one of the basic necessities of life, doesn't mean that's true for me. I'm truly happy with my busy schedule, my boys, my friends and my business. That's good enough for me."

"Boo hiss on good enough. You're only thirty-one. That's like a woman's sexual peak. Good enough is good enough for an eighty year old. You should be going for *great*. And speaking of great, did you notice the fit of his slacks? Probably custom-made to hug that nice bum of his. What do you think?"

Angel groaned. "In the case of Mister O'Grady, it is not a question of what he does or does not have in his pants. I was almost mutilated today because of him."

"Baloney. It was an accident and you know it. You can't hold him personally responsible."

"Then there's the rather important matter of his being

the politician I would most like to see run out of office—a man with whom I am in complete opposition."

Becky smiled. "You know what they say about opposites...ooh, ooh, I've got another one—politics makes strange bedfellows. At any rate, I'm putting my money on him winning whatever debates you two have over dinner Friday night."

The reminder made Angel's stomach flutter—a sign that usually preceded a bout of clumsiness, but she chose to ignore it. "Why do I keep letting you in my house?" With a half-smile, she balled up a dishtowel and pitched it at Becky. Instead of hitting her target however, it caught the edge of the wicker napkin holder, which then flew over the edge of the table, causing its paper contents to go floating throughout the kitchen. Angel immediately began scrambling around the floor, picking up napkins, but Rolf thought it looked like playtime. His big front paws landed on her back and she ended up sprawled flat on her stomach. Rolf barked twice, licked her cheek then lay down beside her.

"You're right, Angel. Who needs a man when you've got a mutant puppy to roll around on the floor with you?" Becky gathered up a handful of napkins and put them on the table as Angel got to her feet.

Before either could say another word, the eight-year-old twins burst in through the back door with tempers flaring.

"Ma-a-aw!" Josh cried out first. "He kicked me right in the privates."

"Did not!" Jeff retorted even more loudly. "He got in the way of my foot." He tried to grasp a handful of his brother's auburn hair but Angel grasped his wrist before he could do any damage.

"Stop it, both of you. If you fight, you get hurt. The end. Now, wash your hands and faces while I see what's keeping Chris. We're going to be late for soccer practice again."

* * *

"Are you happy, Shamus? I behaved like you instead of me."

Ah, but how could ya resist such a foin bit o' fluff?

Occasionally, when Sean was particularly bewildered or frustrated by some problem, he imagined himself talking it out with his dearly departed Irish grandfather.

Of all the dumb things to do, asking out a female constituent ranked in the top ten. A date could turn into a relationship, which could end in hard feelings when she discovered he wasn't looking for a wife. And there was no telling what a disappointed woman might say about the man responsible. When the man was a political figure, it could ultimately damage his career. Of course, Shamus never understood the need for so much logic, especially if it involved a *foin bit o' fluff*, like Angelina Cheswick.

Sean had truly loved his Grampa Shamus and had spent every childhood summer with the laughing Irishman, listening again and again to his tales of The Little People and hidden pots of gold. It often crossed Sean's mind that Grampa was an overgrown Leprechaun himself.

After Gramma passed away and Alzheimer's disease began to erode Grampa's mind, Sean didn't hesitate to offer his assistance, rather than subject the fun-loving old guy to the care of strangers. Shamus's children, including Sean's father, all had homes and businesses in other states, while Sean had been roaming the globe without any goals, in the aftermath of his personal tragedy. Eight years ago, he moved into Shamus's Coral City home to be his companion and caretaker, and a week later, he took over the management of Grampa's beloved Shamrock Construction Company rather than letting it fall apart.

Even in the late stages of his disease, Shamus's eyes frequently twinkled with mischief. He wanted to see

Sean having fun with his life, but Sean had not felt lighthearted since the day his dreams turned to dust. Shamus also wished to attend Sean's wedding and to bounce Sean's children on his knee before he died. His grandson had not been able to grant those wishes either. Perhaps that was why Sean sometimes imagined hearing his grandfather's voice prodding him to do and say things he wouldn't, or shouldn't, as the serious, very respectable mayor of Coral City.

But a date with the fiery Angel Cheswick? He couldn't deny being attracted to her flashing dark eyes and lush body. But she clearly had an irrational temper, a total lack of political savvy and a lifestyle that only a masochist would elect. So why didn't he simply call her back and cancel their…He stopped himself from even thinking of Friday night as a date. It was an appointment. Nothing else.

Nothin' else? Are ya sure about that, boyo?

In the privacy of his mind, Sean could admit that he wasn't at all sure about what he had arranged with Angel. What he *was* sure about though was that he hadn't felt that kind of instant attraction since he was ten years old.

Vicky had been in third grade and he in fifth the first time he asked her to marry him. And she accepted. He still remembered telling Shamus that he was in love and they were going to get married. Rather than making fun of his grandson's first crush, Shamus had informed him that he was following a family tradition. All O'Grady men fell in love with their future wives the first moment they set eyes on each other.

Sean and Vicky's love for each other withstood every storm life tossed at them in the years that followed. They firmly believed they would still be holding hands when their grandchildren got married.

She was only twenty-three when Sean got the call. He hadn't even been in the same state as she that day. His complete obsession with establishing a secure career for their future had him spending a lot of time in California. A car accident, his mother told him with tears strangling her throat. Vicky had been passing through an intersection when another driver ran a red light. She was in critical condition. Hurry home.

He had taken the first flight he could get, but he arrived too late to say goodbye.

"I heard he's a gigolo."

"Christopher Cheswick!" Angel scolded her ten-year-old son. "Where did you learn such a word?" She continued folding the laundry at the kitchen table.

He shrugged. "It's what they call a man who takes a woman out and makes her pay for his dinner. He must have heard about all the money Dad left you. He'll probably move right in here and then kill us off one by one."

"That does it. No more television. No more internet. You're getting way too many crazy ideas in your little brain. Mayor O'Grady is a very respectable gentleman and I'm pretty sure he has a lot more money than we do. Your father left us comfortable, but we're hardly rich enough to be killed for our money. Besides, this isn't a date. I already explained that to you. He owes me a new bike and he's letting me pick it out myself. We are then going to have a *very brief meeting*...about Coral City."

"But Scott said he's taking you out to dinner." Christopher accented his whining voice with a pout.

Scott said. How many times a day did she have to hear those words? Becky's son, Scott, was Chris's best friend, but sometimes she wished they'd never met. "People often have meetings over a meal. Here," she directed, handing him a stack of his folded clothes. "Put these away then get moving on that book report you have due."

As he stalked off, grumbling all the way, Angel

gathered up the rest of the laundry. Christopher had taken Warren's death so much harder than the twins. That had to be why he objected so vehemently to her going out with a man. Last year, she had accepted an invitation to meet for coffee with a man from church and, between how nervous she'd been and how upset Chris had gotten, she had cancelled and decided not to bother trying to date again. This time, she had carefully explained that this evening was not a date but he still reacted badly.

Every one of the hundred times over the past four days when she'd picked up the phone to cancel, she repeated that litany to herself. *This is not a date.* Then why wouldn't her stomach settle down? And why was she worrying about what she would wear? The answer was logical. This evening was important...to the future of her hometown. He had promised to discuss her complaints and she was going to see to it that he heard her point of view.

Two hours and three dress changes later, Angel was as ready as she would ever be. Her straight black skirt and tailored, white blouse gave her the businesslike look she thought appropriate for the situation. She had started out letting her thick, wavy hair hang loose then tried a hairband in it to keep it off her face, but that still seemed too casual, so she tied it up in her usual ponytail and nixed that as well. Finally she settled on clipping the sides and top together with a filigreed silver clip, while leaving the back hang down. The only makeup she put on was a touch of tinted lip gloss. Nothing special needed to go into her appearance.

This wasn't a date.

Yet, the fluttering in her stomach had multiplied tenfold, warning her that she would have to be extra cautious in her movements until she relaxed a little.

Becky was in the kitchen waiting for her when she came downstairs.

"Oh, hi," Angel said with forced cheerfulness. "I was going to send the boys over in a few minutes."

"I know. But His Honor isn't due here for about twenty minutes and I wanted to give you a little present to commemorate your first date." She handed Angel a dress-size box prettily wrapped in silver foil with a large, purple lace bow. "You're so out of practice, I figured you needed some help."

Angel took the gift and efficiently removed the wrapping. "So help me, Becky, if this is a sexy black negligee, you can take it right home and wear it for Larry tonight."

"It's not a negligee. It's—" She stopped short as they both heard the doorbell.

Abruptly, a chorus of boys' voices yelled, "I'll get it," and a fight broke out in the foyer.

"It's my turn!"

"You got it last time."

"I'm the man of the house. I have to check him out first."

Angel dashed from the kitchen with the box still in her hand. At the same moment, Rolf joined the fray by the front door. Beyond the boys' shouts and the dog's barking, she vaguely heard Becky demanding she bring back the box.

Angel never saw which boy got to open the door because Rolf's hard head jerked up under the box, knocking it out of her hand. When she tried to catch it, the lid flew off and the box turned upside-down in mid-air, tumbling the contents all over the slick tile floor.

Sean caught the tail end of Angel's juggling act as the door was yanked open and the noisemakers all took off in the face of certain punishment. Without hesitation, he knelt down beside her and began picking up the items on the floor and returning them to the box.

Suddenly their hands froze as they each realized exactly what those items were. While Angel held a box of fluorescent condoms, Sean had possession of a black lace brassiere with the cup centers cut out. Contraceptive foam, flavored lubricant and a freakishly large, purple dildo were the other objects Sean immediately recognized. The neighbor, Becky, had mentioned that Angel ran her own business, but she hadn't said what sort of business that was.

He folded the lingerie and placed it gingerly in the box. "I know I'm a bit early, but it looks like you're, uh, all set."

CHAPTER 3

"Good heavens," Angel muttered after the first shock wave subsided. As if her fingers had abruptly caught fire, she threw the humiliating box away from her and bolted to her feet. "Becky! You're a dead woman!"

Knowing a sincere threat when she heard one, Becky hurried to the back door, yelling, "I think I hear the boys calling. See ya later."

"Excuse me," Angel murmured with as much dignity as she could gather, then took off down the hall and ducked into the bathroom.

Sean took a few seconds to decide his next course of action. He couldn't leave, although that was probably what she was hoping he would do. He also didn't know her well enough to go after her and offer comfort or understanding. It would probably be best to pretend it hadn't happened and that approach would require getting rid of the evidence. He quickly gathered up the items on the floor, put the lid back on the box and took it out to the kitchen.

He realized his attempt at humor had pushed Angel's blush from pink to crimson, but he'd been unable to stop the words from exiting his mouth. This really was a unique way to greet a date. Considering her horrified reaction and her murderous threat to Becky, the box of goodies couldn't have anything to do with her business. He wasn't sure if that thought relieved or disappointed him.

When Angel didn't return after a few minutes, he followed the path she'd taken and stopped by the only closed door. "Angel? Are you all right?"

There was a long pause before she replied. "No. I...I don't feel well. We'll have to make it another time."

Sean stared at the closed door. She was probably right. He should leave and sign a note at the bicycle shop to pay for whatever she picked out on her own time. But he imagined hearing Shamus's reaction to such a cowardly retreat.

Don't ya be shamin' me now. When I was your age I could charm a colleen roit oot of her pantaloons. Surely ya can charm this one oot of the necessary.

"I'm not leaving, Angel. It could be another month before you have any free time again and I want to get this matter of your bicycle cleared up."

Charmin', boyo. Truly charmin'.

"Angelina?" He thought he heard an acknowledgment. "I gather Becky had something to do with that, uh, collection. And probably a private joke is involved." This time he heard a definite groan. "I promise, if you'll come out of there, I won't ask what the joke is. In fact, I'll erase my memory of everything that happened from the moment your front door opened until now."

The door opened slowly and she stepped out. "I can't believe I just hid in the bathroom. My ten-year-old handles himself better than that." She lowered her lashes so she wouldn't have to see the laughter in his eyes.

True to his word, however, he dropped the matter. "You look very..." His gaze skimmed the prudish blouse buttoned snugly around her throat. "...nice. Shall we go?" He gallantly offered his arm to escort her down the hall but she quickly stepped away.

A few minutes later, she had located her purse and locked up the house. Her heartbeat had returned to normal but she could still feel an abnormal amount of heat in her face and her stomach felt like she'd swallowed a tankful of eels. When they reached his dark blue, American-made sedan, he opened the passenger door and held out his hand to assist her into the seat. Still preferring to avoid his touch, she tried to duck her head and step inside in one move.

Thud! Her forehead slammed against the edge of the car's roof. Flashes of color burst behind her eyes as she rebounded back into Sean's chest.

"Geez, are you all right?" He turned her to face him, tugged at the hand she had reflexively pressed to her head, then inspected the injury. "I'm afraid you're going to have quite a bruise. We'd better go back inside and put some ice on it."

"It's not that bad. Let's just go." All she wanted was to get the evening over with as quickly as possible and, to do that, the evening had to get started.

After several minutes of silent driving, Sean attempted to draw Angel into a conversation about the merits of dressing casually in south Florida. She assumed it was his way of explaining why he was in a short-sleeved sports shirt instead of a jacket and tie. Their opposite choices of attire gave evidence of how differently each had defined the evening. Fortunately the trip to the bicycle shop ended shortly after they exhausted the scintillating topic of the weather.

When she saw how the sales clerk stared at her forehead, she murmured, "I must look like Cyclops."

"Nonsense," Sean assured her. He moved a few hairs

of her bangs back and forth. "No one can see it with your hair like that. Besides, it could have happened to anyone."

Angel gave him a skeptical look. She knew differently, but she couldn't explain about her little accidents without letting him know how nervous he made her.

Although he steered her toward the most expensive, state-of-the-art touring bicycle, she saw the one that would suit her on the other side of the store—an old-fashioned one, with pedal-brakes, fat safety tires and a wide, comfortable seat. The only thing fancy about it was the candy-apple red color of the framework.

When Sean was convinced she was not simply trying to save him money, he paid for it and gave the clerk instructions for delivery. He had the feeling the type of bike she chose told him more about the lady than she would willingly reveal. Perhaps beneath her conservative black-and-white exterior, there was a little candy-apple red dying to get out.

The restaurant he had chosen was not the well-lit, family type, nor could it strictly be termed cozy and romantic. An artificial white tree trimmed with blue and silver ornaments—the traditional south Florida Chanukah bush—had been added to the lobby, all the help wore red, velvety Santa Claus hats and the planter surrounding the booth they were seated in was filled with potted red and white poinsettia plants. As soon as they had both ordered, Angel was ready to get on with what she chose to believe they'd come here for.

"Well now, Mayor O'Grady, as—"

"Sean. Call me Sean or I don't have to listen."

She narrowed her eyes at him. "You didn't say there were any conditions to our dinner discussion."

He raised an eyebrow at her. "I didn't say there weren't either."

"I see. All right...Sean. As I mentioned, there are

several issues facing Coral City that I'm very concerned about."

"Another condition is that you must wait until after we've finished eating. Political debate tends to flatten the taste of a good meal."

"*Hmmm.* Are there any other conditions I should know about?" The light from the hurricane candle on their table gave his eyes a silvery glint. His mouth wasn't smiling but his eyes hinted at a humorous thought.

"I'll let you know as I think of them. Right now I need you to tell me about yourself. The more I know about you, the better I'll understand your complaints. Do you usually fill every minute of every day with some kind of activity?"

She shrugged. "Not intentionally. I just do whatever has to be done. The police department needed a crossing guard at that busy intersection for an hour in the morning and the afternoon and no one applied. So I offered to do it. By spending time in the boys' classes, I always know what's expected of them by their teachers and how they're progressing. My volunteer work at church is a way of paying back what the church provides for us. The neighborhood boys wanted to be Cub Scouts, but none of the other parents had the time—"

"So naturally, you offered to be the den leader. Do you ever do anything just for Angelina Cheswick?"

"Of course I do," she answered defensively. "I have my business."

"Oh, yes, Becky mentioned that. Are you going to tell me or should I start guessing?"

The silver glints flickered again. Was it a telltale sign that he was suppressing a sarcastic comment? What kind of business could he be thinking she had? "I make hair ornaments called Angel's Haloes. You know, decorative headbands, clips, combs, ties and so on. I converted the laundry room into my work area."

Sean shook his head. "I don't know how you find the time for all of it."

"I make the ornaments while the kids are in school or after they're in bed. A few stores are regular customers now, so there isn't much selling involved, except for the occasional craft show. Actually, it's just a matter of being very organized and time-conscious. Warren was a stickler for organization."

"Your husband?"

She nodded.

"When…how did he…Sorry. You don't have to talk about him."

"That's okay. It's not so difficult anymore. He died of a heart attack a little over two years ago. He was quite a bit older than me and after the children were born…well, he worked much too hard, and…it was all too much."

Sean could hear remnants of sorrow and something else he couldn't quite identify. Thinking to comfort her, he reached over the table and placed his hand over hers.

Instantly she jerked her hand away from his and right into the full wine glass at her place. Pink liquid splashed all over the white tablecloth between them. Without missing a beat, Angel moved the hurricane candle aside, sopped up the extra liquid with her linen napkin and continued the conversation as though nothing unusual had happened.

Sean started to signal to the waiter, but stopped as he realized she would probably rather not have more attention drawn to her. He righted her glass, refilled it then handed her his clean napkin. "Losing a loved one under any circumstances is one of the hardest things about life."

The quiet way he said the words let Angel know they were expressed from personal experience. She couldn't help but recall what Becky had said about his fiancée.

In between courses he asked her about what sports the boys played and how they did in school. She never had any trouble talking about her children.

"Josh and Jeff are doing fine now that the school agreed to let them remain in the same class. They prefer to split twins, especially identical ones, but mine became so withdrawn and uncooperative when they were separated, the principal agreed to make an exception. Twins are unique children and should be treated as such. I'm certain they read each other's thoughts, even if they're not aware of it yet. They fight, like all kids do, but they're also extremely close. Outsiders rarely come between them.

"Christopher's the one I worry about. He gets straight A's, excels in every sport and seems to get along with other children. But he doesn't smile very often. I'm afraid he really believes Warren left him in charge of the family."

"Has he told you that?"

"Not in those exact words. He won't talk about his father at all. I keep hoping the day will come when he'll want to share his feelings with me."

Sean's forehead creased with concern. Remembering how hard Vicky's and Shamus's deaths were for him to accept as an adult, he could not fathom how little Christopher felt about losing his father. "Maybe something will happen to force him to express his feelings. If not, you may want to consider counseling."

Angel's chin lifted defensively. "My child does not need counseling. He just needs time and a lot of love."

Sean knew when to defuse a bomb. "We would probably all be better off with a little of that remedy. It's a shame you didn't have one girl. Three boys must really keep you on your toes."

Mollified, she entertained him with a few of her favorite kid stories, but she remained prepared to change the subject to politics the moment he swallowed his last bite. When he ordered coffee for them both, she excused herself and headed to the ladies room. She was congratulating herself for only spilling one glass of wine and not getting a single drop of food on her white blouse, until she caught sight of herself in the mirror. There, in the center of her forehead, was the biggest, bluest golf ball she had ever seen.

All through dinner Sean's gaze had skittered around the room or focused on his food. She had wondered why he kept asking her questions yet didn't meet her eyes when she answered. Now she knew he had been doing his best *not* to look directly at her face. He probably would have burst out laughing.

Darn! The squiggly eels were back, and on a full stomach too. It didn't matter. She intended to say her piece, he would take her home and this whole night could be forgotten.

Weaving her way back to their table, she mentally reviewed the points that needed to be covered. Her thoughts took flight when a young waitress stepped into her path carrying a huge tray of dirty dishes.

"Excuse me," the girl blurted out at the same moment Angel bumped her arm. Glasses jiggled. Plates rattled. But the waitress's excellent balance prevented a disaster. Angel was about to heave a sigh of relief when the girl directed her attention to the floor.

As Angel's gaze followed the waitress's, she noticed several diners turning their heads away from her. Then she saw the reason for the furtive smiles. Caught on her heel and trailing behind her was at least a foot of toilet tissue. She sighed, recalling how Becky had once compared Angel's life to a slapstick comedy. At least she was accustomed to this sort of mishap. Wordlessly, she bent over, removed the tissue from her shoe and dropped it on the tray of dirty dishes. She thanked the waitress as she continued on her way.

One look at O'Grady's mouth working hard not to smile

told her he had witnessed this latest embarrassment. On the positive side, she felt certain he would never want to be seen in public with her again. Knowing there was no way to explain her little problem, she simply slid into the booth, cleared her throat and began her prepared speech. "Mayor...*Sean*, you did promise that I—"

"I'm all ears."

His smile looked real but his eyes still didn't meet hers. They focused on her mouth instead. Angel found that equally unsettling, and when he leaned toward her, she automatically inched back a bit and straightened her spine.

"There are two issues I wanted to talk to you about. I admit that I may not have been as involved in local politics as I should be. However, I do know I don't like what I see happening to Coral City.

"The development of vacant land is an atrocity. There should be much stricter controls on what is being built and where. Someone broke ground last week for another shopping center, but the new one two blocks away is still half empty. And those little matchbox houses on the corner of Shelton Road are bound to bring the market value of the whole community down. You're letting developers do whatever they please with our town. I realize construction is your business, but I don't think that should affect your decisions."

She took his serious expression and slow nod as understanding, if not agreement, and went on. "Also the children desperately need a neighborhood sports complex." His head tilted a bit and his one brow lifted, as if with curiosity, but the silver glints in his eyes had turned to shards of glass. "Well?"

"Well, what?" he asked in a flat tone of voice.

"What do you have to say about all that?"

Sean stroked an imaginary beard on his chin. "Let's see. As to your complaint about the development, I'll have to give you a short lesson on city planning. Thirty-three years ago, a master plan was laid out for Coral City. Parcels of land were designated for certain uses at that time.

"If a developer buys a piece of property that has an existing commercial zoning, the city cannot prevent him from building a shopping center on it. We can only discourage him by charging prohibitive fees for the additional impact that the new construction will have on the city's utilities. We do have the power to turn down a request to *change* a zoning on a parcel, and if you had taken the time to investigate the matter, you would have learned that the present council has not approved a single variance request that would have increased the development originally intended."

Angel felt her cheeks flush. As an interested citizen, she should have known how the system worked. She swallowed hard and made herself meet his eyes. "Oh," she said softly, but it didn't spare her from the rest of his lecture.

"Realizing just how uninformed you really are, I should probably ignore your insinuations against me personally, but why stop now?"

His voice had raised a notch with annoyance. Angel glanced around, but all she saw were poinsettias and diners concentrating on their meals. She wondered if anyone would notice if she simply slid under the table and crawled out of the restaurant.

"Please note that the mayor is a voting member of the city council. I am not omnipotent. What powers we have were given us by the voters…like yourself. And lastly, in order to prevent anyone from accusing me of a conflict of interest, Shamrock Construction *never* bids on a job within the city limits.

"The mayoral election is in March. If you have any other questions about my record or my platform for re-election between now and then, please don't hesitate to ask. Now, unless there's some other accusation you need to sling at me, I'd just as soon call it a night."

Already having paid the check while she was in the ladies room, he slid out of the booth. His manners prohibited him from walking out ahead of her, but he didn't bother to offer her his assistance as she rose.

The drive back to her house seemed endless. A thunderstorm had erupted outside, but the tension crackling between the two people inside the car competed with that of the lightning. Neither attempted to speak until they were parked in Angel's driveway.

"I sincerely apologize," she said as he turned toward her. "I do things like this—get worked up over something, then go shooting my mouth off without having all the facts. I should know better by now, but..." She shrugged, not able to think of a reasonable explanation. "I'm sure you've been a very good mayor, and I'll probably vote for you again in March. Thank you for the bicycle. And dinner." As she fumbled for the door handle, he shifted to the center of the bench seat, captured her hand in his and halted her exit.

"Wait," he said quietly, much too close to her ear. "You'll get drenched. It'll probably slow down in a minute and I want to say something."

And he meant to, but he couldn't think of anything except how good she smelled. Her face turned toward his and a flash of lightning revealed more than a little nervousness in her big dark eyes.

Give it up, boyo. Ya've wanted a taste since first ya seen her.

A roar of thunder muffled Angel's gasp as Sean's lips touched hers. A kiss was totally unexpected, completely inappropriate. He must have thought the same thing, because he abruptly pulled back and scrutinized her face as though it were the first time he had seen her.

Angel felt the hand that had been holding hers graze its way up her arm, stroke her cheek then cup her neck. The masculine eyes that had shown momentary confusion softened and warmed in their appraisal of her. Angel wondered at the heaviness filling her body, preventing her from doing the rational thing. *Move*, her mind demanded. *Stay*, her body argued. *Again*, her eyes requested.

He complied with the last.

Where his mouth met hers, a tingling sensation began as a spark and intensified as it coursed through her limbs and exploded in her fingertips. To ease the odd feeling, she molded her hands to his shoulders and soon found it got even better when she stroked his neck and hair. His lips slanted over hers and she tucked her head in his arm to accommodate them both.

An unfamiliar liquid heat energized and drained her at the same time. The desire to explore, to discover more, overcame any last remnants of rationality. She just wanted to feel all there was to feel. *Immediately.*

His tongue begged access and she granted it without hesitation. When his hands skimmed over her, too urgently to do more than relay his need to get past the barriers to bare flesh, she dragged one knee up over his lap. A murmur of approval escaped her throat as his fingers slipped beneath her skirt to caress her stocking-covered thigh.

Flash! The high-intensity security light over the garage door glared through the car's windshield like an evil eye and Angel's sanity returned with a jolt. Sean's took a few seconds longer.

"Good heavens," she whispered. "Oh, dear God!" came out with considerably more volume as she pushed against his chest.

"Angel..." His palm teased the outside of her thigh on its way out from under her skirt.

She couldn't think of anything intelligent to excuse her outlandish behavior, so she did the only thing she could think of—escape. Oblivious to the pouring rain, she shoved the car door open and bolted. But she didn't get far. Her heel caught on the seat belt strap and broke off with a loud crack. The sudden release of her trapped foot threw her off-balance, hurtling her forward like a rock from a slingshot. The next second she was face down in the soggy grass.

By the time Sean reached her, she was back on her feet, holding the remains of the broken shoe. Soaked to the skin and smeared with dirt and leaves, she lacked the energy to stop Sean from helping her hobble toward her front door.

The door flew open before they reached it. Seven pairs of eyes stared at her in shock until Christopher broke away from the group. With all the strength his seventy-eight-pound body could muster, he walloped Sean in the stomach.

"You creep! What'd you do to my mom?"

CHAPTER 4

Angel switched on the lamp next to her bed then picked up the novel she had started several nights ago. Sleep was clearly out of the question.

After convincing everyone that she had merely had another little accident, she had sent Sean and Becky on their respective ways.

Becky's curiosity would have to wait to be satisfied until daylight...after Angel figured out what had happened herself. And what to do about Christopher? He shouldn't have hit Sean but how could she punish him for being protective of her?

Of course, Christopher's attack hadn't been nearly as awful as her own. Even if she had been justified, which she now knew she hadn't been, her disapproval of Sean could have been voiced in a more cautious, tactful way. But those two adjectives had never been associated with Angelina Santieri Cheswick. Words like impetuous, hot-tempered and passionate described her much better.

Passionate? She mulled the word over in her mind.

Yes, she had always considered herself passionate when it came to a cause she believed in. When she cared deeply about something, energy built up inside her like a volcano until it spewed the fire and lava from her system.

Unfortunately, fire and lava burn. Usually she only hurt herself, in the form of embarrassment or little mishaps, but occasionally someone else got singed. In those cases she always made a sincere apology immediately after she regained her composure…as she had with Sean.

Was it a crime to care so much about her community that she felt passionate about it?

Passionate. Her Sicilian heritage struck again. She doubted that either of her parents would willingly accept responsibility for her wanton reaction to Sean's kiss. Perhaps the evil spirit of some demented nymphomaniac had taken over her body. There, now that's rational thinking. She could write the mayor a letter and explain how supernatural forces had been at work.

She would have liked to put the blame entirely on him. He started it. But she not only encouraged him, she had been all over him like a kid let loose in a giant toy store. How could she have done that? She didn't even know the man. What she did know was that he made her lose control and that made her extremely uncomfortable. One didn't have a schedule like hers without a tremendous amount of discipline. When one was juggling as many obligations as she, one couldn't afford to relax even for a second, or else everything would come tumbling down at once.

Chemistry. That was another tricky word. It was the only possible answer to what had happened however. Naturally she had heard, and read, about the phenomenon, but firsthand experience had always eluded her. Never would she have imagined that it could

indiscriminately strike its victims without any prior
warning—like lightning—nor did she realize it could
transform a straitlaced mommy into a world class...She
wasn't even knowledgeable enough to come up with the
right name for what she'd momentarily turned into in
Sean's car. Out of a lifetime of little embarrassments,
this was the first one she was certain she would never
overcome.

What she had felt with Warren was the way it *should*
be between a husband and wife—comfortable, secure,
respectful. One month after Angel graduated from high
school, she and a girlfriend declared their independence.
Suffering through countless New York winters helped
them select Fort Lauderdale as their destination. Within
a week they had secretarial jobs and an apartment
outside the oceanfront city.

Warren Cheswick, the senior vice president of a
national credit card company, was her first boss, her
first male friend and, a year later, her first, and only,
sexual partner. He was a dynamic businessman who
regularly put in seventy-hour work weeks. She was a
bright, highly skilled whirlwind who found him and his
orderly ways of working and living much more inviting
than the dating scene her roommate endorsed. Warren's
wife had divorced him for the same character traits
Angel appreciated in him.

Their friendship had flowed naturally from the office
to the bedroom. She was nineteen and he, forty-nine,
when they married. Stress and chain-smoking had
begun to take its toll on him even then. His once auburn
hair was nearly all gray and worry lines permanently
marred his pale complexion, but she loved him for how
he treated her, not his outward appearance.

Angel had given him her virginity as an engagement
gift, not so much because she had carefully protected it,
but because none of the boys she had dated during her
teens had stirred any desire in her. For that matter,

neither had Warren. From the beginning, their relationship was built on respect and friendship. That didn't change much after they shared a bedroom...except on Saturday night. Then, after the lights were out, Warren would occasionally join her in her twin bed for five or ten minutes.

Though he had no desire to father more children since his were grown, he knew how much Angel wanted them, and he wanted to give Angel everything she desired. Although their lovemaking was neither frequent nor earth-shattering, it was effective. Christopher arrived two years after their wedding day and, as planned, she had her tubes tied following the twins' birthday eighteen months later. After that, Warren shared her bed less and less often, and she hadn't given that more than a fleeting thought. Their life had seemed so perfect, until the morning Warren didn't wake up when the alarm clock went off.

The encounter with Sean O'Grady explicitly suggested a way she may have been less than an ideal wife for Warren. Maybe he had never stirred her passions because she had never stirred his. Discovering she was capable of acting like a sex maniac with a virtual stranger made her more aware than ever of how selfish she had been.

Had she been as considerate of him as he always was of her, if she hadn't added to his stress by having three rambunctious children, perhaps he would still be alive. She couldn't go back and change what had happened, but she couldn't seem to ignore the guilt either.

Sean truly did not want to rehash the events of the past hours. Why bother? None of it could possibly happen in the real world. Someone like Angel Cheswick simply did not exist in the life he knew. All evening he had expected to see a cameraman filming the reality show he must have unknowingly been part of.

He couldn't remember anyone ever putting him through such a kaleidoscope of emotions in so brief a time span. Even without Shamus's imaginary goading, he would have had a devil of a time maintaining his mature, gentlemanly persona. It had been a monumental struggle not to laugh out loud at her string of accidents, to argue at the top of his lungs over her twisted, uninformed, yet passionate, opinions...to discover just how far that passion could have taken them if they'd had five more minutes in the dark.

The trouble was, she made him want to do it all over again.

Shamus watched his grandson tossing and turning on his bed and smiled. *Finally.* It had taken a lot of energy to whip up that thunderstorm but it had been worth it.

Sean and Angelina had kissed. The rest should move along without the need of any more of his shenanigans.

But something told him to stay vigilant. His help might still be needed to get the deed done before Christmas.

"You turned him down? How could you?" Becky made it sound as though Angel had betrayed all of womankind with her refusal.

Angel tried her best to meet her friend's glare of disapproval but ended up watching Rolf's tail slap the kitchen floor. "I can't imagine why he even called this morning. After last night he should have had his fill of the entire Cheswick family. I certainly have no intention of going through that kind of torture again. It was the most humiliating experience I have ever had. And for me, that's saying a lot. Anyway, wouldn't I have appeared too available if I had been free for dinner again tonight?"

"*Hmmph.* I can almost understand you putting him off for the next couple of weeks because of Christmas but what was your excuse for New Year's Eve?"

"I promised the boys they could each have a friend sleep over that night."

"And I'll bet my shoe money the boys haven't heard *that* good news yet. Listen, kiddo, playing hard to get is fine when you're twenty, but—"

"*Hah!* Listen to yourself. The other day I was at my peak at thirty-one, and today I'm too old to turn down a date."

Becky clucked her tongue. "Not just any date. Sean O'Grady is—oh, never mind. If you can't see what a unique specimen he is, nothing I say is going to open your eyes. Since you're so indifferent to his charms, how about letting me enjoy them secondhand. I demand a minute-to-minute account of last night. *Something* good must have happened."

"After your cute little joke box, you don't have the right to demand anything." Her expression turned to complete self-disgust. "Let's just say it went downhill from there and I really don't want to recall a single minute of it."

Angel may not have wanted to recall any of her encounter with Sean but he simply refused to stay out of her head no matter what she was doing. It didn't help matters that he called again on Sunday afternoon.

"How's the busiest lady in Coral City?" he asked as though they were old friends.

"Up to my elbows in ribbons and lace," she answered in an equally friendly, but hurried tone. "And hours away from completing an order I promised to deliver by tomorrow morning."

"I just thought I'd check your schedule again. Any chance you're free this evening?"

"No. Sorry."

"Then how about tomorrow night? I'd like to take you to dinner and *not* talk politics. I'll pay for a sitter for the boys."

Angel took a deep breath. "I'm sorry. I really can't."

"Angel? Are you seeing someone?"

"What? Oh, gawd no," she responded quickly, surprised that he leapt to that conclusion, but it helped her come up with her excuse. "No, it's not that, really. I'm afraid I'm just not...comfortable about...going out. I still...well, Warren...and then Christopher gets so upset...I just can't. I hope you can understand."

Understand? He hadn't understood a single thing since he met her, but he recognized rejection when it hit him between the eyes. "Sure. I was only trying to make up for causing you so much...*discomfort.* Don't forget the city council meeting Tuesday night. If you can rearrange your Cub Scouts for one night, maybe you'll discover something interesting."

Angel waited for the relief to wash over her after she hung up. He wouldn't be calling anymore. She wouldn't have to jump every time the phone rang. There would be no more fretting that he might talk her into being alone with him. Wasn't that terrific?

When it took her more than a heartbeat to answer herself, she decided that, although she wanted to attend a council meeting, maybe she would wait until January, or February. Or after the election. Sometime after the memory of his hand beneath her skirt stopped making her blush.

Good, Sean told himself. She's definitely not interested. I can get on with my life. Before he even finished the thought he imagined hearing Shamus's sarcastic retort to that.

Not interested, ya say? That's a wee bit hard to believe, considering how she melted when ya kissed her.

How could she not be interested? Kissing her had been all the proof he'd needed to know that his attraction to her was out of the ordinary. There was so much chemistry between them, it was a wonder his car hadn't blown up.

But damned if he was going to beg. He would simply have to put her out of his mind.

Shamus rubbed his chin through his thick gray beard. Obviously, understanding the way the female mind works wasn't one of the powers granted him when he became an angel. The kiss had been enough to push Sean into the proper frame of mind, but not Angelina.

It looked like a bit more meddling was called for after all. Considering the fact that there were only twelve days left until Christmas—twelve more days to take advantage of his extended powers and Gabriel being too busy to watch him every second—Shamus knew he had to come up with a humdinger of a plan.

But what more could he do?

Thinking he could use a bit of the old magick, he recalled the political discussion the couple had had over dinner and an idea popped into his head. All he had to do was whisper a few words in the right ears.

"We need a show of support from the parents. Please Angel, say you'll be there."

Angel sighed. Perhaps it was time to enroll in a "How to Say No" class. This was hardly the first time the president of the Parent-Teachers' Association had asked for help, but it was the first time she needed to refuse.

"I'm sorry, Pam. I have the Cub Scouts tomorrow night."

"No problem. The boys can earn a badge in civic awareness or something. Get their parents to meet you with their boys at City Hall. The issue isn't on the agenda but if enough of us are there, the mayor won't be able to ignore us. We want some answers. Now, not next month!"

Angel knew her priorities. The children's welfare always came before her own fears. She couldn't say no, as usual. "All right. I'll bring the troop." She disconnected then started making the necessary calls.

She would attend, but this time she would have all the facts before she opened her mouth. No one, especially not His Honor the Mayor, was going to accuse her of being uninformed again.

"Shamus! Was that your doing?"

Shamus smiled innocently, "Why Sara, me darlin'. You're looking particularly lovely t'night."

"Don't try to charm me, you old rascal. I've been working for a month to give my granddaughter Pam a peaceful Christmas, and you've gone and gotten her involved in another cause. That vacant land issue wasn't supposed to come up until late January."

"Now ya know as well as me that your Pammy is happiest when she's all stirred up over something, and ya've got me solemn word that the whole thing will be over with afore Christmas gets here." He hung his head in shame. "I know 'twas wrong, but I couldna come up with another way ta get me grandson a sweetheart. I guess I'm just an old romantic fool."

Sara clucked her tongue at him, but her expression softened. "All right. You're forgiven. This time."

Shamus partially lifted his head to peek at her. "Then ya won't be telling Gabriel what I done?"

"I suppose not," she said, then slowly grinned. "But now you owe me one, you old coot."

Tuesday night, seven of her twelve scouts showed up with their parents at City Hall. Pam's telephone network had been so effective, Angel's group had to stand along the back wall, which was not the best way to keep young boys from fidgeting or wandering off. Besides, it would have been better for her to sit as well, preferably behind a very large person or two. Perhaps Sean wouldn't notice her. In her sneakers, she was barely five foot two and she could scrunch down a little more. Besides, it was a fairly large room, maybe he was nearsighted.

She heard his voice calling the meeting to order and, while he was busy doing whatever mayors do, she decided to hazard a glance toward the raised platform in front of the room. Like every other place in town, the hall was decorated with a combination of holiday regalia meant to include all beliefs and not offend any individual.

As the reading of the minutes droned on, she took the opportunity to study the people who represented her and made a startling discovery. All four members of the council were well over the age of sixty. Sean was half their age but had no wife or children. How could these members of the community possibly empathize with the needs of a young family?

Her gaze clung to the one person she had intended to ignore. Why did he have to be so darn good to look at? The floodlights illuminating the dais also enhanced the lighter streaks in his thick blond hair. The somber dark suit he wore was tempered by a light blue dress shirt and plain, dark tie. He had the kind of lean build that carried a suit well. When her wicked mind automatically progressed to thoughts of how those shoulders had felt beneath her hands, she forced her eyes back to his face.

He was intently listening to the City Manager's report, his head turned to the side. What a marvelous profile. He could have been a model or the lead in a romantic movie. She couldn't tell from that distance whether his tanned face was freshly shaved but she recalled the light brush of stubble against her throat when he...

Caught! His gaze latched onto hers and clung with velvet hooks—one eyebrow lifted slightly, an imperceptible nod of his head...Was he greeting or taunting her? She felt a wave of dizziness sweep over

her and realized she had forgotten to breathe. Inhaling
sharply was her next mistake. He couldn't possibly have
seen the movement of her chest, yet his slow grin
implied he had. His ego must thoroughly relish the
knowledge that he could unnerve her so easily.

For over an hour, Angel managed to avoid looking at
Sean and concentrate on the proceedings. The boys,
who'd been given permission to sit on the floor, rose
and applauded the part where one of their classmates
received an award for the best bicycle safety poster.
However, the seemingly endless series of tedious issues,
like business license requests, had them begging to go
home.

She sensed Sean's attention return to her again and
again but only verified her instincts once. When she did,
the same light-headed feeling filled her. It had to be a
trick of some kind. He was sending suggestive messages
with his eyes and making her think about…about things
that didn't belong in her head while flanked by her
children.

Finally the floor was opened to any other new
business and Pam swiftly popped up with hers.

"Mayor O'Grady, we heard a large piece of property
has been deeded to the city. Would you tell us what
plans have been made for its use?"

He smiled and turned his seductive eyes on the PTO
president. "Your information sources have beaten me to
the punch again, Mrs. Kaplan. But you're a bit
premature. For those who haven't heard about the land
grant, let me offer some background. Last year we
passed a resolution regarding new development in Coral
City. Because of the impact that additional residences or
businesses have on the city's utilities and services, the
developer must now pay a fee. The expenditure of that
fee must go toward public improvement.

"In the case of one developer, we agreed—*just
yesterday*—to accept a parcel of undeveloped land in

lieu of the fee due. The members of this council haven't had time for more than a preliminary discussion, but the land will probably be best utilized as a passive park, leaving most of the property in its natural state."

Angel pressed her clenched fists to her sides. She wanted to speak out but her vow not to open her mouth without knowing the facts, combined with not wanting to bring his focus directly onto her, kept her silent. Thankfully, one of Pam's other supporters picked up the ball.

"I heard the property contains over twelve acres, more than enough for a sports complex. We already have two passive parks. The people, the *children*, need a place to play baseball, football, soccer—"

"Right now," a third parent broke in, "they have to be driven all the way over to Petrie to share their facilities. Both towns have grown so much that scheduling those fields for games for all the teams has become next to impossible. Just because children can't vote doesn't mean you should ignore their needs."

Voices of approval rose around the room but Angel could hear the grumbles of dissension as well. She surveyed the dais and was dismayed to see the elderly council members frowning and shaking their heads. It looked like they had already decided firmly against a sports field of any kind. Mayor O'Grady's smile remained fixed but Angel felt certain his mind was already made up as well.

When the noise level in the room rose to deafening proportions, the mayor pounded his gavel then said. "I see this is going to be more sensitive than anticipated. If the council agrees, I suggest we hold an open forum on this issue. A public notice will be posted and the forum can take place at the end of January's regular council meeting. Mrs. Kaplan, you'll recruit one person to present the case for the sports complex. I'm sure I'll have a volunteer to do the same regarding the passive park."

The meeting was adjourned soon afterward and Angel herded the boys outside without another glance toward the dais. She had a lot to consider, like how she could actively support the group demanding a sports complex without having to be in the same room with Sean O'Grady.

Sean lost sight of Angel's dark hair amidst the sea of taller exiting citizens. Had he honestly thought he could simply forget her? How could he possibly forget a woman who could put him in a semi-aroused state from across a roomful of people, most of whom were looking at him? Her passionate nature had literally reached out and enticed him. He had felt her straining to get on her soapbox. Why had she held back? Surely their encounter hadn't frightened her speechless. Impossible. There had to be another reason for her reticence.

Mayhaps ya were roit afore. She's just not interested in ya.

Sean flinched as though someone had just elbowed him in the side. He had imagined hearing Shamus's voice from time to time since the beloved man's passing but lately it had seemed like he was standing right beside him full-time.

Not interested, huh? He had willed her to look at him throughout the meeting, but she had done a fair job of pretending she didn't notice. After the first visual contact, he knew her avoidance of him was definitely *not* due to lack of interest. She had practically devoured him with her eyes.

So, what do ya intend to do aboot it?

One thing was certain. He couldn't let it drop just because she wasn't *comfortable* around him. Hell, comfortable wasn't the way she made him feel either, but their mutual discomfort took them in opposite directions. At the very least he believed they should spend one more evening together to see if they had anything more in common than spontaneous combustion. And if the next date should head in the same explosive direction the first had, he would make sure they were somewhere a lot less cramped and infinitely more private.

He would call and politely ask her out once more. If she refused again, well, he'd simply have to launch a pro-active campaign to wear her down.

By noon the next day, he had her refusal.

"Why not?" he asked merely to hear what excuse she would come up with this time.

"I already told you."

"I didn't accept that as a rational explanation. Are you afraid of me?"

"Don't be ridiculous."

"Then meet me for lunch—someplace full of people, completely unromantic and casual. We need to talk."

All she could think of was how little the roomful of people had mattered to her composure the night before. "No."

"We'll talk politics, I promise."

"You've used that promise already, Mayor. I really don't have time to talk now. I have an order to get ready."

"You know, Angel, maybe I just need a clearer explanation about why you don't want to go out with me. Tell me that you don't find me even slightly attractive, that you can't stand talking to me and that kissing me completely turned you off, and I won't bother you again." Her very long pause was enough to have him imagining how hard she was trying to say any of those criticisms without success.

The only response he received was an audible, frustrated sigh.

"All right, Angel. I accept your challenge."

"I am *not* challenging you. I just want you to stop calling me."

"Sorry, I don't believe that. And I'll tell you something

else you won't like to hear. You should have accepted the lunch invitation. Now I won't stop until I've gotten everything I want."

"What are you talking about?" Angel's voice had the edge of worry he was hoping for.

"Surrender, Angel. Total, unconditional surrender. And *that's* a campaign promise you can count on."

CHAPTER 5

Sean hadn't planned to be so melodramatic with his challenge but Angel may as well have thrown her virtual gauntlet at his feet. He felt the adrenaline pumping through his system and laughed to himself. Damned if he wasn't having the most fun he'd had in ages.

During his college years, he discovered he had a strong aptitude for political science, with a particular fascination for analyzing successful campaigns. Running for mayor of a small town had not taken a genius of campaign strategy, but the knowledge remained with him.

Angel had initially thought she didn't like him because of his record as mayor, but she had admitted being wrong about that. She said she didn't want to go out with him, but she couldn't deny that she had liked his kisses. If he could seduce her into his arms again, he was certain she would also admit she was wrong about not dating him.

Have ya considered a good old-fashioned blind side, Mr. Know-It-All with your fancy education?

Not a bad thought. He knew most of her crazy schedule. He just had to figure out which activity he could infiltrate.

Angel hustled her boys out to the car as soon as the dinner dishes were cleared away that evening.

Within ten minutes of walking in the house after the meeting last night, Pam Kaplan had called. She was having a meeting the next evening at her house to help organize a campaign for the sports complex and she knew Angel would want to be involved.

Pam's living room was already packed with supporters when Angel and her boys arrived.

"Oh, good!" Pam exclaimed when she saw her. "Now we can get started. Boys, go on to the family room. The rest of the kids are having some sort of video game contest." That was all they had to hear to leave their mother's side. Pam called the impromptu gathering to order a few seconds later.

"For anyone who missed last night's meeting, let me review the situation."

Angel had never mastered the art of speaking in front of a large audience—a classroom full of children or a scout meeting didn't count—so she truly admired how Pam held everyone's attention and spoke with such authority. In no time, she had given a summary of the land deal and mapped out a strategy to prepare for a professional and impressive presentation in January. There was research to be done on timing of such a project as well as estimated expenses and fundraising possibilities. There were petitions to be drawn up and signatures to be solicited. Someone needed to take responsibility for door-to-door canvassing, phone calls and preparing press releases for the local news venues, while someone else could take on the higher-tech informational sources such as setting up a website and blog.

This being such an emotional issue, hands immediately went up when Pam asked for volunteers. Angel repeatedly raised her hand but Pam passed her over every time. She began to wonder why Pam had even asked her to come if she didn't want her help on any of the committees. And she definitely wanted to help. Not only because of the strong need for the complex, but also because it was the opposite of what the mayor wanted.

After his nonsensical call that day, she kept trying to think of what she could say or do to convince him to leave her alone.

"Well Angel, what do you say? Will you do it?"

Angel blinked at Pam. What had she been asked to do?

"Someone has to do it. And it should be someone with a familiar, friendly face, like the city's favorite crossing guard. Someone everyone likes, regardless of which side she's on. I'd do it, but I tend to get a little pushy and I have been known to rub some people the wrong way."

That caused a ripple of jovial laughter throughout the room which turned into encouragement for Angel to accept the job.

"What exactly would I need to do?" she asked cautiously, hoping no one could guess she'd been daydreaming.

"Just be your concerned, passionate, super-involved self," Pam said with a bright smile. "Everyone else will do the legwork and gather statistics. I'm sure we'll have a volunteer or two to help write the actual presentation." Several voices instantly offered their assistance. "You see? All you'd have to do is be the official spokesperson for the group and present our case at the next council meeting."

Angel's eyes widened in shock. "*Spokesperson?* I'd

have to get up and give a speech in City Hall?"

Everyone in the room seemed to think she was the definitive choice...except her. She wanted to help, she really did, but wasn't there something else she could do more comfortably? Something less noticeable? Pam's usage of the word passionate echoed in her ears. Lately, that personality trait was getting her into more trouble than usual.

Suddenly it occurred to her that this could be the ideal way to turn off the persistent mayor. He couldn't possibly want anything personal to do with the spokesperson of the group going against him on such an important issue.

Without giving it another thought, she announced, "I'll do it."

Angel didn't normally work on Saturday mornings. At least one of her boys always seemed to have a sports event at that time and she felt it was important that she always be there to cheer them on. It may have been different if their father were alive. He might have gotten interested in their activities now that they were older. *May have. Might have.*

She shook her head and sighed. Warren had been on her mind a lot lately...ever since a certain someone's hand had crept under her skirt. She gave her head another shake. "Enough!" she said aloud.

The reason she was at home, instead of at Chris's soccer game with Becky, was because of the order she had unexpectedly received from a ladies' accessory shop at the mall. They wanted to try some of her holiday-themed and extra-sparkly items but they needed them *immediately*. If Angel's Haloes did well there, it could mean a lot more orders. Although Warren had left them financially secure, she wanted to be self-sufficient. It was a matter of pride. And neither memories of Warren nor thoughts of that other man were going to distract her from getting this order completed.

She heard Rolf barking several seconds before the doorbell rang. She considered pretending she wasn't home, since she normally wouldn't have been, but that would have been like telling a lie. Besides, it could just be a neighbor who needed to borrow something.

"Quiet, Rolf," she ordered as she walked to the door and pushed the big dog out of her way. His tail was wagging happily and his bark had been one of recognition. She didn't hesitate to open the door.

"Good morning," Sean said with a wide grin.

Angel frowned and made a mental note not to trust Rolf's barks and tail wags ever again. A lifetime of good manners forced her to reply, but not to smile. "Good morning." She kept one hand on the door and stood in the opening, the way she would if he were a stranger. "May I help you?"

His wide smile flattened under her formality. "I heard you're going to be the spokesperson for the group in favor of the sports complex."

"That's right," Angel said stiffly, without opening the door any wider or moving aside to let him in.

"After the meeting Tuesday, I got to thinking that it wasn't really fair for the council members to have access to more information than the concerned parents. I had already decided the ethical thing to do would be to pass along any facts we have to the other side, regardless of who their spokesperson turned out to be. Since that person is you, I just thought I could stop by and discuss the matter with you this morning."

Angel grimaced. She needed all the ammunition she could get to help their cause. What if he knew something that the sports complex group did not? "That's very considerate of you, Mayor. But I'm afraid this morning is impossible. I have a rush order to fill. Perhaps I could call your office and make an appoint—"

"I don't have a single opening all week…which was

why I thought I'd bring my notes by this morning to go over with you...but I understand. You're busy, I get it. Just give my office a call." He turned and started walking back to his car.

"Wait!" Angel called quickly when she saw the folder in his hand. Apparently his intention was honorable.

He turned around but stayed where he was.

"Would you be willing to talk while I work on the order?"

"Of course." His expression remained serious as he took a step closer.

As soon as she opened the door and moved aside, he entered...and smiled...just a wee bit. He gave Rolf a vigorous ear scratch that ensured his total adoration.

As she led him to her workroom, he asked, "Where are the boys?"

"Petrie's Field. Chris is playing soccer and Josh and Jeff went to watch. Becky drove them all so I could work. Of course, if we had a field here in Coral City, they could have ridden their bikes to and from the game."

"Don't the parents go to watch the game anyway?" Sean questioned, clearly not grasping her point.

She sat down at her work table and motioned for him to take the folding chair Becky used when visiting. "No. Unfortunately, not all parents have the time or inclination. Under those circumstances, the children are cheated out of a chance to play because they don't have transportation."

"Car pools?" Sean suggested.

She shook her head. "To be part of a pool, a parent has to be willing or able to drive every so often." She chose several narrow red and white ribbons, nimbly tied them together in the middle with a wire then squeezed a dollop of tacky glue onto a ceramic tile. As her fingers attached a row of red satin rosettes to a plastic barrette, she reiterated the other points that had been made at the council meeting, such as the overcrowded schedule at Petrie Field.

As she talked and her hands worked, she noticed Sean's gaze moving back and forth between her face and the hair ornament. She was fairly sure she was getting through to him, which should have given her a sense of confidence, but with each passing minute, his nearness was making her more self-conscious.

She shouldn't have brought him into her workroom. There simply wasn't enough air in there for two people. Becky was okay but the room was much too small for someone his size. And the limited space was definitely getting warmer by the minute. She finished the first barrette and began on its mate. "Your turn," she said when he had no further questions on anything she'd related.

For more than a heartbeat, Sean couldn't comprehend what it was his turn to do. He'd been intently watching her hands and fantasizing about having those talented fingers threaded through his hair again, roaming over his body and bringing parts of him alive the way she turned a few strips of ribbon and wire into a thing of intricate beauty. "That is really fascinating. Do you mind if I get a closer look?" Before she could refuse, he scooted his chair next to hers and leaned forward so that he could better watch each movement of her fingers.

She swallowed hard and did her best to keep working. His warm breath wafted over the back of her hand and a smell that she already recognized as part aftershave, part Sean, filled her senses. Only the fact that she had made this particular barrette hundreds of times allowed her to finish it.

"Beautiful," he said, looking into her eyes. "Hurry up. Let me see you do a different one."

Pride in her work had her choosing to create a more complicated arrangement of braided ribbons and rhinestone strands for a large hair comb but his close scrutiny was unnerving. She took a breath and started again.

"Would it help if I held this part together while you gather the other pieces?" he asked innocently as he tightened his fingers around the part she was still holding. The movement brought his arm along hers and his chest against her shoulder, as his other arm casually relocated to the back of her chair.

Angel felt the temperature in the room increase by another several degrees and fought to maintain her composure. "That's not necessary. I have a tool to do that." She picked up a tiny clamp and closed it around the ribbons she'd been fumbling with. "I should have done that to begin with." She waited for him to ease his body back to a safer distance. Instead, he turned her face toward his and leaned closer.

His mouth had almost touched hers when she jerked back. "I thought you came here to give me information." She meant to be stern but the soft tone of her voice betrayed her weakness.

Sean brushed his thumb across her lips and they involuntarily parted for him. "What are you afraid of, Angel?"

She straightened her spine, but only accomplished drawing his gaze to her t-shirt-covered breasts. "I'm…I'm not afraid. I told you, I'm not comfortable—"

"With dating. That's what you told me you're uncomfortable with, although I still don't understand your reasoning. At any rate, I wasn't trying to *date* you just then. I was trying to kiss you."

"Why?" she asked quite seriously.

He wasn't sure what answer she wanted to hear, so he stuck to the truth. "Because kissing you the other night was way too good not to repeat."

She frowned at the realization that she couldn't argue with that, so she changed direction. "I've been thinking you might be one of those men who gets more interested when a woman turns him down, which probably never happens to you. I know for a fact there's a plethora of young, beautiful women you could call up who'd be thrilled to share more than kisses with you."

"A *plethora*?" he repeated with a chuckle.

"At least a plethora," she answered seriously. "So it must be my rejection that has you coming after me. Why else would you keep pursuing someone like me?"

His grin vanished and he sat back in his chair. "What do you mean *someone like you*?"

She got back to busying her hands so she didn't have to look at him as she spoke. "You know exactly what I mean."

He shook his head. "Sorry. I don't have a clue. The first time I saw you I thought you were very attractive. Some weird things happened the night we went out but I admired the way you handled yourself no matter what went wrong. Kissing you turned me inside out. And now I know you're not only devoted to a whole *plethora* of worthy activities, you're incredibly artistic as well. Why the hell wouldn't I want to pursue someone like you?"

She clucked her tongue and took a slow, deep breath. "Because...because I'm such a *mom*, and you're prime beef. Becky's words, not mine."

That made him chuckle. "All right, for argument's sake, let's say I'm only pursuing you because you've turned me down for a second date. In that case, if you really want me to leave you alone, all you'd have to do is go out with me. Instead of pushing me away when I try to kiss you, you should take the initiative. Push yourself on me and kiss me the way you did the other night. If you're right, I'll quickly get bored and that'll be the end of it."

Could it be that easy? Angel heard a grain of male logic in his scenario. Had he just told her how she might be rid of him once and for all? The thought of kissing him on her own terms made her feel strange and warm inside. She very much wanted to kiss him again and following his suggestion could be a way to do it while still maintaining a smidgeon of her dignity. Suddenly she had the nerve to accept his dare.

She shifted in her chair to face him, placed her hands behind his neck and drew his head to hers. Then she saw the silver glints twinkle in his eyes and she retreated again. "You're up to something."

He blinked at her in surprise. "I beg your pardon?"

"Your eyes give you away. What was your plan in coming here? So far I haven't heard any useful information. Are you trying to seduce me into telling you our plans?"

He laughed out loud at that. "I won't deny wanting to seduce you but there's nothing you can tell me that I don't already know. I really did come by to give you information, but...I admit to finding you distracting." He handed her the folder. "A copy of all the pertinent facts of the land deal are in here with a few notes I made."

She glanced inside then set the folder behind her. "You could have handed this to me at my front door. Have you got something else to share with our group?" She swiveled her chair back toward her work and picked up where she'd left off. "Like I said, I really am on a tight deadline."

"Right. So, here's the bottom line. The primary argument against the sports complex is the expense. It's not just a matter of clearing land. Electric, water and sewer lines need to be put in. Bleachers, bathroom facilities and concession stands have to be constructed, parking areas paved, and so on. Then there's the upkeep and management. That means employees on the city's payroll. Who's going to pay for all that? Nearly half of our community consists of retirees on fixed incomes. We have to consider how a tax hike would affect them. We owe our elderly all the consideration we can give them."

Angel could see this was no rehearsed campaign

speech of his. He truly felt very strongly about what he was saying. She listened to the rest of his arguments in favor of the passive park and made notes of points she'd have to discuss with Pam and the other parents. The start-up and maintenance costs were already at the top of their problems-to-be-resolved list and he gave her a few more red-tape items they hadn't thought of.

"Thank you," Angel said sincerely. "I'll share your information with the group. But you may as well know, we have some very knowledgeable people on our side and if there is any way to make this happen, we're going to fight for it."

He grinned. "I have no doubt about that. And now that the business is out of the way, we need to settle a personal matter." He leaned forward.

"I really don't have any more time—"

"Five minutes. Give me five minutes of all your attention and then I'll help you with your order. I can see there are some little things I could do to speed up the job."

Although that was true and his offer of help was tempting, the last thing she wanted was for him to stay in the cramped workroom any longer than necessary.

"Please?"

She set down the piece she was working on and turned toward him.

"I want the truth. Did you like kissing me?"

She stared at her lap. "You know I did."

"Then why don't you want to repeat it?"

"Because kissing—the kind of kissing we did—leads to...other things. And I'm really not ready for...other things."

He was quiet for a long moment then took both her hands in his. "Please look at me." She raised her eyes. "I believe you are a very special woman. And I'm pretty sure you're as distracted by me as I am by you. But staying away from each other doesn't seem to be the answer to getting *un*-distracted. The only answer is to spend time together and see if whatever flared up between us burns out just as fast. And to show you how understanding I am about your concern, I will make you a promise. If you'll agree to go out with me at least one, no, *two* more times, I will make sure that, *if* there is a goodnight kiss, it will stay in the nice zone, far, far away from the naughty things you're not ready for."

Angel's eyes widened in surprise. It sounded rational. "And if you can't live up to that promise?"

"I'll stay away, whether I want to or not."

His eyes gave him away again.

"What's the catch?"

"No catch. I just wonder whether…never mind."

She narrowed her eyes at him. "What do you wonder?"

He shrugged. "Maybe my memory is playing tricks on me but, I seem to remember that *you* were responsible for our first kiss racing into the naughty zone. If I'm going to make such a huge promise to you, I'd like some assurance that you'll be able to keep it nice and not tempt me into breaking my promise."

"That's ridiculous," she said rolling her eyes.

"Really? Prove it."

"What?"

"Prove it. Show me that we can kiss and you can resist the temptation to drag me over to the dark side."

"You're crazy. C'mon, you said you'd help me."

"One kiss. That's all I'm demanding in exchange for my promise."

"Fine." When he didn't come closer, she cocked her head in question.

"You're the one with something to prove."

"Oh." She leaned toward him and pecked him on the mouth.

He smirked. "Seriously? I can get more than that from Rolf."

Clucking her tongue, she determined to be done with his nonsense. She would give him the kiss he requested but she would prove that *he* was the one who'd taken them to the naughty zone, not her. Maybe, if she kissed him well enough, he would break his promise even *before* the date he wanted. And, in the meantime, she'd get to experience being passionately kissed one more time.

She inched to the edge of her chair, wrapped her arms around his neck and brought their mouths together. The kiss began as she'd intended—slow, tender, undemanding. But then he made a sound that let her know just how deeply he was being affected by the simple caress. That was a little surprising, but how her body reacted to that sound with a soft moan of need was even more unexpected.

His hands slid up and down her bare arms and that strange, warming sensation flushed through her body. His tongue touched her lips and she opened her mouth to him. A flicker of common sense tried to get through the wave of sensation pouring over her. It was happening again. Just like it had with him before. And again, she was anxious to find out where the building heat would take her.

She felt a surge of relief when he pulled her onto his lap and their bodies were no longer separated. Yet the need for more contact increased. Her hands craved the feel of him. *More*, she thought, without really understanding what she wanted more of. When his palm scraped up her denim-clad thigh, over her hip and stopped at her ribs, she moved his hand up over her breast. And still, it was not enough to stop the rising pressure to do something more.

Sean suddenly knew how it felt to be caught between heaven and hell. And an Angel had taken him there. Her hands were everywhere but where he wanted them to be. Her mouth was sweeter and hungrier than he remembered. Her breast filled his hand and swelled with its need for attention. He wanted to be rid of the layers of clothes and to feel her skin against his, but he didn't dare take more than she was willing to give.

Despite his challenge, he hadn't really expected her passions to take over so swiftly. He hadn't really expected to have to be the one to put on the brakes. He could only hope this would prove to her that she shouldn't deny herself the pleasures that could be found in each other's arms. For the sake of his mental and physical well-being, he hoped she'd come around to his way of thinking sooner rather than later.

"*Mom!* Hey Mom, we won!"

Christopher's exuberant voice shattered the spell in the small workroom. It took Angel a millisecond to leap from Sean's lap onto her own chair.

"Did you hear me?" Chris asked, skidding into the tiled room in his socks. His joyous smile faltered the instant he saw Sean. His expression darkened even more when he took a good look at his mother. "What's the matter? You look all sweaty. And your hair's all messed up, like you were in a fight or something."

Angel forced a smile in spite of how badly her insides were quaking. "Nothing's the matter, honey. It's just a little warm in this room. Mayor O'Grady and I have been discussing the sports complex I told you about."

"You said you couldn't come to the game because you had a big order to do." He turned and ran off before either adult could say a word.

Sean reached for Angel's hand, but she jerked it away.

"Angel, I—"

Just leave. Please."

Sean had no choice but to quietly accept her dismissal. On the way home he reviewed his strategy. Blindsiding her combined with seduction had definitely proved effective in tearing down her defenses but it was obviously going to take a lot more than hot kisses to convince her to let him into her already overcrowded life.

For his part, this second kiss was more than enough to convince him to keep up his campaign. His heart might be a bit rusty, but he still recognized all the symptoms of falling in love when they were upon him. This time, however, he wasn't going to put things off until a more convenient time.

"Got any brilliant ideas, Shamus?"

Count on The Little People, me boyo. They always show up to help when an Irish son's got himself a wee bit o' trouble.

CHAPTER 6

Shamus watched Christopher run as fast as his young legs and stockinged feet could carry him, away from the house, across the street and down the canal bank. Given time, the boy would adjust to the idea of his mother having another man in her life, but Shamus didn't have that much time. And it was very clear to Shamus that Angel would not accept Sean if her children didn't.

Luckily, the twins were ready and willing for a father figure to join their family, so Shamus felt he could concentrate on their older brother. He had tried whispering positive thoughts about Sean in Christopher's ear, but the boy was holding in too much resentment to hear him. It was quite obvious that he was going to have to pull out all the stops.

Shamus had never tried to assume corporeal form but he had seen others do it during special times, so he knew he could if the need was great enough. With his mind focused on his wish, he pictured himself as he was, before the illness robbed his health and his memory. It took much more energy than he'd expected but a few seconds later, he was standing on the canal bank behind Christopher. He blinked and two fishing rods, already baited, appeared in his hand.

As Christopher hurled a rock into the water, Shamus mentally switched to a speech pattern the boy would find familiar. "It's much easier to catch a fish with one of these." He sat down on the grass a few feet away from the boy and held one of the rods out to him.

Christopher looked sideways at the man. Never, ever talk to strangers, his mother's voice echoed in his head. And never accept a gift from someone you don't know.

He's just a lonesome old grampa who misses his own grandson and is looking for someone to talk to, another, gentler voice countered.

Chris felt a sense of complete safety flow through his body and he relaxed a little.

"I don't know how to fish," Chris admitted with a glance at the rod that said he wished he did.

"Nothing to it," Shamus said and placed the rod in the boy's hand. Remembering the day he taught Sean to fish, Shamus gave Christopher his first lesson. They sat in comfortable silence for a while until Shamus felt the boy's fears melt away.

"It must be mighty hard on you," Shamus began.

Chris glanced up at him. "What do you mean?"

"Why, being ten years old and having the whole world on your shoulders." Chris gave him a curious look and Shamus elaborated. "We old folks don't have much to do but gossip, and your mom's a pretty well-known lady. It's a real shame, you being so young and having to take care of her. And those twins seem like a real handful."

"They're not so bad. They kinda look out for each other."

"But I'll bet you still have to keep an eye on them. Your mom's probably too busy to bother."

Chris turned and glared at the older man. "That's not true. My mom's never too busy for us. She does stuff for us all the time!"

"Oh?" Shamus raised his brows. "And what do you do for her?"

"Lots of things. I help a lot. You can ask her."

"Because you're the man of the house, right?"

"Right."

"Why didn't your dad ever take you fishing?"

Chris shrugged. "He had a very important job and he was kinda tired all the time. He said he didn't have time for nonsense."

Shamus was indignant. "Nonsense? Why fishing's one of the necessities in a man's life. Keeps us healthy, you know."

Chris gawked at him. "It does?"

"Absolutely. Take my friend, Sean O'Grady. There's not a man around with more responsibility, but he always finds time to cast a line or two. I can't help but notice that face you're making son. Have you got something sour in your stomach?"

"Naw. It's your friend that gives me a stomach ache."

Shamus looked shocked. "Is that so? And here I thought he was such a good man."

"He keeps bothering my mom."

"Ah, I see. And you don't want your mom having any men around but you and your brothers, right?" Chris narrowed his eyes and Shamus let him think about that for a moment before continuing. "Tell me, who's your best friend?"

"Scott," Chris answered easily.

"Okay. What if Scott moved away? Forever. You'd probably miss him a lot at first, and there'd never be anyone else to take his place in exactly the same way. But sooner or later, you'd get lonesome or bored and want to find another friend to keep you company. Wouldn't you?"

"Maybe," Chris slowly admitted.

"Sure you would. It's the same for your mom. She needs to find a new man-friend, one to fill the empty spot your dad left." Shamus couldn't be certain he'd made his point, but at least Chris was listening. "You know, if your mom had a man-friend, you might get to enjoy his company too. Especially if he liked to fish and go camping."

"Camping?" Chris asked with wide eyes. "My dad never took us camping. He said it was a waste of time."

"He said that, did he? Why, if my friend the mayor heard that, there'd be an argument for sure."

"The mayor? You mean Mr. O'Grady likes to camp too?"

Shamus laughed as he felt the boy's interest rising. "Almost as much as he likes going to Disney World. Too bad he doesn't have a boy of his own to have such fun with." He felt his energy fading and knew he had to go. He reeled in his line and got to his feet. "It doesn't look like the fish are fooled by our bait today, so I think I'll be heading home."

When Chris tried to give him back the rod, he waved him off. "You hold onto it for now. I have a feeling you'll get lots more use out of it than I will."

"Wow, thanks," Chris said with delight.

"But in return, I want you to think about something. If I was your dad, sitting up in heaven looking down on my family, I might be wishing I had more fun with them while I had time. And I might be wanting to see my oldest boy having some fun like a boy should instead of acting like a little old man. I'd know that you hadn't forgotten me just because you were smiling once in a while. And I'd be wanting your mom to find a good man to keep her company, so she wouldn't be so lonely all the time."

"You think my mom's lonely even with all the people around her?"

"I know she is son. And if you'd open your heart to her needs, the way your dad always did, you'd know she is too." Shamus placed his hand on the top of Christopher's head and applied just a wee bit of pressure. "God bless ya, boyo. And may the luck o' the Irish be on ya."

Angel found Christopher exactly where she knew he'd be, but it surprised her to see him casting a fishing line into the canal. Her surprise increased tremendously when he looked up at her with a world-class little-boy smile. It was enough for her to forget everything she'd intended to say to him.

"Hey, Mom, look what I got. This neat old guy gave me one of his rods and showed me how to fish."

Angel was completely bewildered. Her first instinct was to question who the "old guy" was but the fact that Chris was smiling stopped her from going down that rabbit hole. In fact, if she wasn't mistaken, Chris's whole demeanor seemed to have undergone some sort of metamorphosis. If she had known a fishing rod could make this much of a difference, she would have bought one a year ago.

"Here, try it," Chris said, holding up the rod.

She sat down beside him and let him show her what to do. Fishing was one of those hobbies she never understood the allure of, but as she curled her fingers around the grip, a sense of peace came over her.

Chris seemed content to let her hold the rod for a while as he lay back on the grass and stared up at the clouds. "Have you ever gone camping?"

"No, but I'd give it a try if you wanted to. The troop's been invited to the weekend jamboree in May. We could all do that."

"But who would show us what to do?"

Angel smiled at her little worrier. "I'm sure someone would come to our aid."

"Mr. O'Grady knows about camping."

Angel was certain her ears were playing tricks on her until Chris went on.

"I been thinkin'. Dad wouldn't want you feeling lonesome forever. I don't think he'd mind if you, you know, like went to the movies or something with Mr. O'Grady."

Angel scrutinized the rod in her hand, wondering if it had some sort of magical powers. How had Christopher gone from being jealous of Sean to accepting the idea of her dating him in one hour? And why in heaven's name would he think Sean knew about camping?

She remembered suggesting a camping trip to Warren shortly before he died. She'd thought it might help him relax. Instead, the mere thought of such an adventure nearly did him in. Throughout most of their marriage, she managed to restrain her energy and youthful impulses, knowing how much more sedate he was, but occasionally it got the best of her.

There were times that she just felt like busting loose, skipping rope with the kids, racing them to the car...*going camping.*

Sean would do those things with ya.

She glanced at Chris, thinking he had spoken, but he was totally preoccupied following an ant's progress up a blade of grass. Her ears *were* playing tricks on her. It wasn't fair to compare Warren with Sean.

Had Chris really said that his dad wouldn't want her feeling lonesome forever? Where would he have come up with such an idea?

He wouldna want ya feeling guilty neither. He passed on 'cause 'twas his time, not for anything ya did or didna do.

Now Angel knew her brain had slipped off track somewhere between the house and the canal bank. Hearing her own little voice in her head wasn't unusual, but never had she heard herself thinking with an Irish accent. Despite the voice, however, she knew Warren had worked himself to death trying to provide for his young family.

Pshaw! The man worked hisself ta death 'cause he loved his work. He knew very well what he was taking on by marrying a girl half his age. And if he didna want the children he could have done something ta keep from fathering 'em!

So, what's your point, she asked the foreign voice in her head, as though it weren't her own subconscious talking to her.

Me point is this, 'tis time ta let go o' the life ya had with Warren and get yourself hitched ta Sean. Now there's a young stud who'll be able ta keep up with the four of ya!

Angel dropped the fishing rod on the ground as if it had burned her hand. She had no idea why she was arguing with herself in a man's Irish-accented voice, but to tell herself to marry Sean, who she barely knew, proved that there was something very weird happening to her brain.

Shamus scratched his whickered cheek. He'd gotten lucky when Angel accepted the rod, which allowed her to hear him, but he couldn't count on her picking it up again. With a shrug, he decided he'd done as much work on the two of them as he could at the moment. Angelina wasn't completely convinced yet, but he figured another nudge or two would do it. At least he hoped so; there were only five days left until Christmas.

After what happened between them Saturday morning, Angel assumed Sean would start badgering her to go out again, despite his promise not to. Considering Christopher's drastic change of attitude, she had even decided, if Sean asked nicely enough, she would agree to a date…at some future time, after the holidays perhaps, or maybe after the council presentation.

She had also given a lot of thought during the night to everything the weird voice in her head had suggested. Although she had never heard of such a strange thing happening during self-analysis, it seemed to have worked for her. She definitely felt better about herself when she woke up in the morning.

But Sunday flew by, then Monday, and Sean still hadn't called. Not that she had time to talk to him in the midst of Christmas preparations. She barely had time to talk to Flora Gelbert, the sweet lady from the Senior Citizens Auxiliary, who called to invite her Cub Scout troop and their parents to their Christmas party Tuesday night. When the boys heard there would be refreshments and Santa Claus would be there with a gift for every child who attended, every one of the scouts was ready to go.

By Tuesday afternoon, she accepted the fact that Sean wasn't going to call again. He had simply gotten tired of being turned down and moved on to his next quarry—probably someone younger, thinner, taller, prettier, blonder, and without children who punched him in the stomach—someone not at all like her.

The rec center was filled with people when she, Becky and their boys arrived that evening. Flora Gelbert was at the door to greet them.

"Thank you so much for inviting us," Angel said. "This is the first year you've done this, isn't it?"

"Yes, but we've already decided to make it an annual event. Sean thought it was high time the seniors and the children of Coral City do a little mixing."

"Sean?" Angel asked needlessly as Becky gave her an elbow in the ribs.

"Sean O'Grady, the mayor."

"Is…is he here tonight?" The mention of his name triggered a hot flash within her.

"Of course, dear. That's him up there."

"Don't you think he makes the most adorable Santa Claus you've ever seen?"

Angel scanned the crowd but couldn't see his sun-streaked head. Angel's mouth dropped open as her gaze lit on the jolly, fat man situated center stage in the red suit with the dressed-up little girl on his knee. *Sean was playing Santa Claus?* While she tried to absorb that, Becky took off after the boys before they could assault the refreshment table, leaving Angel to converse with Flora alone.

"Of course, our Sean's adorable no matter what he's doing. Everyone agrees that he's the best bingo caller we ever had. Never gets his numbers backward the way Charlie used to."

Angel wondered if her mind was back to playing tricks on her again. "Did you say Sean is a bingo caller?"

"Oh yes. Every Wednesday night. Why do you look so surprised, dear?"

Angel shook her head in wonderment. "I guess I just don't see him as someone who would, uh, spend his evenings like that."

"Then you don't know our Sean very well. Whenever any of us seniors needs anything, he's right there with a helping hand. Somebody even nicknamed him Saint Sean a while back. He not only organized the senior transportation corps, he was one of the original volunteer drivers." When Angel looked at her curiously, Flora explained. "A lot of the elderly in our city don't drive so when they need a ride to the grocery store or the doctor's office, all they have to do is call the transportation line in the mayor's office and a volunteer driver is sent to that person's house. It's a wonderful program."

"Yes, it certainly is." Angel was too shocked by her own ignorance to say more. "I'd better go help Becky with the boys. Thank you again for inviting us."

How could she not have known about the programs for seniors? Easy. She was always totally occupied with the programs for children. Why hadn't Sean told her about his volunteer work? Easy again. He didn't need to boast about what good deeds he did any more than she would.

How did he do it all? Mayor of the city, owner of a construction company, volunteer? He must not have any free time to—

She stopped cold as the realization hit. He wasn't much different from her, filling every minute of every day with some sort of activity. Could it possibly be that they had something in common? Could he possibly be as lonely as she? Her mind flew back to the rumor Becky had tried to tell her the day after he first came to her house. Someone he had loved had died. Could it be—

"Angel! Have you gone deaf?" Becky asked, laughing. "I want you to come take a picture on Santa's lap with me."

"Oh, no. I can't." In spite of her protests, Becky managed to drag her all the way to the stage, but that was as far as she would go. Santa's gray eyes met hers and she knew there was no way she could sit on his lap in front of all these people. Just recalling the last time she was on his lap stole her breath away.

Becky gave up on her and had a photo taken with her boys instead. After the picture was taken, Angel watched Santa draw Becky close and say something that made her laugh and give him a thumbs-up sign. But when Angel asked her about it, Becky insisted it was just a joke. No big deal.

The joke, however, was apparently on her, for when it was time to leave, Becky and all five boys had already departed.

"Will you accept a ride home in Santa's sleigh?" Sean

murmured from behind her, causing her to jump. He had gotten out of his costume but he still had a Santa-like twinkle in his eyes.

"*Hmmm*. How lucky for me that he hasn't left yet. I just happen to be stranded."

"I noticed," he said sympathetically, as if he weren't the one who conspired with Becky to put her in that position. "It's quite convenient actually, since I wanted to talk to you about the park issue."

She was relieved he gave her a legitimate reason to be pleased about having to go home with him.

As they said good night to the group of seniors on cleanup detail, she noted that everyone had a beaming smile for Sean and called him by his first name, but more important, he was able to do the same with each of them.

"I'm very impressed," she admitted once they were on their way home.

He grinned at her. "Shows you how dumb I am. Here I was trying to impress you with kisses when all I had to do was put on a Santa suit."

"And call bingo numbers every Wednesday night, and be the hero of most of the people over sixty in Coral City. They call you Saint Sean for crying out loud!"

He shrugged off her compliments. "It makes me feel good. You, of all people, should get that."

Of course she got it. She just hadn't realized he had understood *her* from the beginning. "Oh, you missed the turn," she said as he drove by her street.

"Intentionally. I want to show you something." He drove for several minutes then pulled off the road. "This is the property."

"Oh! I'd been meaning to check it out, but…well, you know how it is." She got out of the car to get a better look and he came around to her side. "I hope you didn't bring me here to convince me that this land should be kept in its natural state because, even if I have changed my mind about you, I—"

"You've changed your mind about me?"

"Well, yes, I—"

"What about going out with me?"

She sighed. "Some things happened and I think I'd like—"

His head dipped down and his mouth cut off the little speech she had prepared in her mind. If only his kisses didn't make her feel quite so good, she might have protested. But with the lightest touch of his hands on her back, he stimulated every nerve in her body and her prepared speech gave way to a more physical response.

His mouth moved softly over hers in an undemanding, yet thoroughly seductive manner. She could no more resist parting her lips for him than she could stop breathing. Her tongue caressed his as he deepened the kiss and their sighs of pleasure drifted into the sounds of the night.

Without breaking the hypnotic kiss, he repositioned their bodies so that he was leaning against the car and she was standing between his spread legs. Angel instinctively reacted to the urging of his hands sliding down her back and over her hips to move closer to his heat. When those same guiding hands covered her bottom, pressing and lifting her more intimately against him, the kiss abruptly turned hungry.

And just as abruptly, he withdrew his mouth from hers. "Do I still make you uncomfortable, Angel?"

Unable to speak, she shook her head, no.

"We're about to slip over to the naughty zone. Is that okay with you now?"

She nodded then pulled his head down so they could get back to kissing. They had kissed like this twice before but she was unprepared for the shock of what it would feel like to have his desire teasing hers. It was electric and exciting and a little scary all at once. So *this* was the feeling Becky talked about. A need so powerful, a lifetime of modesty and discretion was erased in an instant. A lack of experience meant nothing. She knew without a doubt what she wanted...and she wanted it immediately.

But when she slipped her hand between their bodies and found his belt buckle, he quickly moved his hands up her back to change his hold on her from desperate need to a comforting hug.

"Easy, love," Sean whispered. "I'm sorry. I didn't mean for this to go quite so far, at least not here or now, but I failed to take into account how easy it is for you to make me forget my good intentions."

She eased her hand away from his belt and settled it on his chest. "It's very nice of you to try to take the blame, but it's pretty obvious which one of us has a problem controlling her passionate nature." She took a slow, deep breath then turned around so her back was against his chest and his arms were beneath her breasts. "I don't suppose you'd believe that I've never...um, that what happens to me when I'm near you—"

"Hush," he murmured and hugged her more snuggly against him. "Your horrified reactions have been quite believable I assure you. And I couldn't be more flattered." With the lightest touch on her cheek, he got her to tilt her head back for a lingering, but undemanding, kiss.

"Did you really have something to tell me or did you just want to make sure I'm still unable to control myself around you?"

He chuckled and gave her another kiss. "Both. The truth is, after what happened with your son the last time, I thought it was best to stop...pushing you. When I saw you tonight though, well, there was something different in the way you looked at me. And apparently I was right."

"Like I said, some things happened and I decided going out with you would be...okay."

"Just okay?"

She smiled up at him. "Maybe a little better than okay."

"Good. Next item on the agenda. Although we are both admittedly anxious to give in to your passionate nature, I'm not going to be satisfied with a stolen hour once a week…at least not on a long-term basis. I want to be able to spend whole nights in the same bed with you. And there's only one way that's going to happen without causing gossip which would be hurtful to your boys."

"And what way is that?"

"We get married."

Angel's eyes opened wide and she swiveled around in his embrace. She blinked twice but he was still standing there, smiling at her like she was the most beautiful woman he'd ever seen. That settled it. She'd entered an alternate dimension where none of the usual rules applied.

"Of course," he continued, "I realize we need to give your boys a chance to get to know me, but that shouldn't take too long once I start my campaign to win them over. How does St. Patrick's Day sound? My grandfather, Shamus, would have liked that a lot."

"*Sean!* Stop it. I don't think this is funny."

He stopped smiling. "I'm completely serious. I doubt if there were ever two people more equally matched or more in need of a supportive partner. In case you missed it, that was political speak for I'm crazy in love with you."

His words made her insides quiver. "But…but we hardly know each other."

"We know everything that's important. Besides, getting to know the less important things about each other will help us keep our minds off what we'd rather be doing for the next, um…" He used his fingers to count. "Twelve weeks."

There were a lot of words swimming around in her head and she opened and closed her mouth several times, but none of them came out.

He tipped her chin up with his finger then kissed her nose. "I can see I've caught you unprepared again, so I won't insist on your affirmative vote tonight. Instead, I'll tell you my news. Before the party tonight, the president of the Senior Auxiliary told me their group had an emergency meeting about the disposition of this piece of property."

Angel's mouth turned down in anticipation of what he had to say.

"It's not what you think. They're excited about the idea of a sports complex. It turns out there are quite a number of seniors who would like to play softball and a lot of others who would like to get involved on a volunteer basis to be umpires, referees, even concession operators. They wanted me to know they're in favor of the idea and would support a bond issue to pay for it if we put it on the upcoming ballot."

Angel was so surprised, it took a few seconds for it to sink in, and when it did, she gave him an exuberant hug. "That's wonderful! I can hardly wait to tell everyone."

She started to move out of his arms, but he held her still. "I know exactly how you feel, and it would be my pleasure to help you spread the news. However, I would like another kiss before I take you home. That is, if you can promise not to drag me over to the dark side with you again."

Angel gasped, but his smile and the silver glints in his eyes let her know he was teasing. She shook her head and sighed. "Has it occurred to you that there's something very strange about how we came together?"

Sean gave her a squeeze. "I heard Angels can wish for anything they want at Christmastime, and they can't be turned down."

"So you think I wished for you?"

"Who else?"

Who else? Shamus repeated as he watched his grandson and future granddaughter-in-law kiss. *Who else, indeed.*

THE
PERFECT GIFT

Christmas Presents Series
Novella Two

MARILYN CAMPBELL

CHAPTER 1

Full-time handyman needed urgently. Room, meals, allowance included. Retired gentleman only.

Leanne Shepard's urgent need seemed to have been granted in the form of the man who had just entered her office. After two weeks of interviewing unsuitable prospects—most of whom were neither elderly nor gentlemen—this applicant was almost too good to be true.

Frazzled, shoulder-length gray hair stuck out from beneath a battered, wide-brimmed straw hat. A bushy gray beard covered the lower half of his face and dark sunglasses shielded his eyes, leaving exposed only a very tan nose and two slashes of cheekbone. A wooden toothpick jutted out from the beard, about where his mouth would be.

He wore a loose, short-sleeved shirt patterned with parrots and jungle flowers faded from too much sun or too many washings, and his threadbare jeans looked a size too large. Old, leather sandals completed the Ernest Hemingway look-alike image.

Actually, if the hair and beard had been white and the toothpick were a pipe, he might have passed for a Key West Santa Claus. Considering her Christmas Eve deadline, that seemed to make him the perfect man for the job. The only thing left was to find out if he had the skills for it.

"Zachariah Gibbon?" she asked, mentally crossing her fingers that he was the one who had called that morning.

"Yup."

She held out her hand to him but withdrew it when he made no move to take it. Perhaps he was one of those old-fashioned men who didn't approve of shaking hands with women. "I'm Leanne Shepard. As you can see, I'm not quite settled in yet," she explained, with a wave of her hand at the stacks of storage boxes crammed inside the small, street-front office. "Please have a seat." She motioned toward the metal folding chair she had brought in from home, then perched herself on the corner of the desk.

As Mr. Gibbon stepped closer, it occurred to her that he had probably been quite tall in his youth. Even with his back hunched from age, he was still a head taller than her own five feet five inches.

He shuffled forward slowly and, with a muffled groan, settled his large frame on the small chair. "Might's well get one thing straight right off. No one calls me Mr. Gibbon. Zachariah'll do just fine." His speech was grated out through jaws clenched around the toothpick.

She couldn't help but wonder if he was as unfriendly as he seemed. Since he would be living in her home, she preferred an arm's length relationship, but he would need to be able to accept her supervision. "Excuse me, Mr.–er, Zachariah, but would you please take off your sunglasses? It's difficult for me to judge someone when I can't see his face."

The toothpick bobbed up and down rapidly within its

coarse, gray nest. "Rather not. They're prescription. I'm a mite nearsighted, an' I lost my regular pair."

"Just for a moment then. And I'll come closer if it really makes you uncomfortable." He still didn't comply. She was about to force the issue when she came to her senses. It wouldn't do to antagonize the only decent applicant she had had. "Never mind. It's not that important. Where are you from, Zachariah?"

"Born in Tennessee. Lived there all my life, 'cept when Uncle Sam needed me, of course. But the last few winters have been mighty hard in them mountains. Got me hankerin' for some warmer weather."

Leanne smiled. "Well, there aren't many places warmer in the winter than the Florida Keys. I must say, you remind me a little of my Grandpa. He was a Conch...lived all his life right here in Key West. He passed away two months ago, at the end of September, and left me his house." She let out a soft sigh as a loving memory came to mind.

"You can't imagine how many people advised me to sell it. Oh, I know that would be the logical thing to do, but I decided against it. Not only because he loved that house, but after what I've been through the last—" She stopped before the bad memories had a chance to resurface. "At any rate, are you...in good health, Zachariah?"

"Fit as a fiddle, accordin' to the doc at the VA. Not quite as fast as I used to be, an' I don't last quite as long, an' like I said, the eyes ain't so good, but everythin' still works well enough."

Had he been a younger man, she might have assumed his comment was suggestive, but there was nothing about his tone of voice to make her suspicious. "That's good to hear. I'm afraid the house is in pretty bad shape, and it does have two stories, three if you count the attic. When you called this morning, you mentioned that you did construction work before you retired. How are you with plumbing? Nothing works in the bathroom upstairs."

"No problem."

She let out the breath she'd been holding. "Electrical wiring? I can't tell you what's wrong, but most of the outlets are dead."

He nodded and gave her a thumbs-up sign.

"Wonderful. Once those two necessities are taken care of, there are a lot of less urgent things like replacing rotten wood, refinishing cabinets and sanding floors. You know, general renovation work. Oh, and the yard needs a good clean-up and some landscaping. Will that be all right?"

"Yup."

Again, she exhaled with relief. "Excellent. As I mentioned in my ad, you would live in the house. The job pays a weekly allowance besides room and board."

"That'll do just fine. Don't need much more than a roof over my head, food in my gut, gas in my truck an' somethin' to keep my hands busy. Just so's you're not tryin' to adopt a granddaddy like some do-gooder."

Although that thought had crossed her mind, she rolled her eyes and shook her head no. "There's just one small complication. In order for me to keep feeding both of us, I need to get my business off the ground and I think I've come up with the ultimate promotional plan. Every Christmas Eve, until Grandma became too ill, the Shepards hosted a holiday event, featuring her famous candy cane cookies and infamous egg nog punch. There was music and carolers and games. Every resident on the island was invited to drop by…and most of them did, even if it was just a quick stop on the way to or from another party or obligation. I think it would be a terrific way for me to reintroduce myself to the community, not as a visiting relative, but as a permanent resident."

He scratched the back of his neck for several seconds

then said, "That's twenty-seven days from today."

She made a face. "I know. But I'm not suggesting *everything* be completed by then…just enough to make some sort of outdoor gathering possible." Since that idea had just occurred, her thoughts took a detour. "Maybe I could rent a portable toilet or two and some picnic tables. But I would still need electricity to be able to string up lights…and hope it didn't rain." She forced her mind back to the immediate need—a handyman to help with everything. "And I'll pay you extra to work on weekends until then."

When he remained quiet, she added, "And I can help with some things, like cleaning and painting and peeling off wallpaper. It's not like I have enough business to require my being in the office all day every day. So? What do you think?"

"Wouldn't like havin' a filly underfoot while I work. Anyways, I won't have an opinion on how long the work will take until I see the house, but I'm willin' to give it a try."

"Wonderful. Do you have any questions…about anything?"

"Yup. Where would I get hold of you when you're not here in the office?"

"Oh, I'm sorry. I thought you understood. I'll be living in the house while the work is taking place."

His nose twitched as though he smelled something foul. "Don't sound like that house is fit for a little slip o' gal like yourself."

She gave him a crooked smile. "I have no choice. My…financial situation is a bit…well, let's just say I have to keep my expenses down at the moment."

"Gotta have my privacy," he added quickly.

"It's a big house and I promise to respect your privacy."

"An' one other thing," he continued. "I ain't about to do none of your cookin' or cleanin' or washin' your unmentionables, like one of them newfangled houseboys. I lived this long without ever waitin' on some filly. Ain't gonna start now."

Leanne stifled the giggle that threatened to burst forth. He was going so far out of his way to prove what a gruff old grizzly he was, she would bet he was probably the exact opposite—a cuddly teddy bear, just like Grandpa had been. "You don't need to worry about any of that, Zachariah. I'll tend to the cooking and laundry for both of us. As to cleaning, well when you see the house, you'll understand why housekeeping is the least of my concerns. I assure you, I need a husband...not a wife."

The toothpick flew out of his mouth on a puff of breath and landed in her lap. "*Husband?* Your ad ain't said nothin' about gettin' hitched!"

"Oh dear, no," she said quickly, no longer able to hold back the giggle as she brushed the toothpick off her jeans. "I only meant that I need someone to do the chores that *used* to be considered a husband's work. Really. It was just a joke...and obviously not a very good one. Okay?"

He dug a fresh toothpick out of his shirt pocket and stuck it in his mouth. "Okay. When can I start?"

"Would this afternoon be too soon?"

"Nope. Got everythin' I need in my pickup outside. Just gimme the address, an' I'll find it."

As she wrote out the directions for him, she said, "I'm determined to make some progress here today, but I should be home in a couple hours. That should give you some time to look around and make your own assessments of the job." Having no doubt she could trust him completely, she handed him a key. "That's for the back door. I don't have one for the front. Can I expect you for dinner?"

Zachariah nodded once and, uttering a groan, he slowly rose from the flimsy chair. At the door, he stopped and took another look around the crowded room. "What is it you're gonna be doin' here?"

She stood and straightened her shoulders proudly. "I'm a financial advisor slash investment counselor slash insurance agent." She heard him inhale sharply and his body seemed to go rigid for a moment. "Zachariah? Are you all right?" She reached out to touch his forearm but he jerked away.

"I'm fine. See you in a couple hours."

Ellwood Zachariah Gibbon Rush—better known as Zach to his immediate family and E.Z. to everyone else—forced himself to continue the old man charade as he headed around to the back of the building where he'd parked his truck.

Of all the damn luck! When he saw the ad in the newspaper, it had seemed like the perfect solution to his most urgent need: a safe place to hide for a while that wouldn't cost him anything. Having to disguise his appearance to get the live-in job made it even more desirable. Even if his employer/landlady was shown a photo of E.Z. Rush, she would honestly deny seeing him in Key West.

He should have realized it was too good to be true. Nothing in his life had gone right lately. Why would this?

The first problem was the fact that his new employer would be living under the same roof with him. Her amicable personality pretty much guaranteed he'd have a hard time avoiding her completely, which meant he would have to maintain the uncomfortable disguise most of the time.

It was already quite clear that he would never be able to tolerate the tropical heat with the extra padding he had donned to conceal his well-toned physique. In New York City, Thanksgiving marked the psychological beginning of winter, with or without snow. In Key West, it was just another day of eighty degrees in the shade. As soon as he was back in his truck he quickly undressed and redressed without the sheet wrapped around his mid-section or the larger, second pair of jeans. He hoped she hadn't paid much attention to his body shape in the short time they had spoken.

He congratulated himself for coming up with a reasonable excuse for wearing sunglasses indoors, but how could he explain the hat? Since the beard was only held on by elastic strings around his ears and the gray hair was attached to the hat, he would have to spend some of the little money he had left for a realistic gray wig.

As he drove along the limited network of streets, he witnessed another major difference between New York and Key West following the Thanksgiving weekend. Christmas lights here were strung on palm trees. The holiday displays in store windows had Santas wearing shorts and flowered shirts, balancing on surf boards. Private yard decorations were similarly altered to fit in with the climate. In front of one house Zach saw a sleigh full of packages being pulled by pink flamingos. There was no question Christmas was celebrated on the island; they just did it with a tropical flair. Since he had just agreed to help get the Shepard house ready for a major Christmas Eve party, he wondered what sort of decorations he would find in the attic she'd mentioned.

Somewhat countering his string of bad luck, he'd barely explored half the island when he saw a costume store with a large "Close-Out Sale" sign in the window. Not only did they have a suitable gray wig long enough to be tied back at the nape, the clerk threw in the matching beard for free.

He felt a little better about his disguise but had to admit that was only one reason to keep his distance from Leanne Shepard. He had done his best not to notice how her breasts stretched the thin fabric of her t-shirt with every breath she took. She had only turned her back on him for an instant before she sat down but he couldn't help but see how nicely she filled out her jeans.

Why did she have to be so appealing? It wouldn't be a problem for him if she were married. He had never been tempted by a woman committed to another. But she wasn't wearing a ring and it sounded as though she were living alone in the house.

Whenever the question of his own bachelorhood arose, Zach always gave the same answer. He was still unmarried at the age of thirty-six because his *perfect woman* had yet to appear. When prodded, he would run down the list of that woman's perfect attributes.

At the top was the requirement that she should have a professional career, even better if it were compatible with his own. She should be around his age, wise as well as intelligent. Independent but socially comfortable, compassionate and considerate of others. Physically, his attraction was roused by a lush figure on medium height, shoulder-length, wheat-colored hair and blue eyes. Her lips would be full and rosy enough not to need additional color and—

Zach shook his head to banish the image. In all the years since he'd first noticed that girls were different from boys, he had never found anyone who had come close to being his *perfect woman*...until thirty minutes ago. Leanne Shepard could have been engineered out of his imagination. Only her eye color was wrong.

Correction. Not wrong, just different. Now that he had seen his perfect woman with brown eyes, he decided to change that item on his list.

How could he possibly sleep under the same roof with her, night after night, and only think of her as his employer? He shoved that question aside even quicker than the first. There were more serious problems to consider, the lesser of which was the exaggeration about his construction skills.

During college he had done a summer stint with Habitat for Humanity, during which he'd learned the basics of carpentry and roofing. He also knew how to fill little holes with white paste and paint over graffiti. And once he'd changed a door knob by watching a do-it-yourself video on his laptop. Basically, he'd always been an apartment-dweller. If something went wrong with plumbing or electrical fixtures, he called the building super and it eventually got taken care of while he was at work. And the closest thing to a yard in his experience was Central Park.

Yet, he had implied that renovating an old house would be "no problem".

He reminded himself that he was a fast learner. Hadn't he mastered the complexities of both the commodities and stock markets before graduating high school? The one instructional video he'd seen assured him he'd have no trouble finding a lesson about whatever he needed to do...if he had a computer, which he didn't. He didn't even know if his new hiding place had wi-fi.

It occurred to him that there must be books containing the information he needed. The third person he asked directed him to a place that sold books and magazines, but its inventory was mainly geared to tourists and beach reading. That clerk suggested he try the hardware store on Duval Street.

Entering BC Hardware was a bit like stepping onto an old, small-town movie set for Zach. To his knowledge, this sort of small, poorly lit store, with its narrow aisles and floor-to-ceiling overloaded shelves had been replaced by corporate megastores long ago. A sole proprietorship simply couldn't compete with their inventory or efficiency. He doubted that this store even had a website.

"Can I help you?"

Zach turned toward the friendly male voice. Two elderly men sat behind the cluttered counter, apparently in the middle of a game of chess. They fit in the setting as neatly as a Norman Rockwell painting.

The man with the deeper tan and least hair grinned and spoke again. "Was there something you were looking for?"

Since Zach was not inclined to spend more than a few minutes inhaling the accumulated dust and mildew that was already tickling his sinuses, he replied, "Have you got a book on home repairs?"

The man shrugged. "Not much call for them anymore. Everything's on YouTube now. But I happen to have one you could look at." He leaned down behind the counter and brought up a thick, hard-cover book. With a quick puff, he blew some of the dust off the front cover. "This one's a basic how-to for homeowners, with a little info on a lot of things. Somebody ordered it a few years back to teach himself how to build a gazebo. Never came back to pick it up. Probably ended up putting in a pool instead."

Zach sneezed three times before he could speak. His allergies demanded he get out of the store immediately. "How much?"

The man's eyebrows raised slightly, "Well, seeing how I've had it awhile and no one else has shown interest…how about five dollars?"

That was a quarter of all the money Zach had left, but it was a necessary investment in his new career. And, after all, he should start getting an allowance in a week.

As the man took Zach's cash, he asked, "What sort of project are you planning?"

Zach sneezed again and picked up the book. "A lot of different repairs…on an old house." He started for the door but the man stopped him with another question.

"On the island?"

Zach was about to lie, but he realized the repairs would probably require his returning to the store for supplies. "Yup." Another triple sneeze kept him from having to say more.

"Two thousand milligrams of vitamin C, lysine capsules morning and night and zinc lozenges. No cold stands a chance against that combo."

Zach waved at him and hurried out the door before the man could make another attempt to involve him in a conversation. Besides acquiring the book he needed, the encounter made him aware that Key West might actually be like a small town where every resident knows every other resident's business. If so, he had one more thing to worry about.

In less than an hour, Zach had familiarized himself with the entire island—its streets, stores, restaurants and sandy beaches. He found the sign that marked the southernmost tip of the continental United States as well as the homes of both Ernest "Papa" Hemingway and John James Audubon. Perhaps, if he stayed long enough to have a little spend money, he'd be able to check out some of the bars that all claimed to be Papa's favorite hangout.

He also observed the eclectic nature of the inhabitants and tourists. Key West could certainly compete with Manhattan in that department. Wandering in and out of a few shops gave him an ideal way to eavesdrop on conversations and listen to answers to tourists' questions about the island, without bringing attention to himself or spending any more money.

The whole time, he tried to avoid thinking about the primary reason he should forget this whole crazy idea...and why he couldn't.

After three months on the run, zig-zagging west, east and southward from New York, keeping one jump ahead of his pursuer—or pursuers, he was never sure about that—he had finally managed to lose them in Louisiana, but he kept moving just in case.

In northern Florida, while perusing a discarded Miami Herald newspaper, he came across the handyman ad. It had felt as though he was being handed an early Christmas gift. He found someone willing to exchange the keys to an old pickup truck, with a temporary license plate, for a ridiculous amount of cash, did a quick paint change on it and headed for Key West.

The situation was exactly what he needed...and it would have been perfect...if Leanne Shepard were a doctor or a beautician or anything besides an investment counselor. He would have enjoyed the irony...if this had happened to someone else. Even at the southernmost point, she would have read about E.Z. Rush's fall from grace, arrest and subsequent vanishing act. She probably saw photos of him.

Like most of the industry, she would have already found him guilty.

And yet there didn't seem to be any alternatives left. Exhausted and out of money, he needed to stop running and come up with a plan to disappear permanently.

If it hadn't been for Dolores insisting he accept a "loan" from her before he'd fled, he wouldn't have lasted as long as he had. Luckily for him, she believed in keeping a supply of cash hidden away for the day solar flares knocked out all technology on the planet. He had always teased her about her paranoia but he now realized how much better his life would be right now if he had prepared for a cataclysm of any sort.

Her last words to him were that she knew he was innocent, that she had a friend who could help her prove it and that he simply had to keep himself safe. That thought had kept him going the first month, but after three, he just wanted to stop running.

Never having been a fugitive, he had relied on strategies he'd gleaned from television and movies to keep himself "off the grid". He made a few mistakes at first, like using a library computer within range of a security camera, which was how someone had tracked his whereabouts. After that, he got warier, avoided places he'd been before, used disguises and hitched a lot of rides. When he absolutely needed a room for a night, he chose a place where no questions were asked.

Despite the risks, hiding in a stranger's house disguised as an old handyman looked like his best option to be fed, sleep indoors and accumulate a bit of cash before taking off again.

He had always had considerable talent when it came to dealing with the opposite sex. Surely he could deceive one woman for a few weeks.

CHAPTER 2

Zach drove into the potholed driveway of the address Leanne had given him and simply stared in amazement. The monstrous house could have come right out of a horror flick.

The yard was overgrown with weeds and littered with trash and dried brown palm fronds. Ancient fruit trees drooped from the weight of broken, moss-covered limbs. One guide wire—which he had just learned was used to anchor the wooden house during a violent storm—remained attached to both the roof and the ground, while two others swayed in the breeze. Zach seriously doubted the house would survive a heavy rain shower, let alone a hurricane, in its current condition. Fortunately, he had also just learned that hurricane season was pretty much over by then.

Warped wooden slats curled away from the main structure, shutters hung by splinters, several posts of the wooden railing around the front porch were missing and one complete length of that railing lay in the yard. The second-floor balcony and the widow's walk on the rooftop appeared to be in the same precarious state. Noting that pieces of wood covered the dormer windows in the attic, he easily imagined bats taking up residence in there.

Despite the deterioration, however, Zach couldn't help but notice the architecture. A half-century ago, this was undoubtedly a very stately home. Now, it would probably take an army of workers and a vault full of money to restore it to a livable condition—neither of which seemed to be readily available to its current owner based on her search for a live-in Zach-of-all-trades.

He glanced at the big book on the floor of the truck and realized a book of magic spells might have been a better purchase. His new employer was clearly hoping he could perform some magic for her...and in record time too. The question flitted through his mind as to whether he would stay through Christmas to help Leanne if the real perpetrators of his crime were discovered and his innocence was proven. There was something compelling about helping to restore the old house to its former glory. There was something equally compelling about Leanne Shepard.

He quickly cut off that precarious train of thought as a very small silver car pulled up beside him. There was no time to brood, too late to change his mind. His new boss had arrived.

As she got out of her car, thoughts of money and home repairs took a back seat to the realization that his imagination and months of celibacy hadn't distorted his first impression of her. Leanne Shepard was the embodiment of his *perfect woman*.

Like a condemned man on his way to the gas chamber, Zach stuck the book in his duffle bag and stepped out of the truck.

"Hi!" She gave him a bright smile that lit up her eyes.

"Didn't the key work?"

"Ain't tried it yet. Just got here." He thought her smile faded a bit with his answer.

"Oh. Well, then we'll go through the house together." As they walked to the back of the house, she confessed, "I wish I could say it's not as bad as it looks but I don't lie well."

"Have you thought of levelin' it an' startin' over?"

"Them's fightin' words, mister," she replied in a deep voice, then chuckled. "I have always loved this house. Grandpa left it to me with a note that gave me permission to demolish it, but I know his real wish was that I would bring back its dignity. Unfortunately, he was only able to leave me enough money to get her part of the way, which is why I had to come up with a cost-efficient plan of attack. Watch your step."

Zach noted the broken wood on the second step up to the rear porch and followed her example of skipping it. As she unlocked and opened the door, he noticed how loose both hinges were. A lock would hardly be a challenge to someone who really wanted to get into this house. But who would want to?

"Welcome to the Shepard mausoleum," she said waving him into a narrow room that stretched the width of the house and barely had a foot-wide walking path between all the boxes and miscellaneous household items from one side to the other.

Three small windows near the roof line might have let sunlight in…if the layers of grime and cobwebs were removed. Rather than an entry foyer, this space seemed to be a combination storage area and laundry room.

"The washer and dryer are operational and the washtub really comes in handy, especially for gardening. Unfortunately, I can't say the same for the shower stall in the corner. It used to be great for rinsing off the sand and salt after a day at the beach but I haven't been able to get it to work."

Zach made a mental note about the shower and followed Leanne through another door. He had heard that love could blur one's vision, but this was ridiculous. His gaze traveled over the kitchen's yellowed wallpaper, cracked paint on the old wooden cabinets and the fifties-style table and chairs. Pieces of silver tape covered rips in the plastic upholstered seats.

Leanne, in her fitted designer jeans and snug t-shirt, did not belong in this setting. She belonged in a sleek, contemporary environment...like his penthouse apartment in Manhattan. He gave himself a mental kick. That was exactly the kind of thought he had to abort before it took hold and had him forgetting the role he was playing. He fixed his gaze on a stainless steel oven and side-by-side refrigerator that were obviously newer than the rest of the room.

"Those, and the washer and dryer in the utility room, were my first purchases when I moved in. Someone down the road was moving north and offered them all to me for a few hundred dollars. They may not be brand new, but they work. Too bad I can't replace everything as easily."

"What about one of them historical groups?" Zach asked, mainly to keep his mind on impersonal topics. "I seen some old houses today with signs in the yards. They was fixed up real nice."

Leanne smiled. "I know. But this house doesn't qualify. It's a lot younger than Key West's oldest houses and no one famous ever resided within these walls...not even for an overnight stay. Plus, it's had so many alterations and additions that it's too much of a mutant for the Historical Society to be interested in preserving it. Why don't you leave your bag and hat here while I give you the fifty-cent tour?"

Zach nodded, carefully took off his hat and set down the duffle bag.

She gave his hair an odd look but made no comment.

"Okay. I'll start with the positive side. An inspection confirmed that the foundation and main structure are solid and the roof was replaced about eight years ago. Any water stains you see are more than likely old.

"Also, most of the doors and windows open and close to some degree, and there are screens, which is very important since the air conditioning isn't working...something connected with the electrical problems I think. Luckily, the stove runs on propane and the refrigerator is hooked into a generator, so they're okay to use."

Zach followed her lead, nodding when it seemed appropriate, as she pointed out what was wrong in each room, which ceiling fans were safe to turn on, which outlets had power and which plumbing fixtures functioned...or didn't.

The house was much larger inside than it had appeared on the outside. From the front foyer, a stairway led upstairs to three rooms, including Leanne's bedroom, and a large, but completely useless, bathroom.

"All the floors are hardwood planking," Leanne told him proudly. "I'd like all these musty old carpets hauled away and the floors brought back to their original condition. And one day soon, I intend to sort through the mish-mosh of furniture and get rid of anything not worth refinishing. And *all* the clutter has got to go."

Grimacing, she picked up a starched doily and a dusty little vase. "I never understood why Grandma felt it was necessary to have so much *stuff*."

"Growing up in poverty might do it," Zach murmured absently as he fingered the silky tassels on a lampshade. "Living through The Depression affected an entire generation."

Leanne stopped in her tracks and stared at him. "Would you mind repeating that?"

The bewildered expression on her face clued Zach into the fact that he'd accidentally slipped into his true speech pattern. He let out what he hoped was a hearty laugh. "You liked that, huh? Heard it on one of them talk shows an' thought it sounded so smart, I kinda memoried it the way the feller said it." She seemed to accept that, but the close call reminded him of his decision to spend as little time with her as possible...no matter how strongly his body kept trying to lean toward hers.

He was in complete accord with her directive to dispose of the musty carpets and dust collectors. The allergy pill he had taken after leaving the hardware store was still working but he knew he'd have to take another before going to bed. At this rate, though, he was going to have to spend the rest of his cash on antihistamines.

To the right of the front foyer downstairs was an archway into a large living room where another archway framed a formal dining room. A short hallway to the left of the entryway led to the room where Zach would be staying, a room being used for more storage and the only bathroom with a working shower and toilet. Unfortunately, the toilet only flushed after filling the tank with water from the shower and lifting the mechanism inside by hand.

At the end of the long hallway directly ahead of the front door was the kitchen, which had a Dutch-door/pass-through to the dining room. The utility room, where they had entered, was aligned beyond the kitchen. The garage was a separate structure next to the house and, rather than a place for automobiles, it was crammed with lumber, hardware and tools.

"Grandpa was always buying supplies to renovate the house, but he lost interest in keeping the place up after Grandma passed away last year. I think he had gotten into such a habit of taking care of things only after she complained about it that, without her, he didn't know what to do first. So he decided to take a trip around the world and forget all about the house."

She took a deep, chest-rising breath that made Zach more uncomfortable than he already was. He tried to put more space between them but only succeeded in knocking over a pile of lumber. At least restacking it gave him something acceptable to do with his hands.

"He invited me to join him," she continued, "but I was too busy with...my own life. He played tourist for nearly four months, sent me postcards from all the places he stopped and always wrote, 'Wish you were here little one.' He had a fatal heart attack in New Zealand. Not a day goes by that I don't wish I had gone with him."

She sounded so close to tears, Zach wanted to take her in his arms and hold her until the grief flowed away. Instead, he said, "I'm bettin' he understood your reasons, whatever they were. I'm also bettin' he's mighty happy with your wantin' to fix up the house. Maybe he's even anxious to see what you do with the old girl."

She blinked the dampness from her eyes. "Why, Zachariah, that might be exactly what I needed to hear. It sounds like you have personal experience with losing someone you love."

Not some *one*, he thought, some *thing*. He'd lost his entire life. Zach had a split-second of weakness during which he wanted to tell her exactly why he understood regret over making the wrong choice. He truly wanted to bear his soul to her and discover what it would be like to be comforted by her...but he quickly came to his senses. "Not like that. I just been around long enough to know that regret never makes anythin' better."

His response seemed to give her an idea. "First thing tomorrow morning, I'll take you to meet Billy Chesterfield. He was Grandpa's best friend. As long as you're staying here, you should have someone to hang out with. He has a boat, by the way, in case you like to fish."

Zach shrugged indifferently, but inside he felt an

attack of anxiety. It was one thing to deceive her, but he wasn't sure he could fool one of her grandfather's cronies. "Um, if you're done showin' me around for now, I'd kinda like to get settled in and maybe take a shower before dinner."

Leanne flushed slightly. "Of course. I should have realized—I only meant to give you a quick tour and I got carried away...which you'll discover is not uncommon for me. You go on. I'll have dinner ready in about a half hour. I hope you like spaghetti and meatballs."

"Anythin' you fix'll do fine," he said as he shuffled away.

Leanne had considered barbecuing a steak but she wasn't sure if Zachariah had any teeth. Though their relationship had progressed since their meeting in her office, she didn't think they were up to discussing something as personal as his ability to chew meat.

She knew salad was in the iffy category but figured if she cut everything into small pieces, he might manage it. On her way home, she had picked up a loaf of Italian bread and a bottle of Chianti. Altogether, she felt she had planned a decent first meal for her new housemate.

As she prepared the food and set the table, she tried to review what she had told him so far to see if there was any repair item she had failed to mention. Instead, it was the little odd things about him personally that kept popping up in her mind.

His insistence on wearing sunglasses indoors was peculiar, but she supposed his eyesight really could be so bad that dark lenses were better than none at all. At least he had shed some of the gruffness he had displayed earlier.

It had to be her imagination but he also seemed to have shed weight. For some reason, she thought he had a stockier build when she first saw him. And her recollection of his hair was that it was extremely unkempt and scraggly rather than neat and well-conditioned as it now looked. Of course, it was now brushed back into a short tail at the base of his neck but still...And hadn't his beard looked like a wild mass of gray cotton earlier? How had he tamed *that* into such submission?

What kept replaying in her head the loudest, however, were the two phrases he had mumbled about poverty and The Depression. She had definitely *not* imagined the change in his voice or his dialect. Even his explanation of the change seemed odd.

On the other hand, both her intuition and her intellect told her she had nothing to worry about. If either of those reliable senses had sent up a red flag, she would never have hired him to work on her home, let alone live in it with her. There wasn't a doubt in her mind; Zachariah Gibbon was her gift for surviving the last three, impossibly difficult, months.

Grandpa's death had been totally unexpected, but the fact that she hadn't seen him in almost a year made the grief nearly unbearable. It was no surprise, though, that she had inherited the old homestead. After spending so many happy childhood summers there, she was the only one in the family who felt the same way Grandpa did about it. She would never sell it out of the family.

She had always imagined using it as a weekend retreat with her husband and children, perhaps even retiring there in their later years. The destruction of that pleasant fantasy had disintegrated three weeks before Grandpa's funeral. It was one of the few times in her life when she'd gone against an intuitive feeling that something wasn't quite right.

That sense had her checking and double-checking the information she'd received, but everything appeared to be in order. Unfortunately, she and many other brokers had been taken in by a very expertly executed—but completely fraudulent—investment prospectus. Because of her endorsement, a number of important clients had lost a great deal of money. The firm's partners didn't blame her; they simply asked for her resignation, *immediately.*

Because of a sleazy con-artist named E.Z. Rush, she'd lost her position at the high-end brokerage firm in Palm Beach where she had worked for six years. If only she could get her hands on that man for five minutes, she'd...well, she had never actually decided what she would do to him, except that it would be painful.

Two of those important clients were her fiancé, Eric Lazarus, and his father. The senior Lazarus had threatened to sue her personally. Eric had declared that "her reputation was permanently blackened among his circle of acquaintances"—several of whom had often trusted her investment advice with profitable results—and bluntly requested the return of his engagement ring.

She was actually quite proud of how she'd handled her response. She hadn't cried or begged for understanding. She had simply taken the three-carat diamond solitaire ring out to the stables on his estate and planted it in a pile of steaming manure freshly provided by his favorite polo pony.

It didn't matter to any of them that she had also invested and lost a sizable portion of her own savings in the phony company.

In less than a month, she had lost her dear grandfather, her husband-to-be and her job. Refusing to give in to despair, Leanne had made a sweeping decision. Her career goal had always been to set up her own brokerage firm but Palm Beach was no longer a viable location. Key West, another magnet for both old and new money, would do just as well. She had put her townhouse up for sale, packed her belongings and headed south to claim her inheritance. The realtor had warned her that, even with a low asking price, the townhouse could take months to sell, but Leanne figured she had enough money to get by for a year, so she refused to worry about that particular *what-if.*

The first problem with her new life plan was the disastrous condition of the house. It seemed hard to believe that it could have deteriorated so badly since she had last seen it, but, it was quite possible that her memories of the place were clouded by the happy times. And as Grandpa's friend Billy quickly reminded her, it takes constant attention to maintain a house in the tropics, and no one had paid attention to the aging house in quite a while. He had offered his assistance but, since he wouldn't accept payment from her, she declined his help. She was determined not to impose on his kindness except as a last resort.

Within a few days she'd discovered how limited Key West's labor force was. The few local contractors who showed up to inspect the property had demanded what she considered ransom-level prices for their services. When she heard that some developers imported their labor from Miami, she tried doing the same, but no one was willing to travel so far for such a "small job".

When she'd told Billy about her idea to hire a retired gentleman like Grandpa, it had been his suggestion to offer less pay in exchange for room and board. Of course, he also suggested he interview the man before she made any final decision.

On the positive side, a surprising number of men had answered her ad. The downside was that every applicant had made a red flag of warning pop up. Some were objectionable because of their youth or obvious bad habits, others just gave her a negative feeling, but her inner feelings about people were usually accurate, so she followed them.

If only she could have met the evil E.Z. Rush in person, instead of through emails and phone calls, she probably would have saved herself a lot of misery. She had no doubt that her intuition would have picked up on his dishonest nature and she would have heeded the worrisome niggle in her mind.

Although she had promised Billy not to hire anyone until he gave his approval, Zachariah was simply too perfect to take the chance of losing him. Besides, he reminded her so much of Grandpa, she was certain Billy would like him too.

To Leanne's disappointment, Zachariah reverted to one-word responses over dinner. No matter what subject she introduced, she could not engage him in conversation. She suspected part of the problem was the difficulty he was having with the spaghetti. With each mouthful he seemed to take in a few hairs of his beard while most of the sauce stayed outside.

As soon as he cleaned his plate, he excused himself and left the house to take a walk.

Zach sat on the beach, watching the ocean ebb and flow until the sun slipped completely below the horizon. When the stars began to appear and he was sure he was alone, he stripped down to his boxer shorts and ran into the warm water. Having noted the abundance of jagged coral rock formations that were known to shelter a variety of fish, including barracuda, he didn't venture far from the shore.

That was okay. All that mattered was, for the moment, he was free of the irritating disguise, free to stretch, free to be himself.

Free. He would never again take freedom lightly. Gazing up at the clear night sky and feeling the waves gently lap against his body, he decided that, if his fate was to get caught and put in prison, at least his last days of freedom would be in paradise. The only thing that could improve his circumstances would be if Leanne were willing to share this time with him...the *real* him, that is.

His imagination immediately ran with that thought,

conjuring her up in the water with him. She was wearing a modest, one-piece bathing suit—He hit his mental delete button. If he was going to have a fantasy, he could do better than that.

Like a mermaid, she emerged from the water a few feet in front of him, wet and sleek and incredibly beautiful. She wore a string bikini that barely covered her nipples and the triangle between her legs.

She smiled seductively. "I hope I didn't keep you waiting too long."

The sight of her rendered him speechless. He shook his head.

"I saw how you were looking at me earlier." She ran her hands up her thighs, over her stomach, and cupped her full breasts. "Is this what you were imagining?"

"Not quite," he answered hoarsely, and drifted toward her. Taking her hands in his, he placed them behind her back. She kept them there as he untied the two strings that held the top scraps of material in place. "This is what I was imagining." He peeled away the skimpy top and let it float away on a gentle wave. His hands moved to—

Something real nibbled at his calf, startling him enough to shatter the vision in his mind. It was just as well. Playing with that sort of fantasy was only going to make it harder to fall asleep when he got back.

When he thought it was late enough for her to have gone to bed, he got back into disguise and headed back to his new home.

His timing was slightly off.

He was seconds away from slipping unnoticed into his bedroom when Leanne stepped out of the bathroom carrying a battery-operated lantern.

The fragrance of freshly bathed woman assailed his senses. Her wet hair was slicked back from a flawless face. Although the rest of her body was completely covered by a long, blue terrycloth robe, his water fantasy was still playing with his head.

He saw her untying the belt and slipping the robe off her shoulders. She was by far the most erotic creature he'd ever laid eyes on.

The vision affected him so strongly, it took him a moment to realize she was also staring at him with a look of amazement.

She forced a smile. "I, uh, I was afraid you got lost...or something." She blinked several times and cleared her throat. "I'm, uh, all finished in the bathroom...if you...whatever." She lowered her head and hurried past him. "Good night, Zachariah."

"Night," he responded and ducked into his room before he could give into the urge to follow Leanne to hers.

Gathering his wits, he remembered that the small lamp on the dresser was the "safe" one to turn on. The first thing he noticed was that his bed had been turned down as though he were a guest in an upscale hotel. The pillow was fluffy enough to be new and the sheets looked crisp and inviting. He only hoped the water stain on the ceiling above the bed was one of the old ones Leanne had spoken of.

His gaze continued to scan the room until it came to a screeching halt at the dresser mirror. Looking back at him was the old man he had created, but one important piece of the disguise was missing—his sunglasses! They were still in his shirt pocket where he'd stuck them when he went swimming.

Damn! Now he knew exactly why Leanne was staring the way she had. With the lantern light glowing right in his face, she couldn't help but see one of the tell-tale features he had tried to conceal.

Those eyes! Leanne could not remember ever seeing an elderly man's eyes like Zachariah's, and she knew a considerable number of octogenarians. Normally, the skin around the eyes was deeply lined, their eyelids drooped, the lashes were sparse to non-existent, the iris color had paled and overall the eyes were watery or cloudy.

In fact, even among much younger men, those eyes would never be considered average.

Unless her mind and the lantern light had conspired to play a huge joke on her, Zachariah's eyes were a vivid blue, clear and bright, framed with noticeable light brown lashes. No drooping eyelids above or sagging flesh below. Just a few lines. In a word, Zachariah's eyes were...*sensual.*

And his head-to-toe appraisal of her with those eyes had made her feel as though she were being undressed.

No. She had to be wrong. It must have been a trick of the lantern light.

And her worrying that some mishap had befallen him.

And too much stress over the last three months. But just in case her intuition had failed her about Zachariah, she locked her bedroom door. She was able to fall asleep by reassuring herself that Billy would pass judgment on her new housemate tomorrow. If there was anything seriously wrong with Zachariah, Billy would figure it out.

CHAPTER 3

Zach was enormously relieved the next morning when Leanne did not try to initiate a conversation, or worse, ask him to take off his sunglasses for another look at his eyes. He hoped it meant she hadn't noticed anything strange last night after all.

"Are you ready to go?" she asked as soon as he finished his breakfast.

"Go?" Was she throwing him out without a discussion?

"To meet Grandpa's friend, Billy Chesterfield, remember? I decided it would be best to get that introduction out of the way before you got started on anything here. Besides, he probably knows as much about this house and what's stored out in the garage as Grandpa did. Of course, if there's anything else you need, Billy would have it at the store and you can charge it to my account."

Zach followed her through the utility room and out the door that led to the back porch. The word "account" raised his curiosity. "What does Billy do?"

She frowned slightly. "I thought I told you. He owns the hardware store."

It took super-human effort for Zach to get into the passenger seat of her car. Concern that his disguise might not pass the scrutiny of an older man was now superseded by an added complication. Assuming Billy Chesterfield owned BC Hardware, that meant they'd already met, and because of his purchase at that store, Billy must have deduced that he was a novice at home repairs.

Despite his need to figure out a way to get through the upcoming introduction without being exposed, he was distracted by how withdrawn Leanne was. Though he'd only met her yesterday, he already knew her well enough to sense that something was definitely wrong. As Zach, he could probably get her to tell him the problem with a little probing, but Zachariah would never do such a thing. He had no choice but to mind his own business.

By the time she pulled into a parking space in front of the hardware store, Zach had a partial plan of action formed. He would simply have to improvise the rest as he went along. "I stopped in here yesterday," he said, as though he didn't realize this was the store she had referred to.

"Really? You must have met Billy then. He's always here."

He shrugged. "Didn't meet nobody by name. Wasn't here that long."

The instant they entered the store, Zach knew Billy recognized him, remembered his buying the how-to book and was suspicious of why he was now there with Leanne.

"Good morning, Billy," she said, giving him an affectionate hug and peck on the cheek.

"Good morning, Punkin'. What brings you by today?"

"I thought I'd bring my new handyman in to meet you, but he just told me he was in here yesterday. I gather you didn't exchange introductions though. So-o-o, Billy Chesterfield, meet Zachariah Gibbon. He answered my ad yesterday and I hired him on the spot."

Billy held out his hand in greeting, but his eyes narrowed as he shook Zach's hand. "How's the cold?"

"Took your advice," Zach told him. "Woke up feelin' fit as a fiddle agin, thanks to you."

The verbal pat seemed to work. Billy grinned. "Any chance you play chess?"

"Used to. A lot. But then this feller I knew back home passed on..." Zach purposely left his sentence hanging.

Billy nodded with understanding. "Leanne, honey, why don't you go on to that new office of yours and leave Zachariah with me. I'll see to it he gets home."

Leanne smiled happily and gave Billy another hug. "That would be great. I'll see you both later then."

Billy shook his head as she walked out of the store. "You'd never know it by looking at her, but that girl has seen more bad luck in the past few months than some people do in a lifetime."

Zach wanted details but Billy changed the subject before he could figure out how to ask.

"Ever been married, Zachariah?"

"Nope, ain't never took a wife. Thought women was too dang much trouble when I was young an' when I got old, seems like I was the one who was too much trouble for them."

Billy snickered. "I know just what you mean. Never married myself, but I've got a crowd of sisters and brothers who did. With enough nieces and nephews to form two baseball teams, I never felt the need to have kids of my own. Tom and I—Tom was Leanne's grandad—we had hoped our girl would be settled down with a husband and a couple kids by now. Instead, she's setting up house with an old geezer like us."

Zach leaped at the opening. "Why ain't she married? Somethin' wrong with her?"

"Hell, no!" Billy retorted, clearly taking the question as a personal offense. "God never made a prettier, sweeter, more thoughtful girl. She just seemed to be more interested in her career than any man she met. As a matter of fact, she *was* engaged to some high-society guy but after what happened...well, I wouldn't be surprised if she never trusted a man her age again."

Zach's curiosity overpowered his restraint. Anyway, it sounded like Billy was enjoying the chance to gossip. "She done picked herself a bad apple, huh?"

"*Hmmph.* The fiancé was just an ass. The real bad guy was the one that started all the trouble. He even had a con-man's name—*Easy* something or other."

Zach's heart nearly stopped. Billy hadn't grasped all the specifics but he related enough for Zach to draw a fuzzy picture. The bottom line was that he was somehow responsible for all the misfortune in Leanne's life.

Abruptly changing the subject, Billy said, "Leanne was supposed to let me check out anyone she wanted to hire, but it looks like she jumped the gun with you. You might as well know, I'm pretty protective of Tom's little girl. Tell you what, let's set up the old board and get to know each other a bit."

For the first half hour, Billy asked the same sort of questions Leanne had and interjected anecdotes of his own experiences. Luckily, he didn't seem to think Zach wearing prescription sunglasses indoors was odd since he'd lost more than a few pair of glasses himself.

Prior to this visit, Zach's old-man charade had been based on a character he remembered from a movie. As he closely observed Billy, he noted a few little details that could make his act even more realistic.

Billy won the first game of chess before Zach even remembered the basic rules. Just when he began to feel confident of being accepted for what he appeared to be, Billy asked the one question he'd been dreading.

"So, why did you buy that book yesterday?"

Zach chewed on his toothpick a bit and purposely moved his knight into a vulnerable position before answering. "I don't like havin' to admit it, but there's times when my memory ain't as good as it used to be. It's been a few years since I done some of the kinda work she hired me for. If it were my house, I wouldn't care none if I made a mistake or two, but it ain't mine, an' I don't rightly figger that house can stand fer no mistakes."

Billy laughed aloud and tapped Zach's knight over. "Check. You're probably right about that house. It sure is going to take a lot of work. And Leanne's just stubborn enough to see it get done."

He paused and his expression grew serious. "I'm not one to beat around the bush, Zach. I think you and I could get along fine. And believe me, I wouldn't mind a new face around here now that Tom's gone. But I can't let you get away with lying to Leanne."

Zach swallowed hard and waited for the axe to fall.

"A handshake tells a lot about a man. For instance, yours was firm and quick, which means you're strong, but you don't feel a need to prove it. That's good. Your palms were a little damp, so I'd guess you were a bit nervous about meeting me. That's good too.

"But I also know that whatever you did for a living most of your life didn't put enough callouses on your hands for it to have been hard labor. What's your real story, mister?"

Zach could only hope one of the several backups he'd come up with on the way there would gain Billy's sympathy. He took a few seconds, as a proud man probably would. "I ain't a liar. I just pushed the truth a bit. Things ain't gone so good fer me the last few years."

He sighed and hung his head. "You're right. I ain't

done much hard labor. Just one construction job when I was younger. I been a cook mostly. A dang good one too. But haven't been able to get work for a while 'cause of my age, an' social security sure ain't enough to live on. Lost a couple friends last winter. Nothin' left to keep me in them hills."

He paused and sighed again before continuing. "Took a vacation in Key West once an' decided this was where I wanted to finish my time. Saw Leanne's ad the day I got here an' figgered it was like a sign from heaven."

Zach gave Billy a moment to consider that much before pushing for a commitment. "I'll understand if you feel the need to tell her I ain't exactly what I said I was, but if you could see your way clear to keepin' it to yourself, I swear I'll do a good job for her." Billy took so long to answer, Zach was sure he'd failed to convince him.

Finally, he huffed and shook his head. "It's a damned shame. That's what it is. A man works hard all his life, but let his hair turn gray and suddenly no one has any use for him." He ran his hand over his nearly bald head. "If it weren't for my owning this store, I'd probably be in the same shape as you."

Zach could hardly believe his ears. He had somehow managed to tell the right lie. He shoved down the guilt by promising himself to make it right someday in the future.

"Okay," Billy said. "I won't tell Leanne she hired herself a cook to rebuild her house. On one condition."

"Anything," Zach said quickly.

"You let me help you fix up the old place, without letting Leanne know."

Zach faked a sneezing spell to give himself a few seconds to think. On one hand, he welcomed the offer of help from someone who knew the difference between pliers and a wrench. On the other hand, he didn't relish spending so much time with Billy. He was far too observant. Sooner or later he was bound to catch on to the really big lie.

"That's mighty kind," Zach finally told him. "And I sure could use the help...an' instructin'...but I can't be the cause of your losin' business here."

Billy laughed. "That's no problem. Paul comes in every afternoon whether I pay him or not. He won't mind covering for me for a while. Hell, the truth is, I miss putzing around that dinosaur of a house. It would be like old times for me...except Tom had an inkling of what he was doing." He laughed again. "I do have one very important question though."

Zach cocked his head. He was still reeling from the double-edged sword he'd just been handed.

"Who's your favorite singer?"

Several contemporary names popped into his head. "*Hmmm.* Let's see. My favorite, huh?" He racked his brain for a name that one of his grandparents may have mentioned and recalled something about George Clooney's aunt being a singer, but he didn't know her first name. It was all he had. "Clooney."

Billy grinned. "As Bogie once said, I think this is the start of a beautiful friendship."

Rather than wait for Paul to show up, Billy called him. In no time, they were on their way to the Shepard house.

They started with an inspection of the supplies in the garage. All that seemed required of Zach was to trail behind and nod or chuckle at various times during Billy's numerous stories. Zach sincerely hoped he had thousands of them stored away. Any subject was fine, just so he didn't have to deal with any more pop quizzes about "the good ole days". He doubted he could pull another *Clooney* out of his memory banks.

"Where did she want you to start?" Billy asked once he'd refamiliarized himself with the garage inventory.

The image of Leanne coming out of the downstairs

bathroom flashed before his eyes. As much as he would love sharing a shower with her, he needed to prevent the unintentional tease. "She's real fixed on sprucin' up the outside enough to have a party on Christmas Eve, like her Grandpa Tom used to do. But I think her bathroom upstairs should be first. She says nothin' works. An' it ain't fittin' us sharin' facilities downstairs."

Billy agreed and immediately headed up there to check it out.

To Zach's delight, Billy really did enjoy "putzing" around, and he seemed to enjoy teaching even more. Zach soon found himself equally enjoying the role of student.

At noon, Zach repaid Billy by making lunch with what groceries he found in the kitchen. That was the one thing he hadn't lied about—he *was* a very good cook.

It was after three when Billy called it a day. "I'd rather be gone when Leanne gets home. You can tell her I hung around awhile, but don't let her know I did any work. She has the foolish notion that she doesn't want to impose on me. She gets it from Tom. He could be a stubborn cuss at times."

Zach saw Billy out then went upstairs to put Leanne's bathroom back in order. Even though he couldn't honestly claim credit, he was quite pleased with what he'd helped accomplish. Drains had been snaked, two cracked pipes, toilet tank innards and a lot of washers and gaskets had been replaced. All the hardware was modernized, including a new massaging showerhead in Leanne's bath.

Billy had noted that Leanne would probably want to replace the floor and wall tile, but for now at least, everything functioned the way it should. All that was left for him to do was put the tools away and give everything a hard scrubbing with the chemicals and cleansers Billy had pointed out.

* * *

Leanne felt quite reassured after her chat with Billy. It was so typical of him to stop by her office before he went home, just to put her mind at ease. As she had hoped, he not only approved of her choice, he *liked* Zachariah, and was looking forward to having a new companion. It was good to know that her intuition was still on target.

On her way home, she picked up a variety of Chinese food that wouldn't require excessive chewing. She wasn't thinking of anything in particular as she opened the back door and nearly bumped into Zachariah carrying a bucket full of cleaning supplies...and not wearing his sunglasses.

"I...I brought dinner," she said, trying not to gape at his beautiful blue eyes.

"Your bathroom's fixed," he muttered, quickly exiting the back door and heading toward the garage with the bucket.

Leanne had to order herself not to follow him. Her initial impression about his eyes had not been caused by a trick of lantern light. They really were unlike any elderly person's eyes she'd ever seen before.

Concerned that her commenting on it might embarrass him, she left the Chinese food on the kitchen table and went upstairs to see what he meant about her bathroom being fixed. For several seconds, she simply appreciated how clean it was. She didn't know how he'd done it but even the rusty stains on the old porcelain sink and tub had been whitened.

"Everythin's workin' now," Zach said from behind her.

She glanced over her shoulder. "*Everything?*" He nodded, but she had to see it for herself. First she turned on the water in the sink, then she flushed the toilet, and as a grand finale, she turned on the shower full blast.

She was so ecstatic, tears filled her eyes. "I can't believe it! You're a miracle worker!" Without hesitation, she launched herself at him, gave him a firm hug and kissed his hairy cheek.

As she stepped back, she was laughing and crying at the same time. "I brought home Chinese food, but after this surprise, I should take you out to dinner to celebrate."

"Chinese'll do fine," he mumbled and shuffled away.

His abruptness instantly dulled her pleasure. Why was he like that with her? According to Billy, Zachariah was friendly and had a good sense of humor. He said they'd had a good visit together.

Suddenly an explanation came to her. Zachariah had never married nor had grandchildren. It had probably been a very long time since a young woman pressed her body against his and he may have been flustered by her affectionate gesture...or he may have even gotten the wrong impression.

With that in mind, she advised herself not to hug him again until he realized the gesture held no sexual implications for her.

Before joining Leanne for dinner, Zach took a brief, but very cold shower.

CHAPTER 4

By the time Billy made his way to the Shepard house the next afternoon, Zach had already replaced the parts inside the downstairs toilet tank, snaked the drains and replaced the hardware, just as Billy had demonstrated. When Billy checked his work and gave a nod of approval, Zach felt a swell of pride.

"I'd say you're ready for something harder," Billy told him.

"Electricity?"

Billy snorted. "Not that hard. Have you noticed how the wall around the tub looks a little wavy?"

Zach frowned. "Is that a problem?"

Again Billy snorted. "Just take hold of that soap dish and give it a little tug."

Zach obeyed and the soap dish came right off...along with a large chunk of the tiled wall. "What the—"

"Uh-oh," Billy said, cutting off Zach's expletive. "That's not good."

Zach stared at the hole he'd created. It looked like

newspapers had been used as backing or insulation but everything was soggy...and black. "Mold?"

"Maybe, maybe not. Definitely mildew. And rotten wood. I saw breathing masks in the garage. Put one on and tear down all three tiled walls around the tub. Down to the studs. I'll run back to the store and get what we'll need to rebuild the wall."

Within minutes, Zach discovered the stress relieving aspects of demolition.

Leanne could hardly believe her eyes. Toilets that flushed with the press of a shiny new handle. Faucets that gave out hot and cold water without squealing or banging in protest. New walls being built around the downstairs bathtub that no longer exuded a musty odor. It took almighty restraint not to hug Zachariah, but she managed to limit her gratitude to verbal gushing.

"Tomorrow Billy's gonna bring over a fiberglass pop-in to finish up the tub," Zach murmured.

"Just make sure he gives you a bill for any supplies you get from him."

"He said it's free, 'cause he picked it up used at a yard sale. He said to tell you it was just takin' up space in his storage unit. An' it's only temporary. When you get to decidin' what colors you want to decorate in, I can replace it with some nice tile."

"Colors? Decorating? What are these strange words you entice me with?" She watched him try to smother a laugh. Perhaps humor was the way to get Zachariah to warm up to her. "Now, how do you feel about hamburgers, sweet potato fries and an ice cold beer for dinner?"

"Purty good, 'specially the cold beer part. I just need to wash up first."

"You're welcome to use my bathroom upstairs—"

"No need. We got the shower in the utility room hooked up."

"We?" Leanne asked.

"Oh, yeah. Billy stopped by to measure for the pop-in...guess he figgered I might not've got it right with my eyesight not bein' so good...then I couldn't stop him from givin' me a hand with that shower."

Leanne chuckled. "That sounds like Billy. I'm glad you two have connected."

"*Hmmph.* I think he was hopin' for a more challengin' chess player. I'm a bit rusty."

"Really? Well, I'm not very challenging either but I have Grandpa's old chess set and I'd be pleased to let you use me for practice."

Leanne's offer to use her stayed with Zach through dinner and the world's slowest chess match. He'd purposefully turned down her offer of a second beer because the one bottle had him thinking *everything* she said was suggestive. *Your move. Gotcha. Go ahead, take my pawn.* The game would never be the same for him.

He'd known it would be a mistake to spend time with her, but she'd made him feel so good about the work he'd done and then she made him laugh and she just kept smiling at him through dinner and telling him funny, sweet little stories about her grandpa.

He could have said he was too tired to play a game. She wouldn't have questioned it if he'd gone to his room right after dinner. But Leanne Shepard was simply too perfect to resist her company.

The strangest part for Zach was realizing that she actually liked Zachariah Gibbon, the cranky old man who spoke fractured English and needed to do manual labor for room and board. He couldn't think of another young, attractive woman who would give that man the time of day let alone her kindness.

Despite a mind full of thoughts of Leanne's attributes, Zach fell into a deep sleep the minute his eyes closed.

Billy arrived with the tub enclosure in time to wave

goodbye to Leanne as she left for her office. Two hours later, the downstairs bathroom was finished and Zach was anxious to learn another skill.

"Sorry, pal. Paul's taking his family up to Orlando for the weekend so I've got to cover the store. I don't open on Mondays at all so I can spend that whole day here...as long as Leanne is busy elsewhere."

Zach felt deflated. "Oh, sure, of course. I was just hopin' to get goin' on the electrical problems. Fixin' the plumbin' sure made Leanne happy an' I figger she'd be doin' flips if'n we could give her some a-c."

"We can take a look on Monday for sure. Meanwhile, do *not* try to do anything about that yourself. In fact, if you don't mind a suggestion of how to put a smile on our girl's face, spend the rest of today and the weekend cleaning up the yard. You're going to have to get to it soon anyway if she's still convinced about having that holiday party. Maybe put in a new plant or two. I remember her always making a fuss over our climbing bougainvillea."

Zach hauled the first broken tree limb to the corner of the yard as Billy climbed into his truck. By midday, he was drenched with sweat and the trash pile had gained some height but he had barely cleaned a quarter of the property. Even without the wig, beard and heavy jeans, the heat would have made this a brutal chore, but he couldn't take the chance of shedding any part of his disguise. He stood in the front yard and tried to imagine what it would look like with a neatly mowed lawn, stone walkway, maybe a trellis with Leanne's favorite climbing plant showing off a brightly painted door...

In an instant he knew what he could do that afternoon to give Leanne a smile without sweating to death himself.

Leanne pulled into the driveway and came to an abrupt halt. For a moment she thought she was at the wrong house, but then Zach came out the front door—*a door painted a very bright red*—and walked across the porch—*a porch on which two white rocking chairs had been placed*—then down the steps *through a white trellis arch that had bougainvillea with red flowers climbing up both sides.*

She was out of her car by the time he reached her. "What...how...it's..."

"Too much?" Zach offered. "It don't have to be red but I got to thinkin' you might like to paint the house white, like it was to begin with, and the Chinese believe—"

"Oh no, no, it's *perfect*! I'm sorry Zach, but you're just going to have to take another hug!" And before he could escape, she threw her arms around his neck and hugged him as hard as she could. "It's like you read my mind. I *love* bougainvillea and I imagined a trellis right there and the door, well, I hadn't thought of it being red, but now that I see it with the flowers, I wouldn't have it any other color."

Slowly she realized he wasn't hugging her back and she gave him his freedom. Glancing around the front yard and seeing the trash pile, she got excited again. "I can't believe how much better everything looks already."

"Barely put a dent in it," Zach muttered. "And most of the wood on the porch and steps still gotta be replaced before you can have company—"

"Doesn't matter," she said still smiling at the progress he *had* made. "Okay, you've inspired me to get my hands dirty. I promise not to get underfoot but I *am* going to help clean up the rest of the yard this weekend. That way, maybe you can start on replacing the wood." When he didn't respond, she worried that the hug had made him more uncomfortable than she imagined. "Unless you really needed to take a day off—"

"Nope. Don't need no days off," he said quickly then

held out a key. "Here. It's for the new lock on the front door. And I wasn't readin' your mind. Billy told me you liked those flowers and he gave me the okay to dig up a couple of plants from his yard. He had the trellis arch in his storage unit. But I did have to charge the paint and lock set to your account."

He was being so humble, Leanne could barely stop herself from hugging him again, but she managed. "I couldn't be happier if I'd spent a thousand dollars for it. In fact, I'm so happy and you have saved me so much money, I'm going to take you out to dinner. Any kind of food you'd like. You pick."

Zach scratched his head and shifted from one foot to another. "Well, I'd have to take a shower first. Been workin' up quite a sweat out here today."

"I'm in no hurry. Any ideas of where you'd like to eat?"

"Well, I saw this place right on the beach that looks mighty temptin'...if you like crab and you're willin' to eat on a picnic bench outside."

"Ooh, you must mean Charlie's Crab Shack. I love their crab cakes and I haven't been there since…well, for a long time. And they make killer margaritas too. This is going to be fun. I'll change into something comfortable and meet you back in the kitchen."

Zach wished he could wash his mind as easily as his body. His plan had worked. It definitely put a smile on Leanne's face. And thanks to his beard, the smile on his face during the long, full-body hug remained his secret.

He believed he had his body's responses to Leanne reined in…until he stepped out of the bathroom and saw her coming down the stairs—hair tied back in a playful ponytail, a loose cotton top that barely came to her waist, running shorts and, thanks to his sunglasses, she was spared his very appreciative appraisal of her tanned legs and sandaled feet. What truly surprised him however was how she froze for a moment when she caught sight of him.

The reason became clear as he realized she was staring at his waist, or more accurately his navel, which was visible above his jeans because he hadn't buttoned up the oversized shirt. As quickly as possible, he rectified his oversight and she finished descending the stairs with her eyes averted.

She drove them to the Shack, as the locals referred to it, and ordered him to relax and enjoy himself, starting with one of those killer margaritas. The crab cakes lived up to their "best in the world" reputation and the Key lime pie was yellow, as true Key lime pie should be. While the sun set on the west side of the island, Leanne insisted they have one more margarita and watch the waves lap the sand, the combination of which had the magical ability to make the worst problem quiet down for an hour.

Neither made an attempt at conversation. Apparently there was nothing she needed to say and he couldn't say any of the things he wanted to. At any rate, silence seemed to be the respectful way to enjoy such a peaceful moment.

Zach inhaled the sea air and looked up at the stars. What brought him to this place wasn't important at that moment. The only thing that mattered was that it was the first time in his adult life that he wasn't worried about a single thing. Maybe there really was a little magic going on here.

Leanne felt pleased that Zachariah was appreciating his evening out. She simply needed to forget what she'd seen. She certainly couldn't *say* anything to him about it.

And yet, she couldn't seem to banish the image of the flowered shirt hanging open to reveal a strip of very firm, very masculine chest and a flat, tightly muscled stomach.

She supposed her blatant stare had been rude, but who could blame her? She knew thirty-year old men who would pay a king's ransom for those abs. Obviously, a lifetime of construction work had the same results as, if not better than, a consistent workout in a gym.

Zachariah was really quite a remarkable man for his age. First his eyes, now this. She wondered what he would look like clean-shaven with his hair cut and styled. She thought of a few celebrities who'd aged handsomely. Their maturity certainly didn't stop anyone from calling them sexy.

Suddenly she saw herself pulling Zachariah out of his self-imposed cocoon and turning him into a butterfly. Surely there were a number of mature, single women on the island who would be interested in making his acquaintance.

That thought led to another that made her giggle. After getting a glimpse of his hidden attributes, she'd bet there were a number of younger females who would be interested as well.

Putting the Pygmalion fantasy temporarily aside, she took another sip of her margarita and let the magical waves take her worries away.

By the time the sun slipped below the horizon on Sunday, Leanne barely had enough energy to drag the rake and garden cart back into the garage.

She'd never been fanatical about exercising but until that weekend, she'd never thought of herself as out-of-shape. Zachariah had really put her to shame with his ability to do physical labor from sunrise to sunset while barely taking a break in between. Even though he'd been doing this sort of work for fifty or sixty years, one would think his advanced age would slow him down a bit.

Massaging her aching shoulders, she watched him drill a screw into the new railing around the back porch and give it a loving pat. In the past two days, while she gathered the remaining trash, dead leaves and broken branches, trimmed bushes and trees, pulled weeds and battled invasive vines, he replaced all the porch steps, railings and damaged wood on the front and back porches.

Whenever she was struggling with something, he was suddenly at her side, giving her a hand, which let her know he was keeping a protective eye on her. In return, he occasionally *allowed* her to use the cart to help move wood from the garage or grudgingly accepted her offer to hand him screws or nails to make a particular job go faster. With a minimum exchange of words, they had eased into a comfortable, supportive relationship and, as a result, the house and yard had begun to show signs of life again.

Certain he was done drilling, she approached and helped him gather up tools and supplies to be returned to the garage. As soon as everything was put away for the night, she stopped him from heading inside the house. "Wait," she said firmly and linked her arm with his. "We need to take a moment to appreciate how much you've done so—"

"*We* done," he corrected.

She smiled. "Mostly you. Come on. Take a stroll around the perimeter with me." She gave him a tug and he grumbled, but let her lead him slowly around the edge of the property. "You were right about repainting her the original white."

"Have to replace quite a bit of the sidin' wood first. An' all the shutters..."

"Which will be painted the same red as the front door..."

"Gotta replace those attic windows too..."

"And we'll string lights *everywhere*," she said, her excitement evident in her voice. "You won't believe how many boxes of Christmas decorations are in the attic! I'm really starting to believe we may pull this off after all."

"*Hmmph.* Won't do much good to hang lights if we don't get the electric workin' right."

She squeezed his arm and gave him a smile. "I have complete faith in you, Zachariah. After this past week, I believe you can accomplish anything you set your mind to."

CHAPTER 5

She was so happy. She finally had everything she ever wanted. Hugging him close, feeling his strength, she could have stayed in his arms forever. But she needed much more than a hug.

She stepped back and fingered the top button of his flowered shirt. It came undone easily, as did all the rest. His eyes softened as she pushed the shirt off his shoulders. It wasn't enough to see his nipples peak in anticipation, she had to touch...and taste. And he let her take as long as she needed.

"It's your turn," he whispered. And suddenly she was standing naked before him.

He lifted her into the bathtub, but as they stretched out, it turned into her bed.

She didn't want to go slowly any more. She parted her legs and moved her hips against his. Gazing up into his beautiful blue eyes, she—

Leanne coughed. Something tickled her nose and she coughed harder. She ordered the annoyance away. She wanted to finish the sensuous dream.

In a lightning flash of double awareness, she realized she'd been having an unacceptable dream about Zachariah, and that *smoke* was the cause of her coughing. In the next second, she bolted from her bed and dashed downstairs. A crashing sound directed her to the kitchen.

A thick cloud of smoke billowed out of that room, momentarily blinding her. Waving her arms in front of her, she could make out Zachariah frantically whipping a throw rug against the wall, knocking over everything in its path. Fiery sparks burst into flames along an exposed wire faster than he could smother them.

Squinting her eyes and holding her breath, Leanne scrambled for the fire extinguisher she'd seen in one of the cabinets. Once she found it, it took her another few seconds to release the safety lock, but then she frantically sprayed the white foam at the burning wall and everything around it. By the time the canister was empty, specks of white floated through the heavy smoke, making the whole room appear victimized by a snowy blizzard.

Leanne's eyes burned, and she began coughing uncontrollably. She had to get the doors and windows open before they were asphyxiated. As she stepped cautiously across the foam-splattered tile, her foot nudged an obstacle in her path. Squinting through the smoke, she realized why Zachariah wasn't choking like she was.

He was unconscious on the floor!

Beginning to feel faint herself, she stumbled through the utility room and shoved open the back door. She took a deep breath of fresh air then hurried back into the kitchen.

"Zachariah!" she cried and shook his shoulders. No response. A little of the smoke was dissipating, but she was certain he would be better off outside. She positioned herself at his head and worked her hands under his arms. To her dismay, bent over in that manner, she couldn't get her footing in the slippery residue and his upper body seemed to weigh a ton.

Laying his head back down, she moved to his feet. Clamping each of his ankles beneath her armpits, she was able to drag him to the open door. She was so intent on what was behind her as she inched her way outside, she misjudged the length of her burden.

Thunk! His head slid over the door ledge and down the short drop to the porch. Leanne abruptly dropped his feet and hurried to check on what additional injury she had caused.

In desperation, she strained to recall the first-aid course she had taken eons ago. She remembered a little about treating someone for drowning, but what was the treatment for smoke inhalation? One thing was certain. He probably shouldn't be moved again; she might have hurt his back or even broken his neck.

Oh my God, she thought. *What if I've killed him?* She thought she should call 911 but her phone was by her bed upstairs and she didn't want to leave him alone until she at least made an attempt to bring him around.

She knelt down and held her palm near his nose, but she couldn't feel any breath being exhaled. Panicking, she unbuttoned his shirt and pressed her ear to his heart. Either it wasn't beating or the pounding in her head was too loud for her to hear. Her fingers searched beneath his beard for the carotid artery. His skin felt cool and clammy, but she found a pulse—a weak beat that nonetheless gave her an ounce of hope.

Mouth-to-mouth resuscitation. That's what she was supposed to do. *Tip the victim's head back and pinch closed his nose.* She prayed she hadn't already broken his neck.

To make her efforts easier, she removed his sunglasses and tried to clear the beard hair away from his mouth. Like a splash of icy water, her mind registered what she was seeing.

Zachariah's entire beard moved…as though it was a single, separate unit. She blinked and rubbed her eyes to remove any smoke residue that might be affecting her vision. That's when she noticed that the gray hair on his head was also a single piece…and it was askew.

Both the head and facial hair were fake. The wig was well secured by hairpins but she was able to tug it away just enough to see that his real hair, although matted down, was thick and dark. She could also see that the beard had strings on each side that wound around his ears. Bewildered, she yanked off the phony beard.

Despite the raccoon mask of soot, she could easily see that Zachariah Gibbon was certainly not an octogenarian. He wasn't even elderly. He was a fraud! She wanted to scream at him, beat him to a pulp, then turn him over to the police.

But first she had to make sure he didn't die on her porch.

No longer concerned about being gentle, Leanne tipped back his chin, closed his nostrils, and opened his mouth. She inhaled deeply, formed a seal over his mouth with her own then blew the air from her lungs into his.

Head up. Press on his chest ten times. Do it again. The procedure seemed right, but it took nearly a dozen more breath exchanges before he responded.

His chest finally rose with a heave and he gasped for air. When his gasping graduated to violent coughing, she helped raise him to a sitting position and pounded his back.

"*Enough*," he pleaded in a hoarse whisper.

For a moment, Leanne was again distracted by the eyes trying to focus on her. But the anger returned as she watched him draw a handkerchief out of his pocket, wipe his teary eyes and blow his nose. His expression revealed the exact moment when he realized his beard was missing.

"I can explain," he began, but only another coughing fit followed.

Leanne sprang to her feet. "Don't bother! I'm sure you'd just tell me another lie. What sort of sick game are you playing? What could you possibly hope to accomplish with this ridiculous farce? Never mind. I don't care. Just pack your bag and get out of my house."

He tried to rise, but didn't make it. Squinting painfully, he pressed his fingertips to his temple and took a raspy breath. She felt only slightly guilty about being the cause of his headache.

"I wasn't playing any game," he whispered. "I just ran out of options."

She was still furious but the look in his eyes was so pitiful, she decided to let him try to explain. "What do you mean?"

"When you've got money and a regular job, everybody's your friend. When you don't, nobody's willing to give you a break. I was hungry and tired of sleeping in my truck. I just wanted a fresh start." He dragged in another breath and coughed out a bit more smoke.

Leanne stared at the man slumped at her feet. Even covered in soot, he looked too good to be true. There was no way he was helpless or homeless. "I find it very hard to believe you couldn't get a job."

"Would you have hired me if you knew I had a prison record?"

Her mouth dropped open and she stepped back a foot.

He shook his head. "See? It wouldn't have mattered if I explained that it was a non-violent crime, or that I was very neatly framed."

"No, it wouldn't have mattered to me, because I was determined to have a retired gentleman, not a...a man, who..."

"Who would rape you in your sleep?" he finished. "I've never committed a violent act in my life, but I guess I can understand your position. I don't suppose you could give me a chance to repay you for lying? Say for a week? Long enough to clean up the mess in the kitchen and maybe get all your electrical problems worked out. There is still the matter of you wanting to host the Christmas Eve party..."

Her better judgment warned her not to listen. This man was a liar and a damned good actor. Maybe he was lying now. How had her intuition messed up so badly? How had he fooled Billy?

Arms crossed defensively, she paced back and forth across the porch. Was there a possibility that both her and Billy's instincts *were* correct? That Zachariah *was* a good man forced to act out a charade for the purposes of survival? And there *was* the Christmas Eve party to think about...

"I could put the disguise back on. You seemed comfortable enough with Zachariah. He kept his distance from you, didn't he?"

She had to admit he had done his best to avoid spending time with her. And he hadn't moved a muscle when she'd thrown herself at him...*twice*. Lord knows, if his ulterior motive was to physically take advantage of her, it would have been easy enough.

Her thoughts skipped to the miracles he had worked in the bathrooms and the lovely surprise he had prepared for her Friday and how much he'd accomplished over the weekend. How was she going to get the rest of the house renovated if she threw him out?

"I swear, if I do one thing that makes you nervous, you can tell me to leave, and I will be gone a minute later, without another word. Please, just give me a chance."

Her mouth pursed and her eyes narrowed as she weighed the risks of letting him stay against getting the electricity flowing. Considering the possibility of having air conditioning again made her ask, "Exactly what crime did you commit?"

"I didn't commit any crime," he retorted without hesitation. "I was framed." He coughed again, though his lungs were obviously clearing up. "For...stealing petty cash from the construction company I was working for."

Leanne looked dubious. "You went to jail for petty cash?"

He shrugged. "It was over three thousand dollars. They used it for bribes, to inspectors and such. But I didn't take it. I think I know who did, but I couldn't prove it."

"What's your real name?"

"Zach Gibbon."

"*Hmmph.* I don't suppose you needed to lie about that. I'll tell you what. Consider yourself on probation for the next seven days while you work on the electrical problems. *But*, if you give me one reason—"

"I won't."

She crossed the porch one more time. Now that the crisis was over, the memory of the erotic dream rose to the surface of her mind. Apparently, her libido had seen through his disguise with no problem. She told herself that the dream meant nothing except that she was feeling a little lonely. Zach was completely undesirable to her—a lying, unemployed ex-convict. Regardless of how lonely she was or that he had dreamy eyes or an attractive body, he was untrustworthy and that was enough to hold her hormones in check.

"All right. As of this minute, you're on probation. Our conversations will be limited to work requests, questions and updates. I'll prepare your meals but we will no longer share a table...or any of our free time. Also, as you suggested, I would prefer you continue to wear your disguise outside of the house. I don't want the neighbors talking any more than they already are. Plus, I would rather Billy not learn of your deception. He would definitely not approve of your staying here with me no matter what your sad story is. In fact, now that I realize you've been conning him as well, I'd rather you not spend any more time with him than necessary. Now, if you'll excuse me, I'm going to open all the windows and turn on the few fans that work. Then I'm going to get cleaned up and have breakfast out. I'm not sure when I'll be home."

Zach sat where she left him for several minutes. He had never told as many lies in his entire life as he had in the last week. Actually, it surprised him how good he was at it for having had so little practice. A number of brokers he had worked with stretched the truth on an hourly basis, a few outright lied to close a deal. To the contrary, he had always gone to the extreme of sticking with the truth.

And yet *he* was the one who'd been accused of bilking clients out of millions of dollars.

Again, he wished he could come clean with Leanne. However, after this morning's second layer of lies, he had no doubt she would turn him over to the Securities and Exchange Commission in a heartbeat.

He was lucky on one count. She hadn't recognized him. He swiped at his cheek to confirm that he was smeared with soot and, from the looks of his clothes and discarded beard, he was well-coated with white residue. He wondered where that came from since he hadn't found an extinguisher in his quick search.

Thinking of the mess awaiting him in the kitchen, he pushed himself to rise and stay upright. Feeling a localized pain in the back of his head, he located a tender swelling and guessed that he'd hit it when he fell.

He hadn't thought to ask what had happened or how he'd gotten out on the porch, but it wasn't too hard to figure out. Through a series of assumptions, he got to the point where Leanne must have given him mouth-to-mouth resuscitation.

So it hadn't been a dream or hallucination. Her mouth *had* been on his. And her breasts *had* been pressed against him when he came to…just like they were when she'd hugged him, only this time there was nothing but her thin cotton nightshirt between them.

The fact that he had been able to keep his gaze above her shoulders while he was begging for another chance was fair testimony to just how desperate he was.

On the other hand, he realized he had once again lucked out. Instead of attempting to resuscitate him, she could have called the fire department, in which case his identity would be uncovered in short order.

Zach still felt a little dizzy as he went back into the smoky kitchen. The damage he encountered didn't help.

One entire wall was burned black, the cabinets and appliances were coated with soot, and the black and white linoleum was a sea of foam, water, coffee grounds and various items that had once been on the counter…before he started swinging the area rug.

All because he'd wanted to have a pot of coffee ready for Leanne when she came downstairs.

He blamed the disaster on his feeling overly cocky from his multiple successes. When he had plugged in the coffee pot and nothing happened, he had removed the outlet cover. He remembered how well cleaning worked for plumbing issues and figured it would do the same for dusty old wires.

When he tried to wipe the sticky wiring with a dishtowel, there was a loud pop. The next instant, the towel and the wallpaper were on fire and sparks were shooting out of the wall faster than he could react. The last thing he could remember was getting sprayed with foam.

Then he woke up with her mouth on his.

Zach knew he couldn't waste any more time thinking about how his carelessness might have screwed up the perfect situation. If he didn't impress the hell out of Leanne in the next week...or if a Christmas miracle didn't occur...he'd have to hit the road again.

His chest felt like he had a fifty-pound weight on it. He went back outside and tried to take a deep breath but that merely generated another bronchial coughing fit. By the time he headed back to the kitchen, the fans and open windows had helped clear most of the smoke but the smell was horrendous. A steamy shower and fresh clothing went a long way toward eliminating the stench clinging to him but only extensive cleaning was going to hide the fact that there had been a fire in the house.

He focused on the one positive bit he could think of. Leanne had *requested* he maintain his disguise outside of the house and not let Billy in on his secret. Keeping his true identity concealed had to remain a priority for him. When he'd glanced into the bathroom mirror before taking a shower, he confirmed that Leanne couldn't have recognized him even if she had had a photo of E.Z. Rush in her hand. Whether she would recognize him when he was cleaned up was yet to be discovered, though he intended to put off that moment as long as possible.

What couldn't be put off was a desperate call to Billy to remind him of his promise to look into the electrical problems that day. Once Billy saw the kitchen, he wouldn't need to be told that Zach had tried to fix something himself, despite orders to the contrary.

CHAPTER 6

Because Leanne was too upset to eat more than a few bites of the breakfast she'd ordered, she took a walk on the beach. When the waves failed to improve her mood, she searched for a distraction by wandering in and out of several stores. She even tried busying herself in her office, but she simply couldn't focus. By the time her stomach reminded her that lunchtime had come and gone, she could not ignore her guilty conscience another minute. Yes, she was angry about Zachariah's—or rather, *Zach's*—deception, but she really should have stayed to help him clean up the mess. After all, it wasn't his fault the electrical wiring was faulty.

That thought led to his asphyxiation and the injury she'd caused him while dragging him outside. She probably should have taken him to the emergency clinic to be checked out. But fear, then anger had muddied up her good sense. What if he had a relapse or a concussion? For all she knew he was unconscious again, lying in a heap on the floor.

In record time, she locked up her office and headed home. Panic set in again when she saw Billy's truck in her driveway and recalled Zach mentioning that he might be dropping by Monday morning. Good heavens! What if Zach had forgotten and answered the door without his disguise? What would he have told him? With no idea of what might be awaiting her, she used her new key to enter the front door.

The house still smelled of smoke but it was bearable. Male laughter drew her toward the disaster area. "Hello? Is it safe to come in?"

"Hey Punkin'," Billy said without looking back toward her.

He was doing something inside the burned wall which was now just wood framing, pipes and wires.

"What are you doing here?" she asked then held her breath for his answer.

"I'd already planned on stopping by for coffee before I took the boat out. Even thought Zachariah might want to take the day off with me. Of course, once I saw what happened, I couldn't walk away."

Leanne clucked her tongue. "Billy, what did I tell you about—"

"You just hush now. You're not imposing on me because you didn't ask. And neither did Zachariah. I'm helping out because it's the neighborly thing to do. Besides, this is my day off so I can use it however I please."

"But where is Zachariah?"

"Here," came the answer from the utility room on the other side of the wall.

She peeked through the opening and saw Zach...in full disguise. At least that was one less thing to worry about. "So what's the verdict?"

Billy answered for both men. "What would you like first, the good news or the bad?"

"I could use some good."

"The main connection from outside into the old fuse box was partially eaten through, probably just age and salt air...or mice...and it looks like most of the wiring inside the box was corroded or chewed on too."

Leanne grimaced. "You consider that good news?"

"Absolutely. Sometimes finding the cause of electrical problems is the hardest part, so now all we have to do is fix it. I remembered Tom had me order a new circuit breaker control box before he went on his trip, so I just had to figure out where he'd stashed it in the garage. Zachariah could have done the switch out by himself but when it comes to rewiring, a second pair of hands makes the job move a lot easier."

"I guess that makes sense. So what's the bad news?"

"This wall will have to be rebuilt and there's a good chance we'll have to punch a few holes elsewhere..."

She laughed. "I don't think that's a serious problem...as long as Zachariah adds patching them to his to-do list. Still, I really don't—"

"Uh-uh," Billy sounded, cutting her off. "We're talking about your safety here. So I'm going to help with this, no matter what you say. Tom would probably start haunting me if I didn't. And speaking of safety, you need smoke alarms and more fire extinguishers. I'll bring some by tomorrow after I close the store."

Knowing she couldn't really win an argument with Billy, she simply shook her head. "Fine. But I want to help."

"No!" Billy and Zach replied in emphatic unison.

Leanne chuckled. "Okay, okay. It's time I start packing up all of Grandma's and Grandpa's things. If you need me, I'll be upstairs."

The rest of the afternoon passed quickly and productively. As daylight waned, however, they had no choice but to put the balance of the rewiring on hold, but at least all of the downstairs outlets had been updated to code and now had power and safe wiring.

Since Leanne insisted Billy stay for dinner, it was well into the evening before she and Zach were alone, and then he immediately excused himself to take a shower.

Leanne was finished cleaning up from dinner and on her way upstairs for her own bath when he emerged from his room. "Are you going out?" she asked.

"No. I was actually going to ask if it would be okay to watch one of the movies in your collection, but if you'd rather I—"

"Oh no. You're welcome to the movies. I was only wondering why you were still incognito."

"I, uh, thought you would be, you know, more at ease with Zachariah."

She shrugged. "I don't think it makes any difference how you look. I'm not going to forget that it's a costume. In fact, it's a little silly when it's just the two of us. Please. Take it off. Get comfortable. Seriously." She climbed a few steps then said, "I'm still upset about being deceived, but you didn't deserve my attacking you the way I did. It was just…a shock. I really don't want you to leave. You got a lot done again today. Thank you. And, by the way, I'm very glad the terrible dialect was part of the disguise."

He nodded and headed slowly back to his room. She thought he'd be relieved by her change of heart and suggestion to take off the disguise. Instead, he acted as though it was the last thing on earth he wanted to do.

After her bath, it took much longer than usual to decide what to put on. She would be most comfy, and most covered, in her velour robe, but she was afraid it hinted at a nighttime intimacy they didn't share. Finally, she donned yoga pants and a loose t-shirt that didn't seem to hint at anything.

"What are you watching?" she asked as she came into the living room and saw him focused on the television.

"*Usual Suspects*. I always heard it was good but I never got around to seeing it."

"One of my favorites," she told him. "Don't mind watching it again and again, even though I know the ending." He was on the sofa so she sat down in the recliner several feet away, despite the bad angle to the screen.

She had no other choice. The sight of Zach, the *real* Zach, was so compelling she couldn't make herself leave the room. She could barely stop herself from sitting next to him on the couch. He didn't just have great eyes. The whole package was devastatingly sexy.

She did her best to stay focused on the movie, but she couldn't stop herself from sneaking peeks in his direction. A few damp curls of dark brown hair fell over his forehead and the tops of his ears. The merest shadow of a beard gave him the masculine touch needed to balance out the gentle eyes and long lashes.

His jeans and short-sleeved, pullover shirt were fitted well enough to confirm that the glimpse of well-toned abs was just the beginning of a body worth exploring.

In one word, Zach Gibbon was Hot, with a capital H!

He's completely unacceptable, she reminded herself.

He's down on his luck, her intuition countered.

He's a convicted felon.

He said he was framed and I think that's the truth.

Hah! He lied about his age. He could be lying about his crime.

That was a white lie, told only to get the job and a place to live, and he is doing a fine job, by the way.

He's—

Billy likes him and that's enough for me.

Okay, but don't say I didn't warn you.

"Are you sure this is okay?" Zach asked without looking directly at her. "You seem…tense."

"Tense? No. Not at all. I'm fine with…*this*. It's just been a tense day, I guess." She shifted into a more relaxed pose in the chair and stared intently at the television.

Zach knew she was lying. His first thought was that she recognized him, but his male instincts were telling him otherwise. He could feel her visual taps and, unless his instincts had gone off-track, she seemed to be a little intrigued by what she saw.

Having a woman be attracted to him wasn't rare. Getting dates was never a problem. But there were three big differences with Leanne. First, his attraction to her *felt* different than his previous experiences. Reasonable impression, since she was in fact, his *perfect woman* in the flesh.

Secondly, he wasn't free to do anything about the mutual attraction. The slightest move on his part could get him thrown out of his hideaway, regardless of how intrigued she was by his looks.

It was the third difference, however, that made the situation unresolvable. It was one thing to stretch the truth about small details that didn't hurt anyone, but his conscience would not allow him to take advantage of the physical attraction without telling her who he really was.

And she despised the man he really was.

The instant the credits began to roll at the end of the movie, they headed for their separate bedrooms, though Zach doubted he'd be able to lose himself in sleep that night.

Her body catapulted into action. If she didn't hurry, he could die, and it would be all her fault. Trembling fingers tore open the buttons on his shirt, revealing a muscled chest. Her hands glided over his flesh and her body demanded more.

But first she had to help him breathe. She bent her head and pressed her lips to his, and her kiss gave him life. In the next instant, his mouth took control, sucking her breath into his lungs, sweeping her mouth with his tongue.

Without breaking their kiss, she stretched out on top of him and his palms covered her bare bottom.

But he was still wearing his jeans and she wanted him as naked as she was. She desperately wanted to feel him deep inside her body.

Her fingers groped for the opening in his jeans, but there wasn't one. She tugged on the denim, trying to pull it down over his hips, but it wouldn't budge.

She searched his dreamy eyes for the answer.

He shook his head sadly and whispered, "I'm sorry. You have to figure it out first."

Leanne let out a frustrated groan that woke her out of the dream. It felt as though her subconscious had just alerted her to something important. Something it had noticed that she'd missed. Unfortunately, she had no inkling of what it could be.

CHAPTER 7

The dream still bothered Leanne so much the next morning, she made breakfast for Zach but left for her office without sitting down and sharing it with him. Until she figured *something* out, she needed much more than a few hundred feet of space between them. And he didn't question her early departure.

Her calendar note stated this was the day she had planned to begin calling all her former clients to let them know she had opened her own brokerage. In the past, she'd often discovered the answer to a troubling problem while focusing on something totally unrelated and the phone calls certainly seemed to fit the requirement.

By late afternoon, she had put a small dent in her client list but the conversations had put a very large dent in her optimism. Of the clients who accepted her call, only one was willing to transfer the handling of their portfolio to her new office. The rest vaguely promised to think about it or turned her down flat. She heard a number of excuses, but she knew the real reason was lack of trust in her credibility and judgment.

How was she to survive without a client base?

She was on the verge of giving up when a conversation with Grandpa came to mind. He believed letter writing was an art lost to the impersonal, high speed world of emails and texting. He had often told her how he could apologize to Grandma until he was hoarse without being forgiven, but a well-written love letter always melted her heart.

Rather than continue making unwelcome marketing calls, she decided to use some of her new, classy stationery and handwrite individualized letters to each of her long-time clients. Although she would subtly mention opening her own brokerage, the primary purpose of the letters would be to offer an apology for any harm done and a token of recompense in the form of free services. She would send the letters by priority mail, which would cost considerably more but seemed much more sincere under the circumstances. She would wait two weeks, and if she hadn't heard from a client by then, she would follow up with a phone call.

Going through her files reminded her of the extent of the losses some of those clients had endured based on her recommendation. She had to admit she needed a better plan than simply being sincere. She might have to insert a gentle, carefully worded reminder of how much she had helped them gain over their years together.

Despite coming up with an alternate marketing plan, Leanne felt herself sinking deeper into pessimism. She was proud of how well she'd coped with all the challenges she'd been hit with in the last three months. But she was no longer certain she could keep it up.

What made her think she was capable of getting investors to trust her again? What made her think she was capable of renovating an old house? What made her think she could pick up the pieces of broken promises and start over?

If Grandpa were here, he'd know just the right thing to say to have her pushing forward again.

But he wasn't.

Remembering Billy's comment about stopping by after he closed the store, she picked up two large pizzas, an antipasto platter and two bottles of Chianti on her way home.

As she pulled into the driveway, she saw Zach dragging a rolled-up carpet out to the trash pile, which was even larger than it had been that morning. She waited for him to drop it and approach her before heading to the front door. He looked exhausted and very overheated. Forcing a smile, she said, "Looks like you had another productive day."

He shrugged. "Had to put off the electrical until Billy could bring more supplies and he couldn't make it today. Said he'd come by tomorrow."

"Oh." She had counted on Billy being there as a buffer. "Well, that's more pizza and wine for us. How about another movie with dinner?"

"Sounds good to me."

While Zach took a shower, she set up their picnic dinner on the coffee table and moved the recliner closer...but still not *too* close. She chose a humorous, action-packed good-guys versus bad-guys flick for its lack of reality and abundance of conversation-prohibiting noise.

Leanne was finishing her second glass of wine by the time Zach—the real, much too yummy, Zach—joined her in the living room. She poured the last of the first bottle into his glass and opened the second.

Her movie choice effectively eliminated any need to chat and her third glass of wine was doing its job of numbing her self-pity. But the fourth glass, or was it the fifth, seemed to be stirring her libido. She couldn't seem to stop herself from ogling Zach, wondering if he was as good at sex as her dreams had suggested. When a strong spear of desire had her on the brink of finding that out, she realized she had to get away from him…immediately.

"Excuse me," she said abruptly and stood up. "Just need to…use the bathroom. No need to pause the movie. I'll be back in a minute."

Zach tried to keep his attention on the movie but as one minute stretched into five without Leanne returning, he became concerned. He was fairly certain she didn't normally consume as much alcohol with dinner as she just had, so he couldn't help but wonder what had happened that she was trying to avoid thinking about. Had something happened while she was at her office? A business problem? Or was it not having the electric work finished as expected?

Or was it just him? The way she was openly staring at him tonight seemed to suggest *he* was at least a part of what was bothering her. Was she thinking he looked familiar after all? If so, why didn't she simply confront him?

He put the movie on pause and took the remnants of their dinner into the kitchen. That's when he noticed the second bottle of wine had been emptied and his concern raised to worry. After confirming she was nowhere downstairs, he headed up to her room, thinking she may have just gone to bed.

Seconds later, his curiosity turned to worry when he realized she wasn't in the house. He descended the stairs two at a time and rushed outside to make sure she hadn't driven off. She was in no condition to take a walk alone, let alone operate a vehicle. He was slightly relieved to see her car and his truck, but a hurried inspection of the property failed to locate her. He imagined her staggering down the sidewalk, falling—Worse, she could try to cross a street and get hit by a truck. Or even worse, some pervert could see her, force her into his car—

He ran back inside, grabbed his truck keys and raced

out the door. Luckily, his first thought was the right one. He found her sitting on a blanket on the same stretch of beach he had walked a few nights before. He told himself to leave her alone. If she had gotten here by herself, she was sober enough to find her way back without his help. His feet didn't obey.

"Zach!" she exclaimed when she realized who had walked up on her. "You scared me."

"Which is a good reason why you shouldn't be out here alone in your condition."

She giggled. "My condition? I'm perfilly fine. In fact, I was just realizing that I obviously had not imbibed quite enough to quiet all the voices in my head."

He knelt down beside her on the blanket. "I don't have any more wine but I have two good ears if you'd like to talk."

She looked up at him with a crooked smile, but as her gaze traveled from his face down to his crotch, she groaned and lowered her head to her bent knees.

Placing his hand on her shoulder, he asked, "Are you going to be sick?"

"Yes," she whined, "But not the way you mean."

He withdrew his hand and sat back. "I don't understand."

She raised her head and stared out at the water. "Neither do I. In fact, I don't seem to understand anything about my whole world any more. I don't understand why Grandpa had to die before I could say goodbye to him. I don't understand how the house got to be in such a mess."

"You know—"

"I don't understand how a person can be called a genius one day and stupid the next. An' I don't understand how a man can give you a ring and say he wants to be with you forever and then ask for it back just because some bastard made a fool of me." She sniffled, a tear leaked out of the corner of one eye, and suddenly there was no holding back the grief.

Zach hesitated for a full second before wrapping his arms around her. Her head on his chest, he gently rocked her until the sobbing was reduced to an occasional sniff.

"First things first," Zach said in a soft voice. "I've heard enough of Billy's stories to know that your Grandpa knew very well how much you loved him. I also know that even though his body is gone, there's a little bit of his spirit in every room in that house. I have no doubt he's looking down on you from those stars up there. If you feel the need to say something to him, say it. He'll hear you."

She sniffled again and the movement of her head on his chest let him know she knew that also.

"I believe the next thing was the problem of the house, but we both know the mess is only temporary and when it's all done, it will be even nicer than when your grandparents lived in it. It just can't happen overnight." She gave him another nod of understanding.

"Moving on. Anyone who would think you're stupid is too stupid for their opinion to matter, and you're better off without them in your life. If you're referring to the people you used to work for, you should be grateful to them. After all, because of their stupidity, you now own your own brokerage, which is much better than being an employee."

She tilted her head up at him. "How did you know about that?"

"Billy told me." He had no ready comment regarding the bastard she'd referred to, but he certainly had a few thoughts about the bastard who'd tossed her away. "As to the idiot who broke your heart, no matter what his reason was, if it would make you feel any better, I would be most happy to confront him and challenge him to a duel."

She laughed. "That is very gallant of you, sir, but

hardly necessary." She straightened, and he reluctantly released her. "Eric broke the engagement and I felt betrayed, but he didn't actually break my heart. After it was all over, I realized everyone else had always been more excited about our upcoming marriage than I was. The truth is, I accepted his proposal because so many people told me I'd be crazy not to. Anyway, no one else had ever come along who..." Her shoulders slumped.

He waited, but she didn't finish. "Who...*what*?"

She glanced at him, smiled, then looked back at the ocean. "Nah. You wouldn't understand. It's a very girly thing."

"C'mon, try me. I've been told I have a very well-developed feminine side."

She sighed. "Maybe I read too many romance novels in my teens, but I always thought I'd just *know*. Our eyes would meet. Bells would ring. Something would wake up inside me that I'd never known was there. I know. It was silly."

He grinned. "What about when he kissed you?"

She shrugged. "Eric wasn't *bad* at kissing. It just wasn't...perfect."

"What would you consider a *perfect* kiss...according to all those romance novels?"

"*Hmmm*," she sounded dreamily. "When we kissed, the whole world would disappear and time would stop."

"Sounds pretty perfect to me too. And what about...when you made love?"

She closed her eyes and took a slow breath. "It would be a journey into the stars."

Zach never wanted anything in his life as badly as he suddenly wanted to accompany her on that journey. "I gather Eric didn't quite...take you to the stars."

"*Hmmph*. Eric barely got me off the ground."

In his mind, Zach jumped up, whooped, hollered and did a victory dance around the blanket. "That proves you're lucky to be rid of him. He wasn't the one."

"The *one*? I gave up on that romantic notion a long time ago. But what about Zachariah Gibbon? Did he ever meet his *one*?"

He waited for her to look directly into his eyes, then he held her gaze until he was absolutely certain about the attraction being mutual. "I've always referred to that elusive one as my perfect woman. And I'm almost positive I've met her. But I can't do anything about it. You see, I made her a promise that if I did anything to make her nervous, she could send me away, which is the absolute last thing I want to happen."

Leanne licked her lips. "What if..." She took another of those deep breaths that nearly unmanned him. "What if you had already made her *very* nervous, and the last thing it made her want to do was send you away?"

He raised his hand to stroke her cheek, but drew it back again. "If that were the case, she'd have to let me know exactly what she would allow. For instance, if it was all right for me to touch her face or hand, she would have to look me in the eyes and smile."

Ever so slowly, her mouth curved into a soft, inviting smile.

Just as slowly, he reached out and touched her nose with his fingertip, then traced the line of her jaw with his thumb. Being allowed that much gave him the courage to move that hand to her shoulder and lightly trail his fingers all the way down her arm. The gooseflesh he felt rise assured him that an attempt to enclose her hand in his would not be rebuffed.

"Hearing any bells?" he asked hopefully.

She smiled again. "Maybe a ping."

He gave her hand a small squeeze and she returned it in kind. "That's certainly encouraging, but I wouldn't want to jump to any conclusions because of a little ping."

"So, what *would* have you jumping to a conclusion?"

"*Hmmm*, let's see." Zach rubbed his chin thoughtfully.

"Well, let's say my perfect woman believes that the perfect kiss would make the rest of the world disappear. Since I'm too shy to initiate anything so intimate, she'd have to give me a sign that she wanted to be kissed." For a moment he thought he'd gone too far, but then she leaned forward, tilted her head, closed her eyes and pursed her lips.

For the first time in his life, he was nervous about a kiss. If he didn't get it just right—He hushed the insecure voice in his head and brushed his lips lightly over hers. A hint of a spark convinced him it was going to be better than perfect. Although a large part of him wanted to dive into the kiss with his whole body, the wiser part demanded he practice restraint.

Again he lightly brushed his lips over hers then, ever so softly, pressed just firmly enough and long enough for it to be a kiss rather than a peck. His mouth moved to her cheek and down her neck, continuously teasing her with baby kisses and warm breaths until he felt her growing anxious for more. Only then did he return to her mouth and outline her lips with his tongue, and when she parted her lips in invitation, he accepted without hesitation.

A moment later however, he abandoned her mouth for a nibble on her earlobe then murmured, "How's your world looking?"

"What world?" she asked in a low whisper.

His mouth eased back to hers, drawing her into a deeper, more intense kiss. He wanted her to know how badly he had wanted to do this since he first saw her. He wanted her to feel the passion she aroused in him. He desperately wanted to ignite a fire in her as no other man ever had. But his personal order of restraint was still in effect.

Leanne had no idea what he was waiting for. But she *did* know what she wanted and how she wanted it and it was taking him far too long to get the hint. As though the wind had shifted, she became the aggressor in a devouring kiss that left him breathless. Her hands moved over his chest, arms and back as though they were feeding on him as well.

Her desire made him feel weak and empowered all at once. And he was more than willing to forget restraint and let her use him until she had her fill. But when her hand moved downward, his conscience dumped a bucket of ice water in his shorts. He reined in the manic kissing and, taking her hand in his, he moved it to a less sensitive area.

Leanne tilted her head back and blinked at him in confusion.

"I can't…we can't…it's wrong."

CHAPTER 8

Leanne gave her head a shake. "I don't understand. How was any of that wrong? You're not married, are you?"

"No. I'm not and never have been married."

"Then what? You didn't like my making a move?"

He groaned. "I *loved* that you pushed me. I *needed* you to let me know you wanted the same thing I did."

She took a deep breath and inched back from him. "Okay, let me have it. This day can't get any worse."

It took him a moment to start. "You had a lot to drink. I didn't want you to wake up tomorrow—"

"Bullshit. I knew what I was doing. The alcohol fog left my brain with the crying jag. Try again."

"We don't have any protection."

"True, but we didn't need protection for what I had in mind. Unless…do you have…a contagious disease?"

That question earned her a frown. "No."

"Try again."

"If I tell you the real problem, I'm afraid you'll hate me."

"If you don't tell me, I'll have to ask you to leave my home. After what just happened, you can't think we could go on living under the same roof. So you have nothing to lose. You may as well tell me whatever it is. Who knows, I may believe you...*again*."

"Will you at least promise to hear me out completely?"

She exhaled heavily. "Sure. Why not."

"I *was* down on my luck and needed a place to stay, like I said, but not for the reasons I gave you. Also, I *was* accused of a crime I didn't commit, but I don't have a prison record."

"Why would you lie about—Were you cleared?"

"No. I ran after bail was posted."

"Oh, swell. I'm harboring an escaped criminal."

"I'm *not* a criminal," he said sharply then quieted his tone again. "I really was expertly framed."

She made a bored face. "Oh, yes. You said that before. But if you were so innocent, why did you run?"

"Because I overheard the real perpetrators—my boss and another broker—discussing the hit man they'd already hired to kill me and make it look like suicide. They had posted my bail to make sure I was in a position to be permanently removed. They had no intention of letting me tell my side of the story. If people thought I'd killed myself, everyone would believe I had committed the crime, and the real bad guys would get off free."

She took a moment to absorb his story before commenting. "Are you telling me that you intend to hide out for the rest of your life? If you're really innocent, you could go to the authorities and demand protection."

"I could, if I had one piece of solid evidence about the crime or my intended murder. All I have is my word against theirs. And if I turn myself in and they put me in jail for who knows how long before a court date is set,

there's a fair chance I could still end up dead. These are
very wealthy, influential men. But Dolores, my
executive assistant, promised to search for something to
prove who the real guilty parties are. She insisted she
knows someone who would be able to help."

"And has she?"

"I really don't know. She has no idea where I am or
how to contact me and I can't put her at risk by
contacting her. I've just been hoping something would
turn up in the news."

Leanne massaged her temples. Between the excess of
wine and the complication of his story, she had a
headache coming on. "Wait a minute. You referred to
her as your executive assistant. Since when do
construction workers have executive anythings?"

He made a face and stared out at the ocean. "I, uh,
wasn't truthful about my former career."

"Hah! Now there's a surprise. Well, don't stop now. I
can't wait to hear the rest of this soap opera."

His mouth twisted from side to side. "I, uh, I was a
stock broker."

"I beg your pardon?"

"And I was very professionally duped into promoting
a stock offering for a new company. They had all the
proper documents and the numbers and expectations
were within reason. They even had credible forgeries of
signatures of impressive names, which were
conveniently confirmed by middlemen.

"All they needed was a highly successful, trusted
broker from a major firm to push it to other brokers,
who would then push it to their clients. In exchange for
a slightly reduced commission, I was offered a short-
term exclusive arrangement. Since I had a reputation for
picking winners right out of the gate, a lot of brokers
jumped on the offering without checking it out
themselves."

Leanne's stomach began to churn. "This is beginning

to sound way too familiar."

"Let me finish. Within weeks, hundreds of millions of dollars had poured in. Needless to say, I had made a fair amount in commissions. Then the inevitable happened. One of those impressive names denied knowledge of the enterprise. As the fraud was uncovered, my name kept coming up as the brain behind the scam. There was even a record of a large deposit into a Bahamian bank account in my name. My frame-up was as brilliantly arranged as the fraudulent company was constructed."

She thought she might throw up any second. She could hardly breathe. She already knew the story he was relating, but that would make him—*No*. That wasn't possible. God wouldn't do this to her. Yet she had to know for sure. "What is your name?"

"I didn't do it, Leanne, I swear."

"Your name, dammit!"

"Ellwood Zachariah Gibbon." He paused then said the name that was as fatal as sticking a knife in her heart. "Rush. My family calls me Zach, but most people know me as E.Z."

She felt the rage build until she could no longer contain it. *"O-o-oh!"* she roared and pounded her fist against his chest. The next instant she was on her feet. "You pig! Wasn't it enough that you destroyed my life? You had to move into my home? You had to make me want you? How dare you touch me?"

She grabbed the edge of the blanket and yanked with all her fury. She was only slightly satisfied to see him tip backward into the sand. "I'm going home to burn this and scrub myself with lye soap. I would order you to leave tonight but I do owe you money for the work you've done. I'll have it for you tomorrow. You can sleep in your truck in the yard tonight but don't you dare come back inside the house."

Leanne walked several extra blocks in an attempt to burn off her anger.

You were warned, her little voice reminded her.

Shut up.

What good is having intuition if you're not going to pay attention to it?

Excuse me? It was my intuition that convinced me to hire him to begin with and give him a chance after I discovered his first lie. Paying attention to my intuition is what got me into this predicament.

My point exactly.

Leanne questioned the lack of logic in her two-sided thought process, but her confused alter-ego had stopped talking.

By the time she walked home and went to bed, the red anger that had muddied her thinking was muted to blue self-pity again. After several hours of wallowing, the little voice decided to start nagging again.

Have you figured it out yet?

Why are you reminding me of that dream?

Why do you think he wouldn't let you have sex with him? If he was really such a bad guy, wouldn't he have kept his secret and taken advantage of you groping him?

Don't confuse me. I hate him.

The more important question is, do you believe him?

Leanne tried to form an instant negative response but couldn't quite manage the two-letter word.

Just for a moment, try to let go of the hurt and anger. Pretend you have no personal stake in the answer. What does your intuition tell you about his story?

I no longer trust my intuition. For some reason, it is completely unreliable where E.Z. Rush is concerned.

Then try putting yourself in his position. You know that what he described could happen.

It occurred to Leanne that her little voice was beginning to sound an awful lot like Grandpa. The suggestion was one he often made with regard to judging other people. With that in mind, she gave it some consideration.

A fraudulent stock offering of that magnitude would take time to set up and would require a lot of people. But hundreds of millions of dollars can cover a lot of payoffs, and there would always be people willing to bend their ethics and the law for a piece of such a rich pie.

She didn't want to believe his story. It was easier to stay angry and keep blaming him for every horrible thing that had happened in her life.

However, she certainly couldn't blame him for the condition of Grandpa's house.

The memory of Zach comforting her as she cried in his arms drifted through her mind. What he had said about saying goodbye to Grandpa was unbelievably sweet and demonstrated a spiritual nature.

He had said she was fortunate to be free of the people who doubted her because it enabled her to open her own business. She didn't completely disagree with that.

And he had proven in a most dramatic way that Eric's kisses were far from the best she could expect.

The biggest argument on his behalf, however, was the fact that he hadn't taken advantage of her while a lie stood between them, even though he knew the truth would end any chance he'd ever have to be with her.

He may have worn a disguise and told several lies, but she might have resorted to the same solution under the circumstances. And his disguise didn't hide the fact that he was willing to work very hard to survive.

The man she had slowly gotten to know and trust was not the type to destroy the careers of colleagues or rob his long-time clients of ten dollars let alone millions.

There was no use fighting it. She didn't hate him. She believed him.

Are you satisfied, Grandpa? Is that what you've been trying to tell me?

She didn't hear the little voice, but she had a strong

feeling Grandpa was smiling down at her from the stars.

Back to following her intuition, she put on a robe and went outside. As she had ordered, he was asleep, or appeared to be, in the cab of his truck.

She reached inside the open window and touched his shoulder. He was immediately alert...and leery. "Come inside, Zach. We aren't finished talking." Rather than wait for him, she turned and headed back to the house.

He was mere seconds behind her. "I never meant to hurt you, Leanne. If I'd had anywhere else to go, I would have taken off the minute I learned what business you were in. My being the cause of your problems and ending up in your home was just a terrible and very weird coincidence. You've got to believe that."

"I do."

He was so ready for another rejection, it took him a moment to absorb her words. "You do? Why?"

"Yes. And I might be totally out of my mind, but I also believe you're innocent." His face broke into a broad smile and he stepped toward her, but she held up a hand to keep him from getting closer. "You're not off every hook just yet."

His frown returned. "Okay."

"Do you believe I am of sound mind, mature enough to make my own decisions and not at all inebriated at the moment?"

"Yes to one and two. As to three..." He squinted at her. "You appear to be sober. Are you?"

She clucked her tongue. "Of course I'm sober. I just wanted to make sure you were clear on those points. Next, are there are any more facts about yourself that you've kept hidden?"

He gave that a few seconds of deliberation. "There are a few thousand details about my life I haven't shared, although I'd be happy to, but I don't suppose that's the sort of thing you mean. As far as anything that would make you want to punch me again...I guess I should admit that I don't know the first thing about home repairs."

"Then how—" She figured it out on her own. "Billy, right?"

Zach lowered his head with sincere remorse. "Yes. I'm afraid I told him a few lies also, and he took pity on me. In my defense though, I had planned on figuring everything out on my own. But then you insisted we meet and he told me how he really missed 'putzing' around Tom's old house but you wouldn't let him. But I always worked…once he told me what to do."

"*Hmmm.* All right. Anything else?"

"I don't think so. Oh, yeah, there is one other thing—it's more of a confession actually—but this probably isn't the best time—"

"I may not give you a better time. Spill," she commanded in a threatening tone.

"Seriously, it isn't—"

"Now!"

He looked down at his feet, as though he were more embarrassed about this confession than all the lies he'd told. "From the first time I saw you, I, uh, had…impure thoughts about you."

She bit her cheek to keep from laughing. "*Impure thoughts?*"

"That's what they were for *Zachariah.*" He looked truly sheepish. "Actually, they weren't so much thoughts as fantasies."

Recalling the erotic dreams and rather wicked thoughts she had been having about him, she took a step closer and asked, "What sort of fantasies?"

His gaze slid down her robed figure and back up to stare intently into her eyes. "Very, *very* sexy ones. They usually involved getting you naked and you begging me to touch you, kiss you, lick you. All over. From head…to toe." His gaze lingered on her breasts.

Her tongue moistened her suddenly dry lips. "I begged?"

He shrugged. "Commanded might be more accurate."

"And where did these fantasies take place?"

"Anywhere. Everywhere. In the ocean. In my truck. In your bathtub. On the back porch. I'd be happy to give you a, uh, blow-by-blow tour."

She could see him holding his breath for her response, but she had no intention of letting him off the final hook that easily, not after everything he'd put her through. "Follow me," she ordered and strode to the stairs.

Once inside her bedroom, she made him wait a bit more while she unearthed a box from the closet and found what she was looking for. Keeping as straight a face as she could, she tossed two condom packets on her bed. "Do you know what those are?"

His curious frown turned into a lascivious grin. "Protection?"

"Exactly. I am not drunk, there are no lies between us, and you have your protection. I believe that takes care of all your objections against having sex with me, unless you have some new ones."

His grin broadened and he shook his head. Glancing at the condoms, he asked, "Two?"

"Too many?" she teased.

"Too few," he countered.

"*Tou-ché*. Then what are you waiting for? A command?" One raised eyebrow was her answer. "Fine. Take off your clothes. Everything. I'm not removing one stitch until you're more naked than I am." As he swiftly shed one article after another, she didn't bother to conceal her appreciation of the fine body she'd only been able to glimpse before. When he finally dropped his shorts and she noted his semi-erection, she quit fighting her smile and closed the distance between them. Brazenly stroking him, she said, "I'm relieved to see that your previous hesitation was not due to any…shortcoming."

"Wait," he murmured and moved her hand. "I want to

see how close my imagination got to the real thing."

She stood motionless as he raised her t-shirt over her head and removed her bra.

"Perfect," he whispered, cupping her breasts in his hands. "Better than I imagined." He leaned over, caught one peak between his teeth and gently sucked. He gave the other the same attention then knelt before her. Slipping his fingers beneath the waist of her shorts, he lowered them enough to apply kisses across her abdomen and tickle her navel with his tongue.

He eased down the shorts until he caught the top of her panties then lowered both a bit more so he could press slow kisses across her lower abdomen.

Leanne was torn between enjoying the adoration and wanting him to move on. Her body was well aware of what was coming and hurried to welcome him. Yet she gasped with honest surprise when he bared the next few inches and intimately stroked her with his tongue. Her fingers clasped his shoulders and he let the last of her clothing drop to her ankles.

As he teased her with his mouth, she alternated between holding her breath and gasping. "Zach, *please*," was all she could manage to utter, but he needed no more words. Two seconds later, his tongue and fingers worked together to give her what she needed.

Her hands continued clutching his shoulders as he rose, partly to keep standing and partly because his fingers were still playing with her, keeping her aroused and wanting. She drew his head down and pressed her open mouth to his as he brought her to another quick release.

"More?" he murmured into her ear as his fingers moved slowly against her.

"Oh my, yes," she answered then moved his hand away from her body. "But we need to even the score a little." Her fingers grazed his chest and crept lower. "I must admit to having a few fantasies myself, especially after I got a sneak peek at *this*." She caressed his abs then let her fingers trail to even harder, more sensitive flesh. As her fingers wrapped around his sex, she continued. "But unlike you, I thought mine were completely inappropriate."

He touched her cheek. "I'm sorry—"

"Sh-h-h. I'm afraid I need more than words to make up for that. I want you to tell me, *in detail*, about one of your fantasies…while I do my best to distract you. If you win, you get to have sex with me in whatever position you choose. If I win, I get to have sex with you in whatever position *I* choose." She bit her cheek to keep from returning his crooked smile of understanding. "Starting now." Her tongue flicked the tip of his shaft.

He twitched in response and complied. "Remember when you gave me mouth-mouth out on the back porch?"

"*Mm-hmm*," she sounded because her mouth was momentarily filled.

"Uh, I, uh…" He took a deep, controlling breath. "I imagined it didn't work and you—" He had to stop for another moment as her teeth scraped their way upward. "And, uh, you pushed aside my shirt and licked my nipples." Another pause had to be taken to appreciate what her fingers were doing between his thighs. "And when that didn't work, you took off my pants and—" His hands balled into fists as he raced through the end of his story. "And you did what you're doing now and that's how you brought me back to life. The end. Good gawd, Leanne, *have mercy*."

She took her mouth from him only long enough to say, "Just let go." And seconds later, he obeyed again.

As had happened with her, however, the first release barely took the edge off his need.

"You won," she said, smiling as she massaged him back to readiness. "Choose your position."

Zach gave her a deep kiss then laid down on his back on the bed.

Leanne wasn't completely surprised, given his fantasies of her commanding him. She took care of the protection then mounted him without further delay. What she hadn't realized was that he chose that position so, while she was riding him back up pleasure mountain, his hands could easily seduce her back to an even higher peak than she'd reached before.

What he was making her feel was beyond her limited experience and they'd barely begun before she was wondering how it could ever be any better than that. The answer came when he rolled them over. She felt him deep inside, on top, all around her. And when she was certain they could go no higher, he repositioned her again and proved her wrong.

Her entire body suddenly flooded with exquisite, liquid happiness, and together, they soared far above the mountaintop...directly up to the stars.

CHAPTER 9

She didn't remember falling asleep, but the sun was beaming through the bedroom window when her eyes opened again.

"Good morning, beautiful," Zach murmured in her ear. "You were smiling in your sleep."

"*Mmmm.* I was having a yummy dream about Ernest Hemingway." He pouted and she gave him a quick kiss. "But then it turned out he was actually a much younger, very sexy man, in disguise."

"Were you angry at him for deceiving you?" He kissed his way from her neck down to her navel.

"Yes," she told him, then drew his head to her breast. "But he was so good at construction work, I decided to forgive him."

He sucked one nipple into a peak. "About everything?"

She sighed as he moved to the other breast. "Yes. About everything. I can't explain why, because it certainly isn't logical."

"I think I know why," he said quietly and snuggled her into his embrace. "It was fate. Pure and simple. Just look at the timing of everything that has happened to each of us to bring us together in this house. If you ask me, I think Grandpa Tom may have had a hand in all this."

She chuckled. "I think that might be reaching a bit too far for an explanation."

"Maybe a bit," he continued seriously. "But you have to admit, it's been rather extraordinary. Most of my life I've known what my perfect woman would be like, but I never met anyone who even came close. Then the entire universe conspired to push me into your office...and I knew that instant. It was almost as though I didn't need to get to know you, because I already did." When Leanne remained quiet, he leaned back to see her expression. Her eyes were damp. "I wasn't going for tears with that speech—"

"They're happy tears," she assured him with a smile. "That was the most romantic speech I have ever heard...or read."

"Good. Then I feel secure enough to finish it. Leanne Shepard, I know I don't have much to offer...and my life is a mess...but I...I think I'm falling in love with you."

Her cheeks flushed. "Well, Zachariah, Zach, E.Z. and Ellwood Zachariah Gibbon Rush...I think I'm falling in love with all of you too."

Their mouths came together slowly with a kiss more reverent than passionate.

After a quiet moment, Zach said, "I also think we may have a problem...other than the obvious one. I'm fairly certain I've never before *thought* I was falling in love. I definitely have never *been* in love. Lust, yes, but not love...at least not the way other people talk about it. You?"

"The same. Like I said on the beach, my expectations of how love was supposed to feel came from reading romance novels."

"So, if neither one of us has ever been in love, how will we know when we go from *thinking* we're in love to definitely *being* in love?"

"Fair question," she said frowning. "We should probably make up a test of some sort."

He grinned. "I usually do pretty well on tests. What do you have in mind?"

She sat up, propped her chin on her fist and wrinkled her nose. A few seconds later, she snapped her fingers. "I've got it. If you're right about our meeting being fated and I'm right about romance novel love, then that should form the basis of our test."

Zach was intrigued but leery. "So…what's the test?"

"A happy ending. One where your name is cleared, my brokerage succeeds and we're free to live together without looking over our shoulders. Oh, and also the house gets fixed up."

He grimaced. "Does the house *have* to be part of it?"

"Absolutely. If you're right about Grandpa engineering our match, he'll continue to stick his nose in it to the very end…and he would definitely want the house to be part of it. Are we in agreement on this?"

"*Hmmm.* Happy endings all around equals true love," he summarized, though he clearly had some unspoken reservations. "I suppose that's as good a test as any."

"Excellent. So, do we have time to take care of some unfinished business or do you and Billy have a date to punch more holes in walls?"

Zach's expression changed to concern and he angled his head at her. "He's supposed to come by with some items we need to finish all the electrical work and maybe get the a/c going. But what unfinished business do you and I have?"

She let him wonder for a moment, then showed him the condom they hadn't used last night. "I believe *you* were the one who said two would be too few."

* * *

By two o'clock Leanne gave up trying to make progress on her letter writing project. She had forced herself to leave the house and go into her office, knowing Billy would soon be there. It wasn't so much that she thought she'd be in the men's way while they worked. She was more concerned that she would somehow give herself, *her happiness*, away to Billy if he saw her in the same room as Zach...*Zachariah*. It was too new, too unexpected, too *deliciously sensual* to keep it hidden. And yet, she had no choice.

However, the urge to go home grew stronger by the minute, until she had to consider the possibility that rather than hormones, it was her intuition tapping her on the shoulder. What if Billy hadn't shown up and Zach had another accident? Leanne was in her car before she had another thought.

As soon as she pulled into her driveway, she scolded herself. Both Billy's and Zach's trucks were there. Nothing was wrong. She took a calming breath and went inside to see what had gotten accomplished in the last four hours.

She walked from the front door to the back then called up the stairs. "Zachariah, Billy, where are you?" Not getting an answer nor hearing any activity overhead, she went outside and found Billy kneeling behind the a/c compressor. "Does this mean what I think it does?" she asked with a bright smile.

He answered without looking up at her. "Not quite. Getting closer though. I was just about to pack up for today. Would you mind making a pot of coffee? I'd love a cup before I head out."

"Sure thing." She started to walk away then tried to sound casual as she asked, "Where's Zachariah?"

"He's, uh, I had to send him on an errand."

Leanne was counting tablespoons of coffee grounds when her intuition stirred again. First, she realized she had seen both trucks. Where would Billy have sent Zach on foot? Second, Billy never drank coffee in the afternoon. The third and most damning proof that something was wrong—Billy didn't make eye contact with her.

By the time Billy came inside, the coffee was finished brewing and Leanne's stomach was in a knot. "What's going on?"

He sat down at the kitchen table and waited for her to take a seat before answering. "He swore you had no idea who he was. Now that could be true but my gut tells me he said that to make sure you wouldn't be charged with harboring a fugitive. Am I right?"

Heat rushed to Leanne's cheeks, immediately revealing her guilt. "I found out he wasn't...*elderly*, the day of the fire. But he only told me who he was...last night. What happened?"

"From that blush, I gather it was quite a conversation, which isn't going to make any of this easier. I need you to hear me out, Punkin'. I only did what I did to make sure you were safe."

Her ears were ringing with alarms. "Go on."

"I'll admit, he had me fooled at first. But his hands and nose gave him away. No thin skin, no liver spots. The wig and beard were obvious fakes but I figured he might have cancer or bad scars or something like that. And when I questioned his lack of skills, he gave a logical explanation. Still, it didn't take long to figure out he was nowhere close to my age and he was obviously hiding from someone or something. On the other hand, you trusted him and he was a hard worker. My gut told me he had a good reason for hiding and that you were okay with him in the house but I needed to be sure."

When he took too long of a pause, she prodded. "What did you do, Billy?"

"Remember my sister's grandson, Shane?"

She frowned. "The one who became a psychiatrist?"

He shook his head. "The FBI agent."

Her eyes widened. "You turned Zach in? Without knowing the whole story?"

Now it was his turn to frown. "You know me better than that. I just gave Shane a call and asked if he knew of any dangerous fugitives who might fit Zachariah's general description. I told him the man I was wondering about always wore one of those hooded sweatshirts so I never got a good look at his face. He seemed to be homeless, sleeping on the beach and so on, but seemed fairly new at it. The only other detail I told Shane was that the man had no callouses on his hands to indicate he was blue collar. He emailed me about two dozen posters. Then he called to tell me that if there was any chance E.Z. Rush was the man, they wanted to offer him protection in exchange for his testimony."

"*Protection?* Are you saying they now consider him a witness rather than a criminal?"

Billy shrugged. "It sounded like that was a possibility. They didn't fill me in except to warn me that he and anyone around him could be in lethal danger."

"Zach told me he overheard his boss talking to another broker about having him killed and making it look like suicide. And he was certain someone had been tracking him. He also said he had someone working on proving his innocence." A hurricane of emotions had her bolting from her seat and pacing back and forth. "This could be good. Or it could be very, very bad. What if the assassin had a connection inside the FBI and found out about your conversation with Shane? He could be on his way here now. What can we do?"

"*We* can stay calm. I never told Shane where the fugitive had really been or how he was disguised. When Shane got to the hardware store this morning, I called Zachariah, told him my truck battery died and asked him to come pick me up. If the assassin managed to learn what Shane and I discussed, then he'll soon know

E.Z. Rush was taken into custody. And if a would-be killer was just hanging around the area on a tip, I put on the wig, beard and sunglasses and drove Zachariah's truck back here. I'll be staying here until Shane tells me it's over. That way it'll look like the old geezer is still here, working on your house. Sooo, as long as you don't admit to knowing who Zachariah was, *we* should be fine."

"How did your truck get here?"

He shrugged. "I took a walk back to the store, wearing one of Tom's old sweatshirts and a big sun hat, and brought my truck here. Shane agreed that we should do everything just as we had been for the last week, which meant two trucks sitting outside and you going to your office for part of every day."

The underlying message of everything Billy had just told her took a few seconds to sink in. "He's already gone?"

Billy nodded slowly. "It had to be immediate. He wasn't given time to think about it. Or to write a note."

"And I suppose his whereabouts are secret." This was certainly not the *happy ending all around* they were hoping for. She suddenly knew exactly what it felt like to have her heart break. "Any idea how long?"

Billy shook his head. "This is a good thing for him, Punkin'. Better than being a fugitive."

Rationally, Leanne knew Billy was right about that but, at the moment, it certainly didn't feel like a "good thing" at all.

"Now, tell me what all you were hoping to have done in order to have the Christmas Eve party."

She closed her eyes and shook her head. "I was thinking I might go back to my townhouse for a while. I don't think—"

"Stop right there. Shane said everything has to move forward as though nothing has changed here. Otherwise, it may look like you were abetting a fugitive after all."

The ringing of her cell phone distracted her from arguing with him. "Excuse me," she said quickly as she hurried to dig her phone out of her purse. "Maybe it's Zach." A glance at the screen made her shoulders sag. "It's a Palm Beach number. Probably one of my old clients wanting to tell me what a wretched person I am." She set the phone aside and let the caller go to voice mail.

"Zach is *not* going to call you. You need to accept that and move on. Tell me about your party plans," Billy said firmly.

Leanne took a deep breath and tried to switch her thoughts to the lighter subject, but she couldn't ignore the fact that someone was leaving a fairly long message. "I'm sorry, Billy. I need to know who called…just in case." As soon as the incoming message registered, she listened to it.

A minute later she set the phone down and took another deep breath. "That was my realtor. He just emailed me an offer on my townhouse. Lower than I'd hoped but not insulting. All cash and they need to close before the end of the year."

Within forty-eight hours, the terms of the purchase were finalized and the buyer's attorney was drawing up the necessary documents.

The unbelievably well-timed offer effectively eliminated Leanne's idea of returning to Palm Beach for a while. The sale also made it possible for her to spend some of her savings to repair and paint the outside of the old house. Since she could afford to pay a professional crew, Billy applied some friendly pressure to his contacts and had the work started a few days later.

Leanne had no more reasons *not* to have the Christmas Eve party…except for the fact that she didn't feel like celebrating or networking the neighborhood for new business. The one person she most wanted to see would definitely *not* be there.

On December 14th, ten days after Shane took Zach away, and ten days before the party, the news reported that E.Z. Rush had turned himself in and new evidence had the FBI looking at other persons of interest. Shane paid his Uncle Billy a discreet visit to let him know Zach was well but would be remaining in a protected situation *at least* until new arrests were made, including that of the person who had accepted the contract to eliminate Zach. However, until they had absolute proof of Zach's innocence and his life was no longer in danger, he would not be enjoying any freedom.

Leanne kept telling herself he was much better off under FBI protection. At least they were *looking* at other suspects. She decided to believe that Billy having an FBI agent in his family was yet another weird synchronicity, like her Palm Beach townhouse selling right when she was about to give up on Key West.

She found herself taking comfort in the theory that Grandpa was somehow behind all of it.

On the other hand, as much as she wanted to believe Zach would soon be free to come back to her and they would get their happy ending, she couldn't force her logical self to hush. No matter how it had felt that last night, no matter what was shared or what words exchanged, they barely knew each other. There was a line from a movie that kept replaying in her mind…something about relationships begun in stressful situations were doomed to fail. Given enough time apart, one or both of them would realize that.

The days zipped by as Leanne hand-delivered invitations and left flyers in stores announcing the return of the Annual Shepard Christmas Eve celebration. Billy kept a watchful eye on the carpenters and painters and drummed up volunteers to put up Christmas lights and decorations all over the property. More volunteers came forward to run games and contests, help prepare gallons of Grandma's egg nog punch and hundreds of candy cane cookies, arrange for donations of toys and wrap them for attending children. Strolling carolers, musicians and magicians were scheduled to perform throughout the evening.

Leanne hadn't needed to *work* at networking the neighborhood or fret that they may not accept her as one of their own. Everyone loved her grandparents and was overjoyed that the young girl who used to spend her summers and holidays with them had chosen to resurrect a local tradition. Although the original Santa Claus—Grandpa—had passed on, Billy assured Leanne he'd consider it an honor to don the uniform.

The huge turnout on December 24th made all the effort worthwhile. Even the weather cooperated with a dry, comfortable temperature and clear, star-filled sky.

Everything seemed to be going incredibly well until a young boy ran up to Leanne and tugged on her sweater. "Santa said he needs you. Right away!"

Leanne turned toward the front porch, which was completely framed by garland and twinkling lights, and saw Billy sitting on the make-shift Santa throne surrounded by children. For a moment she wondered if the boy had been pranking her but Billy looked up and waved for her to come to him. As she walked beneath the trellis archway and up the steps, she realized he was reading a story to his rapt audience.

"Give me just a second children. Santa has something for Miss Shepard. This is her home now and all of us up at the North Pole want to thank her for having this party. Do you agree she deserves a present for that?"

The children immediately shouted out their agreement and Leanne smiled at Billy. "Thank you, Santa, but you know better than anyone, I didn't exactly manage this all by myself."

"Ho, ho, ho," he sounded loudly in reply. "But you get a present anyway." He handed her a shoe box wrapped in red paper and tied with a thin green ribbon. "It's best if you open it inside the house."

She arched an eyebrow at him but he just waved her toward the front door and went back to reading the story. As soon as she was in the foyer and closed the door behind her, she gave the box a shake. It didn't seem to have anything inside it, but there was only one way to be sure. She pulled off the ribbon and paper and lifted the lid. A piece of folded white paper sat in a nest of crumpled red tissue. Her heart began to race as she set down the box, unfolded the paper and saw a handwritten note. Her gaze lit on her name at the top and the phrase at the bottom. She had to wipe away tears before she could read the message between.

> *My dearest Leanne,*
>
> *I am so sorry I haven't been able to write before now. I was told it was for your safety. I am also extremely sorry I couldn't say goodbye. I was told that was for my safety.*
>
> *I constantly think about our time together, especially the discussion we had that last morning and I have something important to tell you—*
>
> *I know I love you.*

Clutching the letter to her chest, she sat down on the floor and gave into the wrenching sob she'd been holding back all day. The note was so short and said so little. He hadn't even been able to sign it.

"I wasn't going for tears..."

She blinked, swiped at her wet eyes and saw a pair of men's black shoes, then slacks and by the time her gaze reached his beautiful blue eyes she was on her feet and in Zach's arms. "You're really here," she murmured between sniffs. She tilted her head back and stroked his cheek. "How...when—"

He quieted her with a soft kiss. "I just got here,

courtesy of Billy's nephew Shane." He held her close as he continued. "It's basically over. Just so we can move on to happier topics, I'll give you the CliffsNotes version. Between Dolores, who had continued to work for my former boss, and her friend, who turned out to have some less-than-legitimate connections, and Shane and his agency, they grabbed the guy who'd been paid to…get me out of the way. Luckily he was an amateur and turned on his clients for a plea deal."

Zach stroked Leanne's back and kissed the top of her head. "With his statement, the evidence Dolores had compiled and my testimony, the real perpetrators of the fraud, one of whom was my boss, turned on each other. It won't all be public for another day or so, but there was no valid reason for them to stop me from attending your big party."

She tightened her hold around his waist. "Forget the party. I don't want to share you. Not yet."

He lifted her chin with his finger and stared into her eyes. "And I am certainly not in any mood to share you just yet either. But this evening is very important to our future and just because—"

"Did you say *our* future?"

He angled his head. "Didn't you read my note?"

"I read it. That's why I was crying."

"But did you read *all* of it?"

She frowned up at him. "I thought so." She backed out of his embrace and stared at the note she was still holding. He waited expectantly as she reread the words.

On her third read-through, she realized what he wanted her to notice. "You said…you *know*." Tears filled her eyes again.

"It was your test," he reminded. "A happy ending all around equals true love. That was the proof. My name is being cleared, which also covers the part about not having to look over our shoulders. And from what I could see beyond the Christmas decorations, it looks like you've made amazing progress on the house in a very short time."

"My townhouse sold so I could afford to hire some pros...with Billy's help of course. But I believe my brokerage was supposed to be a success also."

"There's no doubt about that happening. Your reputation took a hit but you're gathering new clients. And you are about to hire a major Wall Street hot shot to work for you."

She made a face at him. "I believe said hot shot recently experienced a major reputation hit himself."

"True, but he can be very persuasive...some even say he's charming." He grinned and pulled her close for another, sexier kiss. "So now you just have to say the words and we will be on our way to our happily ever after."

"Merry Christmas?"

He tweaked her nose.

"Fine," she said as though the words he wanted weren't the ones she wanted to say more than anything else. "Ellwood Zachariah Gibbon Rush, I *know* I love you. And I *know* I want you to be a part of my life and share every weird synchronicity that fate has in store along the way."

He leaned down for another long kiss. "And, as I wrote in the note you barely read, I *know* I love you. And I promise to read a stack of romance novels to make sure I *know* exactly what you expect from your lover." That earned him a giggle and a kiss heavy with promise.

"You were right though. I really do need to get back to the party. How would you like to be introduced?"

He didn't give it any thought. "I wouldn't. Not tonight. This is your party. Your night to shine. I might just take a nap...upstairs...in your bedroom."

"A nap is a good idea...especially since you shouldn't count on getting a lot of sleep after all the company leaves."

They shared one more kiss before he headed up the stairs and she went back outside.

"How'd you like your gift?" Billy asked with a distinct Santa-like twinkle in his eyes.

"It was perfect," she replied and blew him a kiss. Before she rejoined the crowd in the front yard, she blew another kiss up to the stars. "Merry Christmas, Grandpa. Your gift was perfect too."

GHOSTS

OF

CHRISTMAS
PAST

Christmas Presents Series

Novella Three

MARILYN CAMPBELL

CHAPTER 1

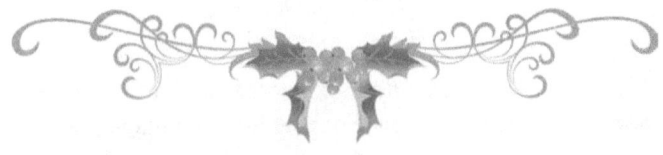

Felicity Flowers eased off the gas pedal of her vintage Volkswagen Bug the moment she saw the sign.

Welcome to Haversham, Vermont
Founded 1710, Population 956

Her first step was to absorb the atmosphere of the town from border to border before examining anything specific at closer range. Carefully obeying the posted speed limit of twenty miles per hour, she spoke into her recorder.

"I'm driving along Main Street. Looks like a typical, very small New England town. The historical architecture has been extremely well preserved. The street and sidewalks are clean. All very quaint, colonial, charming, blah, blah, blah.

"On one side, there's May's, a cutesy diner with ruffled curtains in the front windows. Then there's the Haversham General Store slash Post Office. The City Hall slash Police Department slash Fire Station is on the other side. Next to that is the Haversham Public School.

Pretty small building. Must not be many kids. Opposite the school is Chuck's Garage. No fast food chain in sight."

It was close enough to lunchtime for her to wonder what was on the menu at the diner, despite the ruffled curtains. There were four streets, named First, Second, Third and Fourth Place, leading away from Main. Down those streets Felicity could see a variety of single-family houses. The last building along Main Street was the Haversham Inn. In less than five minutes, she had reached another sign that read:

Leaving Haversham, Vermont
Have a nice day.

She made a U-turn and took another look at that three-story, red brick mansion. Four white columns supported a second floor veranda and three dormers jutted out beneath the gray-shingled roof. Like the rest of the buildings, the old inn was elaborately decorated for the holiday season. It also appeared to be meticulously cared for, unlike a number of the other so-called haunted houses she had visited so far on this trip.

It was just as well that the story she was writing required her to stay there. It appeared to be the only thing in the area remotely resembling a hotel. *Gawd!* It was probably one of those bed and breakfast places where she'd have to leave her room and actually speak coherently just to get a cup of coffee.

She did a brief tour of First through Fourth and their cross-streets and confirmed that all the businesses were on Main. The town was simply too adorable to be natural. There were actually white picket fences surrounding pastel-hued clapboard houses with shutters, window boxes and gingerbread trim.

This wasn't a town, Felicity thought grimacing. This was a set for a Disney movie…or a Stephen King novel. Personally, she was rooting for King. At least that would break up the tedium that had marked this whole project so far.

The fact that every inch of the damn town was decorated with gold and green garland and giant red bows and bells made it even more nightmarish for her. Though it was daylight, she could see that every streetlight and evergreen tree had twinkle lights strung around them. She didn't need the sun to go down for her to imagine how absolutely *magical* Haversham would be at night. The whole town simply oozed Christmas spirit. The only thing missing was fluffy, white snow.

There was nothing in the letter she had received from Wesley Haversham XII, Patron of Haversham, that prepared her for a fairy tale village. His letter had been short and business-like, with just the right enticement.

Mr. Haversham's letter mentioned that he had read her article in *Aware* magazine regarding spiritualists that conned the elderly. He suggested that a visit to his inn the week before Christmas would alter her skeptical opinion of the existence of spirits. As an incentive to get her there, he offered free room and board.

That generous offer, along with her innate curiosity, set her to wondering whether Mr. Haversham had some ulterior motive for wanting her to go to his town at that particular time, which in turn made her more anxious to check it out.

She decided that a story on poltergeists and the living who shared space with them could be a natural follow-up to the article he'd referred to. Soon she had lined up overnight visits at, or near, a dozen places purported to be haunted. To show how *un*-superstitious she was, Haversham Inn was scheduled as number thirteen, the last on her list.

As she drove along, she played back the notes she'd recorded. Her voice sounded the way she felt—bored to tears. When she first hit the road a month ago, she had thought this article might bring back some of the old creative spark. But like everything else she'd tried working on in the last two years, it had failed to do the trick.

So far the story was a dud. And she didn't have the slightest hope that her stay at Haversham Inn would make a difference. However, anything was better than spending another Christmas Eve with family and friends. She preferred to spend that night in a town full of strangers, people who hadn't witnessed the most embarrassing hours of her life and didn't constantly spout phrases like, "poor thing" and "of all the nights in the year". Strangers wouldn't care whether or not she was "getting on with her life" or "throwing it all away".

If Haversham Inn turned out to be more annoying than inspiring, she could always go elsewhere for the next four days, until Christmas was behind her. Maybe Boston or one of the lodges in The Berkshires. Anywhere but home.

She turned into Chuck's Garage and stopped next to the old-fashioned gas pumps to begin step two—personal interviews with the natives. Mechanics in particular were usually interested in her refurbished, baby-blue Bug and she often counted on the old car to act as an icebreaker. Accustomed to self-service, she got out and removed the gas tank cap.

"I'll do that for you, ma'am," a portly, gray-haired man called as he came out of the garage. "Nice car," he said with a smile.

Felicity smiled back and moved aside. "It's dependable. And economical. Fill it with regular, please."

While he got the fuel flowing, she closed the snaps up the front of her brown suede jacket and shoved her hands into the pockets. It felt colder than it did when she started out that morning. At this rate, there would probably be snow for Christmas. Wouldn't that be just peachy.

"Are you Chuck?" she asked to get a conversation going.

"Yep," he replied, keeping his gaze on the pump handle.

"You have a very nice station here, Chuck. I do a bit of traveling and I've got to tell you, those are the cleanest service bays I've ever seen."

Chuck turned to her and grinned. "Thank you, ma'am. I'm proud of it."

"Have you been here long?"

"My father opened this station in nineteen fifty-two. Passed his name and the business on to me."

"I think that's great. You don't often hear things like that in bigger cities. Small towns seem to have more of a sense of tradition, I guess."

Chuck nodded. "Haversham's a town full of tradition. That's for sure."

"Really? Like what?"

He was obviously surprised by her question but, after a moment, he replied. "Lord Wesley Haversham founded this town in 1710, and it's been under the patronage of a Wesley Haversham ever since. The current patron is the twelfth in the line. Now *that's* tradition."

"Patron is a rather archaic title. Is it honorary or does it come with responsibilities?"

Chuck gave her a crooked grin. "Like I said, traditions are a big part of Haversham. But the patron is responsible for just about everything. Kind of like a town manager but more personal I guess."

"Has there ever been a patron not named Wesley Haversham?"

"Nope." The pump clicked off and he returned the handle to its holder. "That'll be eighteen dollars even. Cash or charge?"

"Cash," Felicity said, pulling a twenty out of her shoulder bag. "Where could I get something to eat?"

"May's Diner, down the street. The Haversham Inn serves breakfast and dinner, but no lunch."

He glanced from side to side before adding, "May's the better cook anyway."

She smiled as she opened her car door. "I'll keep that in mind."

"Have a safe trip, ma'am," Chuck said and started walking away.

"Thanks, but I'm only going as far as the inn. I'm staying there for a few days."

Chuck stopped in his tracks and whirled around toward her. "You're staying?" His expression went from surprised to pleased when she nodded. "Then you must be that reporter lady Wesley's expecting. Why didn't you say so? I thought you were just being nosy."

Felicity laughed. "Reporters are notorious for being nosy. But actually, I'm a freelance journalist."

He came back and vigorously shook her hand. "Well, either way, welcome to Haversham. And if you have any other questions, you just stop by and visit any time."

"Thank you, Chuck. I'll probably take you up on that after I get settled in."

Chuck watched her drive away then hurried inside. Within seconds, he had his wife, May, on the phone. "She's here," he told her excitedly. "Seems real nice too."

"How old?" May asked.

"Hmmm, early thirties I'd say."

"What's she look like?"

"Now, May, you know I never look at other women," Chuck protested.

"Baloney. Describe her."

"Well, she was all bundled up and her boots had heels on them, so it was hard to tell about height and weight, but I guess she was about average."

May clucked her tongue. "Was she *attractive*?"

Chuck thought out his answer before he spoke. This was the kind of thing that usually got him in hot water. "Her hair was reddish brown, kind of curly, down to her shoulders. I think her eyes were sort of green and she had some freckles on her nose and cheeks."

"She sounds just right."

"I beg your pardon?" He could tell May was up to something and, as always, she was way ahead of him.

"What's the one thing Haversham needs?"

Chuck frowned to himself then remembered what had been decided by the town council. "A tourist trade?"

"Besides that." She didn't wait for him to guess again. "We need another Haversham! And unless Wesley finds himself a new wife, there isn't going to be a Wesley Haversham the Thirteenth."

"Now, May, honey, you know he's still grieving over Joanne."

"Only because there's no one around to take his mind off her. It's high time for him to be remembering his responsibility to this town."

Chuck didn't really want to know, but he asked anyway. "What scheme are you cooking up in that head of yours?"

She laughed lightly. "Don't worry. You'll hardly have to do a thing."

Felicity turned into the paved driveway on the side of the inn and went around to the rear of the building. Only one car, an American sedan, was in a lot big enough for a dozen. The word, *Registration*, was printed on a small sign above a pair of intricately carved wooden doors. She parked in the space closest to those doors and pulled her suitcase out of the back of her Bug.

With a bit of effort, she lugged her case up the three steps to the covered porch and through the double doors. She found herself in a small foyer tastefully decorated with colonial pieces. On a narrow table were an open guest book and a ballpoint pen with a white feather coming out of its top.

She set her bag down and leafed through the pages. There weren't more than fifty names and addresses listed. She supposed it could be a new book, but the empty parking lot suggested that there was a dearth of guests at the inn. Chuck's instant assumption that she was the "reporter lady" was also a pretty strong clue that visitors here were few and far between.

Using the fake quill pen, she added her name in the book.

"Miss Flowers?"

Felicity looked up to see a very striking man standing a few feet away from her. She wondered how he had approached on the wood plank floors without her hearing him.

"Yes. I'm Felicity Flowers. I have a reservation."

He held out his hand and smiled broadly showing straight white teeth. "Welcome to Haversham Inn. I'm Wesley Haversham."

So, Felicity thought, *this* was the man who wrote her the stiffly formal letter. He was not at all what she'd expected. "It's a pleasure to meet you, Mr. Haversham," she said, returning his smile. "Your letter was quite intriguing."

"I'm glad. And please call me Wes. If you'd like, I'll show you to your room and let you get settled. Then I'll be glad to give you a tour of the house. May I hang your jacket for you?"

Before she had the first snap undone, he was standing behind her to assist. As he hung it in the coat closet, she couldn't resist taking a longer look at him. She had assumed he'd be a stuffy old man with white hair and heavy jowls and a pipe sticking out of his mouth.

Wesley Haversham XII looked more like a model for a *GQ* layout—tall, with nearly black hair brushed smoothly back from his face and just a hint of silver at each temple. Because she was looking at his wire-rimmed glasses, she couldn't tell the color of his eyes, only that they were dark. She'd always thought that glasses made a man more interesting. His white knitted sweater and black dress slacks showed off a lean, fit body. And he seemed to be personable as well. Definitely *GQ* material.

He picked up her bag and led the way up the stairs from the foyer. She thought the rear view was pretty damn nice as well and immediately decided to take plenty of pictures of the inn with him in most of them. If the ghost angle didn't work out, maybe she could sell an article on the owner. If not *GQ*, maybe *Cosmo* would go for it...if he was a bachelor.

"Does your wife help run the inn?" she asked casually.

He momentarily paused then resumed. "My wife passed away several years ago. But my aunt, Louise Ludwig, lives here and keeps everything running smoothly. You'll meet her later."

"I'm sorry about your wife," Felicity said aloud, while thinking that a widower could be considered even more interesting than a bachelor.

He shook his head and smiled. "It's been a while. Here we are." As he opened the first door on the second floor landing, the hinges emitted a loud groan. "Darn. I forgot to oil those. I'll be sure to take care of it later."

He stepped aside and she walked past him into a room that could have been Dolly Madison's parlor. She hadn't expected a full suite, let alone such well-appointed rooms. There was no doubt in her mind that some of the pieces of furniture were valuable antiques.

"This is truly lovely," she declared as she entered the bedroom and saw the fireplace and canopied four-poster. The heavy furniture was dark walnut and the colors were forest green and ivory with touches of red. Through the window she could see the Green

Mountains that bordered the town. Surely this place overflowed with skiers once the snow fell. Valid story or not, this was where she was spending the next four days. "I can hardly wait to see the rest of the rooms."

"Don't you want to unpack?" he asked with surprise.

"I can do that later."

As he escorted her from room to room, words of praise flowed honestly off her tongue. The entire house had been decorated with history and comfort in mind. There were another three suites similar to hers on the second floor, one of which his aunt used. For guests on a budget, there were six small bedrooms on the third floor with two communal bathrooms. Felicity was certain that, for diehard skiers, a discounted price plus the view out the windows was incredible enough to make up for the lack of a private bath.

The first floor had a spacious kitchen, a dining room that could seat twenty, a sitting room with game tables, and Wes's apartment, which faced Main Street.

On every wall of the dining and sitting rooms were portraits of Havershams, the dates of which could be estimated by clothing and hairstyles. The present Wesley bore an amazing resemblance to several of his male ancestors. When she remarked on it, he assured her, for each ancestor, he had a story that he'd be pleased to tell whenever she wished.

She couldn't help but notice how his eyes avoided the most contemporary painting. He was obviously the man in the portrait and the beautiful woman gazing up at him with adoration had to be his late wife. Felicity thought he must miss her terribly.

He brought the tour to an end in the kitchen, where colonial design was skillfully blended with modern conveniences.

"I absolutely *love* this whole place," she gushed. "What a marvelous writer's retreat it would make."

"You really think so? I never thought of—" Wes

looked up at the ceiling. "Did you hear that?"

"What?" she asked, following his gaze.

"That tinkling sound. Like glass wind chimes. It's gone now."

Felicity hadn't heard anything and admitted it.

"They were probably saying thank you for your compliments."

"They?" she asked, already guessing at his explanation.

"My ancestors," he said, with a serious expression. "They don't always make themselves known to strangers so quickly but your appreciation of their home would make a difference. It's always been said that when you hear the sound of the wind chimes, it means a spirit is smiling."

"Well, I certainly hope I get a chance to meet some of them while I'm here. I think I should tell you though, this is the last of thirteen buildings I chose to investigate for my article and I have yet to witness anything even vaguely supernatural."

Wes nodded his understanding. "Spirits are very independent. They choose who they want to communicate with and no amount of pleading will convince them to perform on cue."

"I've been told that before. It's begun to sound like the standard excuse for why nothing strange ever happens when a reporter is nearby."

With a low laugh, Wes said, "I have a feeling your luck's about to change. I'm sure you have a lot of questions but how about some lunch first? Aunt Louise won't be back until about four but there's always something in the fridge."

"Actually, I thought I'd take a walk down to May's Diner."

"Good. I'll go along and introduce you."

Though Felicity would have preferred to talk with some of Haversham's residents without him, she worried that it might seem rude to refuse his company. Before heading out, he insisted on helping her don her jacket. It had been a long time since she'd received such gentlemanly treatment and she decided she liked it. And when his fingers remained in her hair a moment longer than necessary to free it from the collar, she decided she had no objection to that either.

She had only met Wesley Haversham XII an hour ago, but he didn't seem like a stranger to her. She only hoped he wasn't a complete nut-job like most of the people she'd met in the past month.

CHAPTER 2

"Are you sure you wouldn't rather ride?" he asked as he held open the door for her. "It's almost a mile."

"I spent the whole morning driving. I could use some exercise."

"All right. That will give me a chance to give you a bit of Haversham history as we go along."

His hand cupped her elbow as she descended the steps. Even through the suede jacket she felt the strength he could offer should she require it. When they reached the ground he released her, and for just a moment, she had the silliest wish that the parking lot was covered with ice so his steadying support would still be needed.

He began his narration as they strolled around to the front of the inn.

"The first Wesley Haversham was a wealthy British lord. He came over from Yorkshire in 1710 with his wife, Dierdre, and their baby son, who as you probably can guess was named Wesley Haversham the second."

"If he was titled and wealthy, why did he leave England?"

Wes smiled down at her. "Because he was also insanely jealous. Dierdre was so beautiful, every man who saw her fell in love. Her husband fought two duels over her before they left England. He thought if he took her to the New World to live among the savages, he'd have her all to himself."

During the brief seconds Felicity had scanned the family portraits, she had been paying more attention to the men than the women, but it had flashed through her mind that all the women seemed uncommonly beautiful. "Did it work?"

He laughed. "Hardly. Lady Haversham liked people too much to be hidden away. She befriended the Native Americans, organized quilting bees with the women and generally became the center of all social activity in the area. She encouraged her husband to put his energies into building a town and drew up the plans to get him started. Eventually he realized that she freely gave her friendship to anyone who desired it—male or female— but all her love was reserved for him."

"What a nice romantic story. Is it true?"

Wes laughed again. "Who knows? It's been told for almost three hundred years. It's believed that they set the standard for marriages of all future Wesley Havershams. The Haversham men are traditionally jealous, the women have always been beautiful but good-hearted and the stories about them are all of a romantic nature.

"Of course, you have to take into account the fact that the first couple had ten children, all of whom had large broods of their own. Practically every person living in Haversham today can trace their ancestry back to Lady Dierdre and Lord Wesley, so only the positive aspects of the stories get passed on."

Felicity thought he was about to say something else,

something that made him sad, but whatever it was, he kept it to himself.

"Do Dierdre and her husband haunt the inn?"

He waved a finger at her. "Uh-uh. They don't like the word haunt. Or being called ghosts. They're spirits and they reside in the home that was theirs to begin with. But to answer your question, *all* the late Havershams are still around."

"How can you tell?" Felicity asked, making an effort to keep skepticism out of her voice.

"I've seen them."

She withheld the retort that came to her mind. He might be charming, handsome and well-mannered, but apparently he was loony as well. Too bad. She mentally switched gears from interested woman back to professional journalist. "What do they look like?"

"Exactly like they do in their portraits, clothes and all."

"How convenient." The sarcastic words slipped out before she thought better of it.

He stared down his aristocratic nose at her and cocked one dark eyebrow. "You really are a skeptic. No matter. They'll change your opinion soon enough. As I was saying, they're identifiable because of what they're wearing. Otherwise, it would be almost impossible to tell the men apart. As you might have noticed, we all look very similar."

"Are they translucent or solid?"

"Both. It varies."

Before she could ask another question from her mental checklist, they reached May's Diner. He held the door open for her, helped her remove her jacket and hung it up, then led her to a clean table, where he pulled out the chair for her and made sure she was comfortable before seating himself. Whether he was loony or not, she could still appreciate his old-fashioned manners.

Within seconds a waitress came up to them. She was

no more than sixteen, but her body-language and the expression in her eyes suggested she was considerably more mature. "Hi, Wes," she said, handing them each a menu. "You haven't visited us in ages. We missed you." Her words were accompanied by a little eyelash fluttering and a hip shift that brought her thigh up against his arm.

He gave her a pleasant, though non-encouraging, smile as he unobtrusively increased the space between them. "Thanks, Stephie. I've been pretty busy lately."

A short, plump woman wearing a chef's apron came out of the kitchen. Her platinum hair was teased and piled several inches high on top of her head, like an upside-down woven basket, and a pencil was sticking out of one side.

"Stephanie Ann! Stop flirting with Mr. Haversham. I'll take their orders," she said with a dismissive wave of her hand that sent the girl off with a pout. "Sorry about that, Wesley. If she wasn't my niece—"

"No problem," he said, cutting her off with a chuckle. "Let me introduce my guest. May, this is Felicity Flowers. She's researching Haversham Inn for an article she's doing."

Might be doing, Felicity corrected in her own mind. She held out her hand and May squeezed it. "It's a pleasure to meet you. Chuck recommended your cooking to me."

"He better recommend it or he'll be looking for a new place to sleep nights!" She extracted the pencil from her hair and pulled a pad out of a pocket of the apron. "What'll it be?"

They both opted for the vegetable soup and club sandwich special then May headed back to the kitchen.

"In case you were wondering," Wes said in a low voice, "May and Chuck have been married for about forty years."

She recalled Chuck's comment about tradition and

Wes's statement that the people in town could all trace their ancestry back several hundred years. "I hope you don't mind my asking but Chuck told me you're the patron of Haversham and that all the patrons have been Wesley Havershams. Is that correct?"

He nodded. "It doesn't entail much. This is a small town with few problems. My job mainly consists of directing the monthly council meetings. The title of patron started with the first, who gave up his British title of lord but was still expected to lead and support the new town. Thus he was called its patron. Living with spirits for hundreds of years has kept most of the people rather superstitious. They tend to believe that everything will continue to go along fine as long as nothing ever changes."

Felicity thought she understood. "So, a Wesley Haversham is always the town's patron. And Chuck's a mechanic because his father was?"

"Exactly. Most everyone in town works at a trade or profession that was handed down to them through several generations. Chuck's grandfather had a bicycle shop where the garage is now."

Her first impression that she had driven into a Stephen King novel came back to her. "And no one ever changes *anything*? No one ever *leaves* Haversham?" She felt another story angle coming on and this one was accompanied by chills.

It took him a moment to phrase his answer, and when he did, his voice was tinged with resignation. "That's the way it was for several centuries, but even the oldest traditions can face obsolescence. Some of our young adults have moved away in recent years. They wanted more than tradition for their children. I hope they find it."

That could explain the small school building. There really *weren't* many kids in town.

Stephie was still sulking a bit as she brought their

soup and drinks to the table. When she walked away again, Wes said, "Stephie and her friends won't be staying much longer either. There just isn't enough to offer here."

"Maybe they'll come back," Felicity said in an attempt to lighten his mood. "After they've had a taste of the outside world with its crime and dirt and unemployment, Haversham could look pretty good." She could see by his changed expression that she had chosen the right words. As they ate their soup, she took the conversation back to the subject that she had come here to research.

"You told me what the spirits look like, but *when* do they usually appear?"

Wes added a few shakes of salt to his soup then said, "Actual appearances are few and far between. Usually they make themselves known in much less obvious ways."

"Such as?"

"The wind chimes for one, and other noises. Or they move objects. A number of little things. If something is very important, they might leave a message of some kind."

May's appearance postponed Felicity's next question. "Here you go. Two special clubs. Have you told her yet, Wesley?"

Felicity raised her eyebrows at him. May had to be referring to something bigger than he had mentioned thus far.

"I'm getting there, May," he said with a wink. "But she's a real skeptic. Probably won't believe until she sees it."

"Good," May stated firmly. "Then she'll just have to stay through Christmas." She turned to Felicity with a smile. "Make sure he takes you to the Mountaintop Lodge over in Waitsfield while you're here. Chuck and I went there for our anniversary last month. They have a big dance floor and the most wonderful band plays all the old music." For a moment, she closed her eyes and swayed to the music in her head. "And the food's not bad either," she added when she opened her eyes. "You could take her there tonight, Wesley."

"Miss Flowers didn't come here to check out the restaurants in the area," Wes said with a slight frown.

"But she has to eat," May countered. "And your Aunt Louise, as much as we all love her, is a bit lacking in the cooking department."

Wes looked a bit embarrassed as he admitted to Felicity, "It *is* a four-star restaurant with a great view of Camels Hump Mountain.

"I don't want to put you out," Felicity replied without conviction.

"It wouldn't be a problem. I'd be pleased to take you."

May clapped her hands. "All settled then. You'll go tonight. I'll call and make reservations for you." To Felicity, she said, "They dress up a bit there. If you need something, my friend, Bernice owns the women's clothing shop down the street. I'm sure she has something pretty in your size. Then again, with that cute little figure, you probably look good in everything. Don't you think she has a cute figure, Wes?"

He sighed with obvious exasperation. "Did I hear you offer to make reservations for us? You probably should do that...*now*."

Felicity tried to hide her smile behind her hand as May waltzed back to the kitchen.

"I am sorry about that," Wes said. "Are you sure you'd like to go tonight? I could stop her from—"

"I'm sure," she said. "It sounds nice. But I probably should visit Bernice's shop. I didn't pack anything dressy."

"We'll stop by on the way back to the inn."

For a few minutes they ate in silence. Felicity sensed he was still feeling some embarrassment over May pushing them into going out that evening. "If you'd rather not take me I could go——"

"No, no," he protested, quickly cutting her off. "I think it would be nice too. I'm just a little surprised at May."

"Why? Is she usually more subtle?"

Wes laughed. "No. That was normal behavior for May. But I didn't expect her to try her matchmaking tricks on me." He paused a moment, then explained. "My late wife, Joanne, was her favorite niece. Our marriage was the crowning achievement of May's matchmaking career."

There was that sadness in his eyes again. "And you thought she'd never want you to look at another woman, even though Joanne is gone."

Wes shrugged. "*Gone* is a very relative term in this town. But yes, that's sort of what I thought."

Her natural curiosity had her wanting to hear more about his wife, but she didn't feel justified asking about her. Instead she returned to the spirit world. "May asked if you'd told me something yet. What was that about?"

"I was working up to it," he assured her with a slight grin. "Let's see, as I said, the spirits don't often make personal appearances, and there has never been specific way to predict when one might choose to become visible, except for one time." He paused and took another bite of his sandwich.

She gave him a few seconds then prompted, "And that one time is...?"

"Christmas Eve. Or I should say almost every Christmas Eve. They have been known to skip a year now and then, but they've never missed two in a row. Since they didn't visit last Christmas, we're rather certain we can count on them this year."

Felicity had no doubt that when the spirits failed to materialize on Christmas Eve, he would refer back to this conversation, saying he hadn't guaranteed they would appear.

"At any rate, I won't spoil the surprise by telling you what they do, but it will definitely be worth your while to be here on Christmas Eve. As my guest of course."

Though she had already decided to stay through that night, she let him believe his teaser convinced her. As they got up to leave, May popped out of the kitchen again.

"Your reservations are for seven, Wesley. And Felicity, make sure he takes you to Montpelier while you're here. No visit is complete without seeing the state capital and it's such a pretty drive."

Wes ushered Felicity out of the diner before May could think of another excursion for them to take together.

"She means well," he said with a sheepish smile.

A few minutes later they were in front of Bernice's dress shop and Felicity assured Wes that there was no need for him to wait for her. He seemed oddly reluctant to abandon her, but eventually he headed back to the inn alone.

The little bell over the door announced her entrance. From behind a circular rack of dresses a tall, dark-haired woman greeted her cheerfully. "Hello. You must be Felicity."

Felicity's surprise must have shown on her face because the woman laughed and explained herself.

"I'm Bernice. May called and said you'd be dropping by." She stepped around in front of the dress rack and scanned Felicity from head to toe. "I must tell you, I thought May was exaggerating about how pretty you are. And such beautiful hair. It's the same color as my great grandmother's mahogany tea caddy. I have just the thing for you to wear tonight."

As Bernice selected an emerald green turtleneck sweater-dress with long sleeves and hung it in the dressing room, Felicity wondered if the whole town was going to wait up for her and Wes to return from the restaurant to get a minute-by-minute account of the evening. It reminded her of how her family might act if *they* heard she was going out to dinner with an eligible man.

That thought replayed itself while she got out of her clothes and tried on the green dress. Was it possible that these people wanted to see Wes remarry as much as her family and friends wished that would happen for her? She could certainly empathize with him if they did. She had been harassed, nagged and tricked into meeting dozens of bachelors in the last two years.

It wasn't that she didn't want to remarry. She just hadn't met a single man that she couldn't predict exactly what he was going to say or do before he did it. Besides, they all had something about them that reminded her of her ex-husband, which was enough to reject them on the spot. That man was a Pig, with a capital *P*. Not only was he crude and self-centered, what he did to her two Christmas Eve's ago was unforgivable.

As if it were yesterday, she saw herself sitting in their living room with all their family and friends. She had planned a big surprise dinner party for their fifth wedding anniversary. By nine o'clock they ate the reheated dinner. By midnight, all the guests had departed.

He finally showed up at noon on Christmas day, but it was only to pack his clothes. Several more days passed before she learned that he had gone home from the office Christmas party with his secretary...to an apartment he'd spent considerable time in already. This time, however, he had decided to stay. He had actually called it his Christmas gift to himself.

She shook off the anger that still accompanied thoughts of his deceit and studied her reflection instead. Bernice was right; the dress was very flattering. No need to try on another.

Suddenly she heard something that made her freeze.

She waited for it to be repeated but all she heard was Bernice humming a tune. She remembered the door to the shop had a bell. This sound was more like...*glass wind chimes*. She pulled aside the dressing room curtain.

"Bernice? Do you have wind chimes in here?"

"No dear, just the bell on the door. Why?"

"Oh, nothing. I just thought I heard chimes."

Bernice's eyes widened as she noted the fit of the dress. "My, my, that dress is lovely on you. They must have been smiling at the sight of you."

"*They?*" Felicity asked warily.

"My ancestors. Didn't Wesley explain everything to you?"

Felicity's gaze darted around the shop, looking for something that could have made the sound she heard. "Yes, he told me quite a bit already, but I was under the impression that spirits don't move from building to building."

"Maybe they don't in some places, but they certainly do in Haversham. You never know where they might show up to give a nod or do a little mischief. We're all quite used to it though. Now, let's pick out some accessories. May said you didn't bring anything dressy, so I guess you'll need shoes and hose too. What about a bag?"

While Bernice bustled about her shop, Felicity mulled over the idea of a ghost hovering in the dressing room while she was changing. How silly! She didn't believe in ghosts or spirits or anything of the sort.

"I miss you, Jo-Jo." Wes said, staring at the woman in the painting on the dining room wall. He had hung the painting in there after his wife died, mainly because he seldom had cause to go in that room, thus he could avoid looking at it. Once in a while though, he felt the need to talk things out with her.

That wasn't so strange considering the fact that they had been friends from birth. They grew up together, attended school together and, on their wedding night, lost their virginity together. Theirs wasn't the kind of love that exploded with fireworks and passion. Rather, it was relaxed and comfortable and, if fate hadn't intervened, it could have been all Wes would have ever needed.

If only they could have had one child. Not that a son or daughter could have taken Joanne's place. It might have curbed the loneliness, however. But she couldn't conceive and by the time they learned why, the deadly cancer had already gone beyond control.

He no longer asked why fate chose him as the Haversham descendant around whom three hundred year-old traditions would come to an end. Every previous Mr. and Mrs. Wesley Haversham had borne at least three children early in their marriage, then lived happily ever after until they passed on in their old age. His parents, however, had only one child and that was quite late in life. They died within months of each other when Wes was twenty-seven.

He had plenty of Haversham aunts, uncles and cousins in town, but he had never felt as close to them as he had to Joanne. She was all the family he'd ever needed.

And now another long-standing tradition was being broken. In order to save the town from extinction, he had come up with a plan to turn their peaceful, reclusive town into a tourist attraction. And the residents—his extended family and friends—had wholeheartedly backed him. After all, he was Wesley Haversham the Twelfth. He *must* know what he's doing.

Everyone was counting on him to pull this off and whatever it took, even a bit of trickery, he would do it, rather than let down the town.

"I sure wish you could give me your opinion of our houseguest, Jo-Jo. There's so damn much depending on her. She seems very nice, though. In fact—you'll love this—May arranged for us to go to Mountaintop Lodge tonight. Do you realize it will be the first time I've taken a woman out to dinner, other than you?"

It occurred to him that this was really why he came in here—to let her know he would be with another woman. To be honest, it wasn't just that Felicity was a woman, but one that made his insides quiver when he first saw her. One that had him looking forward to the first slow song the band would play tonight so that he could discover what it felt like to hold her close.

Guilt washed over him like a cold draft. Was that fear he was feeling? Or Joanne's way of showing disapproval? Perhaps it was still too soon. Perhaps it would be best to cancel tonight's—

"Wes? Are you here?"

Still wavering between backing out and diving in head-first, it took him a moment to answer Felicity's call. "I'm in the dining room."

She appeared in the doorway a moment later, her arms laden with bags. "Why the hell didn't you tell me the whole damn town was haunted?"

CHAPTER 3

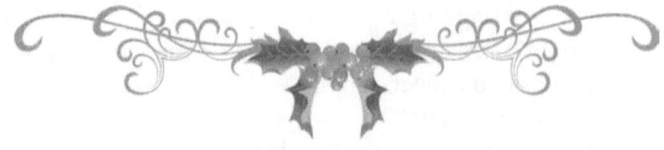

Wes quickly placed his index finger to his lips to hush her. "You'll hurt their feelings."

Felicity sighed and scanned the portraits. "Haunted, shmaunted! What difference does it make what word I use?"

Wes shrugged. "They don't care for profanity, either."

"I beg your pardon?"

"You called it a *damn* town."

Felicity was taken slightly aback. She used curse words all the time and—She aborted her thought when she realized her language had only begun deteriorating after her husband walked out on her. "Okay. I'll be more careful. Now fill me in on whatever little details you failed to mention earlier."

Just then the sound of the outside door closing announced someone else's arrival. "I wasn't keeping anything back. I just hadn't gotten to it yet. But first, let me introduce you to Louise. I'm sure that was her coming in. Just set your packages down in here."

Felicity did as he suggested then went with him into the kitchen. A petite, white-haired woman was coming in from the other doorway carrying two shopping bags that each looked heavier than she was.

"For heaven's sake, Aunt Louise," Wes scolded gently. "How many times do I have to tell you to get one of the boys to help you, or at least call me?"

She set down her bags and lifted her chin. "The day I can't carry groceries into the house is the day I stop buying them. And that day will only come when I'm laid to rest next to Mr. Ludwig."

Wes's exasperated expression told Felicity they'd had this conversation before. "Felicity Flowers, meet the stubborn Louise Ludwig."

"How do you do, Mrs. Ludwig?"

"None of that now. I'm Aunt Louise to everyone in this town, and while you're here, you'll call me the same." She brushed her hands off on her coat then grasped both of Felicity's hands in her own. "How pretty you are, girl. I've always admired people who can turn words into important sentences." Without releasing Felicity's hands, she stared deeply into her eyes for several seconds. "Pretty and intelligent...but sad. Let go of the past child. You have a beautiful future waiting for you, but you can't step into it until you get rid of the anger and hurt inside."

Felicity was too stunned to respond, so she merely looked to Wes to rescue her.

"Aunt Louise is part gypsy," he said with a grin. "She reads tea leaves in her spare time."

The elderly woman released Felicity's hands and shook a finger at Wes. "You better watch your step young man or I'll put a spell on you. Now get out of my kitchen. I have things to do, and it's almost tea time."

They started to go back toward the dining room when Wes stopped. "I almost forgot. You don't need to fix dinner for us—"

"Yes, yes, I know. Mountaintop Lodge. Seven o'clock. Dinner and dancing. Go on now."

Shaking his head, Wes and Felicity left his aunt alone.

"How did she know about tonight?" Felicity asked in a whisper.

With a grin, he said, "She'd tell you she's psychic but more than likely she just came from May's."

"No secrets in a small town, huh?"

"Not one." He picked up her packages and nodded for her to take the lead to her room. At her door, he handed the bags to her rather than go inside. "Aunt Louise and I will be having tea in the sitting room in about fifteen minutes, if you'd care to join us. It's a pleasant tradition that she insists on maintaining."

Felicity promised to be there since he had yet to answer all her questions.

She closed the door but felt no need to lock it. As soon as she turned around to go into the bedroom, the warm beauty of the suite made her smile. This was the kind of environment she imagined would give her the inspiration to write *The Great American Novel*. Someday, she promised herself.

Her smile faded as she entered the bedroom and looked around. Her nightgown and robe were on the bed, her slippers on the floor. She remembered Wes had left her suitcase sitting on top of the cedar chest at the foot of the bed, but now it was gone. She opened the closet door and found the case, but also discovered that her jeans and blouses had been hung up. On top of the dresser were her camera, film and writing supplies. On impulse she checked the drawers and saw that her underwear and sweaters had been neatly stowed away. In the bathroom, all of her toiletries had been put into the medicine cabinet or lined up on the counter.

She had heard of places where the maid unpacked for you, but there was no such maid here. Aunt Louise had been shopping and Wes had been at the diner with her.

But Wes had come back while she was at Bernice's.

Could he have managed all this in the short time they were separated? It didn't look like the unpacking had been done in a hurry. Nonetheless, he had to have been responsible and she didn't like the idea of him going through her things without her permission, even if he did it as a service of the inn.

Quickly, she dumped her purchases on the bed, hung up the new green dress and headed down to the sitting room. He was lounging comfortably in one of the upholstered arm chairs, looking very much like the man in the portrait behind him. In fact, Felicity was fairly sure that the ancestor was sitting in the same chair Wes was. As soon as he saw her, Wes rose with a smile but she was unable to return it.

"Look, I appreciate your unpacking for me, but I'd really rather you—"

"Excuse me?" he interrupted. "I didn't unpack for you."

She frowned at him. "You didn't?" He shook his head. "Well, *someone* did. I assumed it was you since your aunt was out."

"Aunt Louise?" he called. A moment later she came through the door pushing a cart bearing an ornate silver tea service and a tray of cookies. "Did you unpack Felicity's bag while we were out earlier?"

"Are you daft, boy? You were here when I left this morning and you know I just got back. I didn't even know she'd arrived until I ran into Harriet in the grocery store."

Wes turned to Felicity and filled in the blank for her. "Harriet was in May's Diner when we were there."

"Oh," she said, not questioning how he knew what she was thinking. "But then, who unpacked my suitcase?"

Aunt Louise handed her a delicate china cup of black tea on a matching saucer and a linen napkin. "Help yourself to cream or lemon. It was probably your mother, Wesley. You know what a stickler she was for everything being nice and neat and in its proper place."

Felicity's confusion was evident as she sat down in the chair to Wes's left and Aunt Louise took the one opposite him. Only then did he reseat himself. "You didn't tell me your mother lives here with you."

He opened his mouth but his aunt beat him to an explanation. "Of course Wes's mother still lives here. You just can't see her. But she's forever rearranging the kitchen to please herself, knowing full well that I'll just put things back the way I like them."

Wes sighed. "My mother passed away eleven years ago. The two of them have been battling over the household ever since."

"Now wait just a minute," Felicity said. "Are you telling me that a spirit—possibly your own mother—hung up my clothes and put my toothbrush in the bathroom?"

Aunt Louise passed the tray of cookies to Felicity. "Don't fret over it dear. You'll get accustomed to their meddling after a while. If you live in a town full of spirits you learn to expect the unexpected."

Felicity was still certain there had to be a more tangible explanation. Short of calling them liars, however, she had no choice but to let the matter drop. "Speaking of a town full of spirits, I distinctly recall your letter and the only place you mentioned anything about was the inn."

Wes set his cup and saucer down on the table in front of him. "I was afraid you'd think I was a crackpot if I told you the whole story in my letter."

"So Bernice wasn't putting me on? Everyone in town believes their dead ancestors are still hanging around."

"Basically, that's correct," Wes replied.

"And this doesn't bother anyone?"

Aunt Louise chuckled. "The spirits only meddle with people they're fond of and nothing they do is harmful.

They just like to make sure we don't forget about them."

Felicity had never heard of an entire town being haunted. If she could get enough examples of spiritual intervention from a wide variety of residents, this could make a great story after all. And it wouldn't even be necessary for her to believe any of it.

"How is it that no one's ever written an article about Haversham before?"

While Wes's aunt refilled everyone's tea cups, he answered Felicity. "It was always understood that what happened here was our secret and to reveal it to outsiders would be detrimental to both the spirits and the living."

"But you obviously changed your mind now," Felicity pointed out. "Why?" She could tell he was contemplating whether or not to respond truthfully, so she added, "The truth, please."

"All right," he said and got up from his chair to pace a bit as he spoke. "I told you at lunch that some of our young people have moved away. The truth is that *most* of them have left, for one reason or another. At this rate, Haversham could be a *literal* ghost town in thirty or forty years. Did you know that Wyoming is the only state with a smaller population than Vermont?"

She'd read that in her guide book, but hadn't given it much consideration.

"Basically, we can't afford to lose any more people. The town council decided that drastic measures were needed to inject new life into the town, even if it meant revealing our secret."

"Maybe I'm a bit dense, but I don't get the connection."

Aunt Louise spoke up before Wes. "At one time people were spooked by the notion that a house could have spirits in it. But suddenly, television shows have so-called *ghost* hunters out looking for them and millions of people accept the possibility of their existence."

Wes picked it up from there. "There are a number of towns throughout Vermont better equipped to attract tourists for the skiing than Haversham. But none of them can offer what we can—a chance to commune with the spirit world. Besides Haversham Inn, a lot of other old homes could easily be transformed into bed and breakfasts. The economy would improve and our young people might be more willing to stay put."

Felicity could see the rationale but something about it didn't sit well. "And what happens to tradition? Will it all simply be forsaken for commercial enterprise? Will Aunt Louise hang a shingle outside that offers psychic predictions? Or better yet, May's Diner could become a gypsy tea room and Stephie could be taught to read tea leaves to the customers. Of course, Bernice will have to start carrying a whole line of new products—crystals, incense and that sort of thing."

"Obviously, you don't approve of my idea," Wes said, frowning as he returned to his chair.

Felicity sighed and shook her head as she realized she had just done a complete reversal of her initial attitude toward the town, and she had only been there part of one day. *How very odd.* At least now her curiosity was satisfied as to his ulterior motive for getting her here. She decided that evening, when they were alone, might be a better time to probe into his reasoning a bit further.

Seeing that he was still waiting to hear her judgment, she said, "It's not up to me to approve or disapprove. I'm sure it could be very successful. And my writing an article for you would certainly kick it off in a big way. Right?"

Wes and his aunt exchanged a guilty glance. "Right," Wes reluctantly admitted. "I thought if you wrote an article about Haversham's spirits, people would believe it."

"Because I'm a known skeptic?"

Though he looked somewhat uncomfortable, he nodded.

"But then you've got to realize, if I'm not convinced, I could write something negative instead of helpful."

"You won't," Aunt Louise said firmly. "They'll make sure you do what's right."

The grandfather clock in the corner bonged five times, much to Felicity's surprise. She hadn't realized the hour. She asked Wes, "When do we need to leave?"

"Six-thirty will give us plenty of time," he assured her with a forced smile.

"Then I need to excuse myself. Your mother may have unpacked for me, but I think I'd prefer to take a shower myself."

She was almost out the door when she remembered hearing the chimes in Bernice's dressing room.

"They do leave you alone in the bathroom, don't they?"

Wes laughed. "They have never been known to disrespect the privacy of the living."

Felicity decided to take a very quick shower…just in case.

An hour later she stood in front of the full-length mirror in the bedroom and critiqued her appearance. Bernice had talked her into buying a rhinestone-studded comb for her hair, and she had obeyed the woman's instructions about styling it with one side pulled off her face. The result was so complimentary, she'd taken more care than usual with her makeup.

She decided she looked very nice, and it had been too long since she thought that way about herself…as long as two Christmas Eves ago, when she had hoped that looking extra feminine would make her husband notice her again.

The black suede shoes Bernice had chosen had higher heels than she normally wore, but they did make her legs look good. And as tall as Wes was, the added height would make it more comfortable for them to dance together.

If he asked her.

She acknowledged that despite his belief in the supernatural, she found him very attractive and wanted to at least pretend this evening as a date.

The gloomy voice of reality whispered in her mind. *Wesley Haversham had invited her here to help promote a business venture, not for a romantic liaison.* There was a strong possibility that he had lied about how her bag got unpacked. He was probably planning to spend the entire evening telling her fabricated ghost, or rather *spirit* stories to sway her opinion. Besides that, he appeared to still be grieving over his wife. If May hadn't forced this *date*, it may not have happened at all.

Her confident mood effectively crushed, she picked up the little purse that matched the shoes and left the suite.

Some of the confidence returned when she noted that, as early as she was, Wes was already waiting for her. It rose a bit more when his gaze crept from her toes to her hair and his smile grew wider with each inch he progressed.

"Thank you," she said, smiling back. "That was one of the nicest compliments I've received in a while." As he walked toward her, she let her own gaze take in the cut of his charcoal gray suit and powder blue shirt. "You look extremely debonair yourself, sir."

He took her hand in his and placed a feather-light kiss on her knuckles. "Would you care for a glass of sherry before we go?"

She liked the feel of his hand wrapped around hers and was pleased when he didn't release it after his gracious greeting. "No, thank you. I'm not much of a drinker."

"Then why don't we take advantage of the extra time to drive *very* slowly."

His eyes held such sensual promise that she swallowed hard and lowered her lashes. She had been hoping they might dance together that evening, but if she was reading the signals correctly, he was contemplating a considerably more intimate encounter. A flush of warmth flooded her body as she realized that her thoughts had turned down the same seductive path.

As he opened the closet door in the foyer, she grimaced at the idea of spoiling her outfit with her old jacket, but he made that worry disappear as well.

"My mother gave this coat to Aunt Louise and she insists you wear it tonight."

Felicity gasped at the sight of the full-length, mink coat. The rich, reddish-brown color nearly matched her hair. It might have been polite to protest a little, but she simply turned around so that he could put it on her. Wrapped in the magnificent fur, with a gorgeous man doting on her, she felt like a princess.

When they drove onto Main Street and she saw the myriad of twinkle lights, she forgot about the sarcastic thoughts she had had that morning. Tonight she *was* a princess, Haversham was her fairy tale kingdom and, if she was very lucky, Wes would continue to play the part of her prince, at least for the next few hours.

Ghosts and haunted houses, commercial ventures and magazine articles, ex-husbands and deceased wives, could all wait until tomorrow.

During the drive to Waitsfield, Wes commented on various points of interest then gave her a tour through the town. It was immediately evident that Waitsfield was more commercial than Haversham. There were at least two fast food restaurants and a number of tourist-oriented shops. She liked Haversham better.

Felicity didn't know how it had happened, but she had undergone a drastic change since her arrival that morning. Perhaps there really were supernatural forces at work in Haversham…something that had the power to make her want to believe in fairy tales again.

"Are you cold?" Wes asked.

She realized she was sitting there hugging herself and purposely relaxed her body. "Not at all. I was just thinking that there must be a way to save Haversham without turning it into a tourist mecca like Waitsfield."

Wes was quiet for a moment then requested a favor. "Would you mind if we didn't discuss it tonight? The subject of Haversham's future tends to spoil my appetite."

Felicity smiled. *Not* talking business was just fine with her.

The Mountaintop Lodge with its breathtaking view turned out to be as elegant and romantic as May had promised. Heads turned as she and Wes were guided to their table, but rather than making her nervous, it boosted her good feeling a bit higher.

Wes ordered himself to calm down and look at the menu the waiter handed him. His stomach was jittery, his chest was tight and he had the most peculiar urge to throw every man in the restaurant off the cliff outside. How dare they all stare at Felicity that way? Couldn't they see she was spoken for?

Suddenly he realized what was happening to him. He was jealous! Totally, irrationally jealous over a woman he'd only met that morning. It made no sense. He'd never reacted that way with Joanne and she was as beautiful as a woman could be.

He peered over his menu at Felicity. She was very attractive, but that wasn't what was causing these unfamiliar feelings. There was something drawing him to her that couldn't be seen. Something more elemental than physical beauty.

When he took Joanne out, he always felt proud to be seen with her, to have others know he was the one she'd chosen. At the moment, all he could think of was how quickly they could finish dinner so he could have Felicity to himself. The words repeated in his head until he recalled that he had used the same phrase earlier when telling Felicity the story of Lord Wesley and Lady Dierdre.

Could history be repeating itself? Was he being given a second chance to live up to the Haversham tradition? The possibility made itself at home in his mind.

"Do you believe in fate?" he asked.

Felicity angled her head thoughtfully. "I don't know. Maybe. Why?"

"No reason. I was just wondering."

The band struck up an old love song and Wes closed his menu. "Would you care to dance?"

Her practical side hadn't been completely silenced yet. "Shouldn't we wait to order first?"

He stood and held out his hand. "I've waited too long already."

It was hardly an original line and yet, her intuition told her he truly meant it. As strange as it seemed, she felt the same way.

He led her onto the wooden dance floor and she glided gracefully into his embrace. From the first step they moved as if they'd danced together a thousand times before. When his cheek rested against her head, it seemed quite natural for her fingers to stroke the nape of his neck. As if they had done these things before as well. His warm hand caressed the small of her back, bringing her close to him with only the slightest pressure. It felt so right, so *familiar*, that Felicity didn't hesitate to align their bodies so that they each knew the effect they were having on one another.

For several seconds after the band finished the song, they remained entwined. And when they moved apart, Felicity saw her own sense of wonderment reflected in Wes's eyes.

Somehow the waiter got their order, they shared a bottle of wine and ate some food, but Felicity had no idea what any of it tasted like. She had been transported to a dreamy place where all that mattered was the way Wes was looking at her and how he repeatedly stroked the back of her hand with his thumb.

They spoke of inconsequential matters that had nothing to do with what was really on their minds. Eventually they gave up the pretense of enjoying the meal and returned to the dance floor where there was no need for words.

Neither was anxious to give up the pleasure they'd discovered in each other's arms, yet their dancing soon took on an intimacy that was no longer appropriate in public.

"Shall we go home?" he whispered in her ear.

"Please." There was no need to say more.

During the drive back to Haversham, he held her hand, occasionally bringing it to his lips or giving it a squeeze. She didn't allow herself to think about what she was feeling for fear it was only make believe.

The inn was completely dark when they pulled into the lot and parked next to Aunt Louise's car.

"That's strange," Wes said. "I was sure Aunt Louise would be waiting up for us. I wonder why she didn't leave a light on."

"You don't think there could be a crowd of neighbors planning to surprise us, do you?"

Wes laughed. "Not even May would do that. She'll just drop by at dawn for her interrogation."

As soon as they entered the dark foyer, Wes flicked the wall switch several times without the lights responding.

"Probably blew a fuse. Wait right here while I go down to the basement and take care of it."

While he was gone she hung up the borrowed coat in the closet, but she didn't try navigating any further without light. It seemed as though she'd been standing there quite a while when an eerie, flickering light shone from the sitting room. Her heart skipped a beat as her imagination conjured up a ghostly presence.

Taking a nervous step toward the glowing archway, she hoped it was a friendly soul and not his late wife coming to put a damper on their evening.

CHAPTER 4

Felicity gasped aloud as she and Wes nearly collided in the archway to the sitting room. The light was coming from a kerosene lamp in his hand.

"Sorry that took so long." He raised the lamp to illuminate her face. "Are you all right? You look like you've just seen a ghost." His expression and voice were both teasing.

"Very funny," she said with a frown, then realized it *was* pretty funny. "I gather it wasn't just a fuse."

"No. It must be a problem outside. It will have to wait until morning. In the meantime, I'll light a fire in your room." He set the lamp down on the table, so that he could hang up his overcoat.

With the lamp in one hand, he put his other arm around her waist to guide her up the stairs. The sense of anticipation that had built up while they were dancing had faded when they reached the darkened inn, but the moment he touched her, it flared anew. She was uncertain as to how much she wanted to happen between them that night, except that she absolutely had to find out what his kiss tasted like.

She obeyed his hand signals to be very quiet lest they wake up Aunt Louise, but the squeaky door hinges weren't as cooperative. They both held their breath for several long seconds after reclosing the door to see if the noise had roused Aunt Louise.

"Fortunately, she's a bit hard of hearing," Wes murmured after he was certain they hadn't disturbed her.

Felicity stood by the fireplace while he set fire to the logs, then put the kerosene lamp in the bathroom for her.

"Are you cold?" he asked for the second time that evening.

Between the fire blazing at her back and thoughts of how yummy he looked, she was as far from being cold as she could be. "If I say yes, will you wrap your arms around me to warm me up?"

He took a few steps toward her.

"That would be a good excuse to hold you again," he said, removing his glasses and placing them on the fireplace mantle. "Or I could turn on the radio and go back to pretending we were dancing." He closed the distance between them. "Or we could just quit looking for excuses and do what we've both been thinking about for hours."

His fingers stroked her cheek so gently, she sighed and closed her eyes. As his hands tipped her head back, her tongue moistened her lips. By the time his lips touched hers, her pulse was racing with expectation. The tender peck she received did nothing to satisfy her curiosity, let alone her need. She looked up at him and saw restrained desire clouded by confusion. "What is it?"

"If I kiss you the way I want, I'm not going to want to stop there. Part of me knows we just met and it's much too soon to feel this strongly. But another part of me feels like I've known you forever and there's nothing we could do together that would be wrong."

His words melted what little common sense she had left. "I understand. I feel the same way. I hardly ever kiss a man good night on a first date, let alone..." She shyly bowed her head. "Let alone what I want to do with you."

He drew her snugly into his arms and kissed her forehead. "Tell me to go, and I will. I can't promise it won't happen tomorrow or the next day, but it doesn't have to be tonight." As his fingers ran up and down her back and she felt his body changing between them, his words seemed to contradict his actions.

She raised her gaze to his. "I can't order you to leave when I want you to stay so badly. Like you said at dinner, I've already waited long enough."

She slid her hands up the lapels of his jacket and around his neck, then pulled his head down to her. When their lips came together again, she was momentarily overwhelmed by the power she had unleashed. His mouth moved over hers, pressing, withdrawing and pressing again, tempting her with the promise of a deeper kiss only to pull back once more, as if he was afraid to take what he wanted.

Frustrated, she held his head still and took the initiative. With her mouth slanted beneath his, she slipped her tongue between his lips. That was all the encouragement he needed, for a second later he recaptured the lead, diving into an eating kiss that brought them both to their knees. His hands joined the seduction to ease her the rest of the way down onto the plush carpet before the fire.

As demanding as his kisses had become, his touches were even more so. One moment his hand skimmed up her stockinged thigh to knead her hip, the next it captured her breast. He was trying to discover every inch of her at once, and she so wanted to help him. Her sweater dress was already twisted up around her waist and it only took a little maneuvering to get rid of it completely. As she tugged off his jacket and undid his shirt, he bared her breasts to learn their shape and then their taste. In a tangle of arms and legs, the rest of the barriers between them were tossed aside.

"I want you too much," Wes murmured between hot kisses, his body straining against hers. "I should go slow—"

"*No*," she protested and slipped her hand between their bodies to encourage him to act rather than think. "I never needed anything in my life as much as I need to feel you inside of me right now. It's crazy, I know, but I don't care." She lightly grazed his sensitive flesh with her fingernails and he gave in to the primal urge that was driving them both.

What had been desperate need was abruptly catapulted beyond anything definable.

They clung to one another as the raging winds of passion swept them away to a place where nothing mattered but satisfaction. Yet, their hunger was too great to be appeased with one explosive release. Without pause, Wes took them to another, gentler plateau where all their senses were magnified and focused on each other.

When the ultimate pleasure was shared a second time and they lay breathlessly in the sweet afterglow, it occurred to Felicity that what she had just done wasn't very smart. However, she didn't have the energy to scold herself over something so incredibly wonderful. And if she had accidentally gotten pregnant...

Well, would that really be so bad? Her ex-husband hadn't wanted children and she had wanted them badly enough to have them without a husband who cared. No, it wouldn't be so bad if she had just conceived a child by Wesley Haversham the Twelfth.

Wes couldn't fathom what had come over him. In all

his years with Joanne, as much as he had loved her, he had never experienced anything close to what he had just enjoyed with Felicity. Nor had he ever had any interest in experimenting with any other women. What had just happened was proof that fate had surely had a hand in bringing Felicity Flowers to Haversham. Perhaps his being so caught up in the fireworks that he forgot about protection, was another trick of fate. Wesley Haversham the Thirteenth could already be on his way.

He gave her a long, sensual kiss then murmured against her lips. "Marry me."

She smiled and nuzzled his neck. "Okay. Just so I don't have to get up and put clothes on."

He eased her away and waited for her to look at him. "I'm serious."

She blinked at him. "About what?"

"Getting married."

She stared at him long enough to be certain he wasn't kidding. Sitting up, she combed the hair back from his forehead with her fingers. "I didn't think they made men like you anymore. But, believe me, I am a thoroughly modern woman. What we just did—and by the way it was, beyond a doubt, the best sex I ever had—it was by mutual consent. You didn't compromise me or do anything that requires an apology or an offer to make an honest woman of me."

He sat up and grasped her hands. "What if I got you pregnant?"

She shrugged. "It would pose some difficulties, but I could manage. I wouldn't hold you responsible."

"That's a hell of an attitude."

"Careful. We don't want to anger your spirits by getting profane now, do we?"

He gave her hands a squeeze. "Stop it. I'm asking you to be my wife and you're making jokes."

"Wes, please. Be reasonable. Once your hormones

settle back into place you'll realize that we were both simply stricken with a severe case of lust. It will go away, believe me."

His jaw tensed. "It wasn't lust."

"Was it love? Can you honestly say that, in less than one day, you fell madly in love with me? To have and to hold, till death do us part?"

"Yes."

She let out a sigh and mumbled, "I don't believe this conversation." Her mind fought to stay rational despite her emotions telling her to risk everything for a chance at happily ever after. "Look, I can understand how you might be anxious to remarry. It was obviously a good experience for you. But my first marriage was a trip into hell. We mistook lust for love and put each other through torture for five years. I can't risk doing that again. I'm not sure I ever want to get married a second time...to *anyone*. I like my independence."

"I can give you anything you've ever wanted in your life. I'm very wealthy."

"How nice," she said with a laugh. "What's next, do you show me a copy of the results of your last physical? I'm sorry. I know you're not trying to be funny, but you've really thrown me for a loop tonight. Can we just let it drop for now?"

He took a deep breath. "Fine. We can drop it for tonight, but it won't change anything. I love you and I want to marry you."

He got up, walked over to the bed, and turned down the covers.

Felicity rose and went to him. Running a finger down his spine, she asked, "Another service from the friendly staff of the Haversham Inn?" She meant for the double entendre to lighten his mood, but when he turned around, she could see he had taken her remark as an insult.

"Is that what you think of me—a hotel amenity, like a

swimming pool or lounge act? Maybe you're used to calling the concierge to send up a bellboy to service you, but—"

Crack. Her hand slapped his cheek before she could think about it. For several seconds, they stared at each other, breathing heavily.

"I deserved that," Wes finally said. "I apologize."

She shook her head and touched his cheek. "I shouldn't have slapped you. I've never done that in my life."

"And I've never behaved so ungentlemanly. You're the first woman I've been with since my wife died. And there was no one before her. I don't give my love lightly, Felicity. It's important to me that you believe that."

She rose on tiptoes to give him a brief kiss. "I believe you, but that's all the more reason for you to slow down." She kissed him again and this time, he participated. "Will you stay with me?"

"I'd like to, but under the circumstances, it would probably be best if I didn't. Besides, I'd just as soon not have Aunt Louise catch me coming out of your room in the morning. It would be all over town in an hour."

His grin let her know he was going to be okay, and she smiled back. Threading her fingers into the dark curls on his chest, she said, "Maybe you could just lay down with me for a little while."

"I really shouldn't."

She licked his one nipple, then the other.

"I'd probably fall asleep." His protest was not the least bit convincing.

Her hands trailed down his sides and around his waist to cup his firm bottom and she felt his response against her stomach.

"Then again, I don't feel *that* tired."

As his mouth came down on hers they tumbled onto the bed. The third time they came together was much slower, as they discovered the secrets of one another's bodies, but somehow the finish was even more powerful because of it.

Felicity still thought it was lust, though it far surpassed anything she'd ever experienced with her ex-husband.

Wes managed to part from her to spare their reputations and, despite an unreasonable yet profound sense of loneliness, Felicity eventually fell sleep.

She awoke in the morning with the pleasant kind of discomfort that can only be caused by great sex. She had the feeling Aunt Louise didn't need to catch Wes coming out of her room. As a woman, she'd know the minute she saw the smile on Felicity's face.

She stretched and forced her eyes open. To her surprise, a red rose was laying on the pillow next to her. How in the world had he managed to find a rose in the middle of the night in December?

She received two more surprises in the bathroom. First, the power had been restored. Second, the words *Felicity Haversham* were printed on the mirror. The letters appeared to be finger-painted on with some sort of gel.

Wes had the knack of walking around without making any noise, but she wondered how he had opened and closed the door to the suite without her hearing the hinges squeak. She must have been in an extremely deep sleep.

As she descended the stairs, she smelled bacon and coffee and heard a number of voices coming from the dining room. Before she reached the bottom step, however, Wes appeared and detoured her into the sitting room.

She opened her mouth to question why he had done that, but he pulled her into his arms and kissed her for such a long time, she forgot what she was going to ask.

"Good morning to you too," she said quietly. His grin was contagious.

"Now maybe I can handle the crowd in the dining room."

From the way he said that she knew it wasn't good.

He kept his voice low as he explained, "The whole town council just happened to pick this morning to have breakfast here."

"Because of me?"

"Because of us."

"Oh. Are they angry because I'm an outsider? Surely they know I'll be leaving in three days."

He frowned at her. "We'll discuss the matter of your leaving at another time. But no, they're not angry. They're hoping our date last night was successful."

Now it was her turn to frown. "I don't get it. Why would it matter to them?"

Shrugging, he said, "I guess they want to see me happy. Do you accept my proposal of marriage?"

"*Wes...*"

"Not convinced yet? All right, but you'd make this a lot easier if you'd just say yes before we go in there." He held out an arm to escort her. "Shall we go face the inquisition?"

She went with him but she had the uncomfortable feeling there was something going on that he wasn't telling her. "Wait," she said, tugging him back into the sitting room. "Thank you for the rose, but I think the message on the mirror could have been a bit more subtle."

He was completely bewildered by her comment. "What rose? What message?"

"Are you implying that you did not return to my room while I was sleeping, put a rose on the pillow and write *Felicity Haversham* on the mirror in the bathroom?"

His look of confusion was altered to one of awareness. "Was the writing done in a cloudy, jelly-like substance?"

She nodded.

His expression graduated to one of extreme delight. "That's fantastic! They like you. They want you to be my wife."

She rolled her eyes. "*Honestly*. You think your ancestors were showing their approval by writing an ectoplasmic message on the mirror? Look, I'm trying to be open-minded about this spirit business but—"

"It was them. There are no roses growing here in the winter. The nearest florist shop is in Waitsfield. And that substance on the mirror *is* ectoplasm."

She shook her head. She didn't have a better explanation, unless he was lying, and her intuition kept telling her he was a completely honest man. Could Aunt Louise have been her stealthy visitor? That seemed highly unlikely. "I'm sorry. I just can't believe it. Maybe if I actually saw one of them, I'd feel differently. I don't know."

He arched one eyebrow and said, "Maybe one of them will decide to be obliging if that's what you require before you believe you are meant to be my wife."

She felt ridiculously conspicuous as Wes took her into the dining room and introduced her to the group gathering there. She knew May and Chuck—Stephie and her mother were handling the diner—and Bernice and Aunt Louise. Everyone was friendly but openly curious about her background, her career, her plans for the article on Haversham and, of course her opinion of the town, the inn and especially...their patron.

Wes attempted to tactfully request that they respect Felicity's privacy, but his efforts were ignored. If they had been the least bit rude, she would have refused to answer their questions, but they seemed genuinely interested in her and their pride in the town was a pleasure to behold.

"I like Haversham very much," she assured all of them. "And I would truly like to help you, but I can't promise to write what you want me to. What I thought

I'd do is visit with a number of you who believe you have had experiences with spirits, I'll take some photographs and we'll see how it turns out."

"And what about you and Wesley?" May asked bluntly. "Do you two have plans for this evening?"

Felicity couldn't stop the blush as she glanced at Wes. His plans for their evening were explicitly detailed in the steamy look he gave her. "We'll just have to see how that turns out too."

During the next hour, Felicity prepared a schedule of who she would see at what time and where. Wordlessly, Wes penciled himself in from two o'clock on each day.

She hadn't expected him to accompany her to each home or place of business, but she was pleased when he did. It gave her a chance to observe him interacting with his constituents, all of whom were either family or friends. Though it wasn't her primary objective, she also took the opportunity to listen to what the residents had to say about the future of their town. Not a single person voiced an objection to commercializing Haversham, but she picked up the unspoken concerns and fears that they would be losing something very precious in the process. Almost everyone she spoke to used the word "tradition" at some point during their conversation.

By two o'clock she had heard tales of ghostly appearances during times of great joy or sorrow. Wes had to stop several people from revealing what was expected to happen on Christmas Eve in order to keep the event a surprise. She also learned that the spirits could be mischievous or humorous, affectionate or reprimanding. The personality of the living didn't alter when they passed on. Ectoplasmic messages, like the one she supposedly received that morning, were rare, but two people she spoke to had received them when some vital decision had to be made. However, everyone had heard the tinkling wind chimes at some time in their life.

She also learned how well respected Wes was and

how much he cared about each person's welfare. His gentlemanly demeanor went all the way to his core.

"What do you think now?" he asked her when they left the last appointment.

"Boy, you Havershamites sure make it tough to remain a skeptic."

He winked at her. "As someone once said, *you ain't seen nuttin' yet*! Did you notice that the power had been turned back on this morning?"

"Of course. You must have been up awfully early to take care of it."

Wes shook his head. "I didn't take care of anything. *They* did. I guess they figured a fire would be more romantic than electric light." He pulled her close for a lingering kiss. "I think it worked very well."

After all the stories she'd just heard, turning the power off and on was a relatively minor feat for Haversham's spirits. Maybe, just *maybe*, they really were hovering around.

Following May's suggestion, Wes took Felicity to Montpelier for the rest of the day. The historic capitol was as lovely as every other part of Vermont she'd seen so far. As he showed her around, he took advantage of every opportunity to hold her close and kiss her senseless. By the time they returned to the inn, she was weak with desire.

Their lovemaking was no less explosive than the night before and Felicity's resistance took a distinct hit.

"Remember when I asked if you believe in fate?" he murmured.

"Was that last night or a hundred years ago?" She tickled his ear with her tongue and he laughingly repaid her with a nip to her ear lobe before replying.

"I didn't know how you'd react if I told you last night, but after everything you heard today, I think you're ready."

She eased back a bit. "Ooh. This sounds spooky."

He tweaked her nose. "Some months ago, I read your article in *Aware* then I threw out the magazine. Or I thought I did. The next day, I saw it on my nightstand, so I tossed it out with that day's newspaper. The next morning it was beside my bed again, only this time it was open to your article."

"Ancestor intervention again?" Felicity asked. She was feeling less skeptical by the hour.

"What else? At any rate, you know what happened next. The point is, you were *meant* to come here, and the spirits gave fate a nudge. I had thought you were needed to help Haversham, but now I know you had to come for me as well." He kissed her tenderly and she snuggled back into his embrace. "I love you, Felicity, and I want you to stay with me forever. Please be my wife."

It would have been so easy to simply agree. Believe that fate and the spirit world had brought her to Haversham to be with him. But her natural skepticism and a disastrous marriage prevented her from giving in, even while his hands and mouth tempted her with the promise of a lifetime of pleasure. She could not say yes, and yet tonight, she couldn't say no either.

Reluctantly he accepted the small progress he'd made about their future and went back to enjoying the present. He stayed a bit longer that night, but again he returned to his own room.

Felicity drifted off into a peaceful sleep moments after he left her alone.

"Felicity."

She heard her name whispered in her dream, yet it didn't seem to belong there.

"Felicity."

The repetition pulled her out of her dream, but she was too immersed in sleep to heed the call.

"Felicity!"

The whispered demand got through to her and she

raised one eyelid. She didn't remember leaving a light on, but her room was no longer dark. Straining to focus on the source of the light, she was bewildered by what she saw. "Wes?"

He was standing near the foot of the bed, and a soft glow surrounded him. When he made no move or sound, she blinked and squinted until she could see him a bit clearer. It was Wesley, and then again, it wasn't. His hair was parted down the middle and he was wearing a very old-style suit, like something from the twenties or thirties, and no glasses.

She propped herself up on her elbow as she came fully awake. "What are you doing dressed like that?"

"*Marry Wesley,*" he whispered and smoothly glided through the bedroom door to the parlor as though he were floating.

"Wes!" she called, somewhat annoyed at his prank. "Come back here." When he didn't obey, she rose and went into the parlor, only to find herself alone there. She turned on a light and proceeded to search the entire suite, looking behind furniture and drapes, inside closets, even places he couldn't possibly be hiding.

Had she only dreamed that he was there, dressed up like a character from *The Great Gatsby*? Considering all that had happened in the last two days, it was possible that her dreams had become more vivid than usual.

No. He had definitely been there—and vanished—leaving only an odd smell behind.

CHAPTER 5

Felicity quickly put on her robe to go pay Wes a return visit. As soon as she opened the door to her suite and heard the squeaky hinges, she was back to being confused. He couldn't possibly have been there and left without her hearing his exit.

A few seconds later, she was downstairs, knocking on his door. When he didn't answer immediately, she knocked a bit louder and called his name. "Wes, it's Felicity. I need to talk to you."

The door opened and, for a moment, she forgot why she was there. He looked positively delicious. From his tousled hair and sleepy eyes, to his sexy body dressed only in a pair of low-slung boxers, he had clearly been sound asleep, but gave her a welcoming grin nonetheless.

"Couldn't sleep?" he asked, stroking her cheek.

"No. Yes. I—" She forced herself to think past the desire he had so easily reignited. "Were you in my room a few minutes ago?" she asked despite the evidence to the contrary.

His fingers slipped behind her neck and urged her closer for a slow, sensual kiss. "A few minutes?" He moved his lower body against hers. "I feel like I haven't been with you in days."

She closed her eyes as his mouth returned to hers and his hands sought out the sensitive places he had found earlier.

"Let's go back to your room and I'll put you back to sleep," he said, lifting her into his arms.

That slight interruption was enough to remind her of why she had awakened him. "Wait. I have to tell you what happened. I woke up because I thought I heard my name being called. Then I saw you, or it looked like you, but different. And there was a strange light around you."

He set her on her feet and peered at her very intently. "Did the man you saw say anything?"

She made a face at him. "Yes. He...*you* said, 'Marry Wesley,' and then you disappeared."

"Come with me." He led her by the hand into the sitting room and turned on a light. Waving his arm at the portraits on the walls, he asked, "See anyone familiar?"

What he was implying abruptly dawned on her. Her mysterious visitor was one of his ancestors! As crazy as it sounded, she was no longer able to deny the possibility. Her gaze scanned the painted images until she saw who she was looking for. "That's him," she declared, walking up to a portrait of a man with the same hairstyle and wearing the same suit as the man who had awakened her.

Wes smiled. "That's my great-grandfather. The only time he ever makes an appearance is on, um...on a special occasion , which proves how important it is for you to accept my proposal."

She sighed and shook her head. Spiritual endorsement or not, it was all too much, too fast. "I don't know what to think any more."

"Then don't think. Just give in to the inevitable." He pulled her into his arms. "Say yes."

She looked up at him and the adoring expression on his face almost convinced her to say the word. Her heart was ready. But her mind was clinging to practicality.

Now it was his turn to sigh. "All right. Tomorrow is Christmas Eve. I can wait until then."

"A couple people I interviewed mentioned Christmas Eve. What is it that's supposed to happen tomorrow night?"

"Something that will change the mind of the worst skeptic," he said with a teasing smile. "Tomorrow night, at the stroke of midnight, you are going to witness a miracle."

"A *miracle*?" she repeated with a chuckle. "What do you call your great-grandfather's appearance in my bedroom? An everyday occurrence?"

"You'll see." He swept her into his arms again and headed for the stairs. "For now, let's just see what we can do about putting you back to sleep."

Nestled in his arms, she wanted him to understand why it was so hard for her to jump into another marriage. She told him about the very rocky relationship she and her husband had, and how and when it had ended.

He kissed her then and promised that soon she would have a new Christmas Eve memory to help her forget the bitter one.

As it turned out, it was nearly dawn when Wes left her again.

By the time she came downstairs the next morning, Aunt Louise was the only one in the dining room.

"Good morning, sleepyhead," the older woman said with a broad smile. "Would you like breakfast or lunch?"

"Just coffee, please. I have an appointment in fifteen

minutes with the Barringers."

"Not any more you don't. Wesley let everyone know that all appointments were pushed back to this afternoon. He's out right now taking care of that."

"Oh. That was very kind of him."

"*Hmmph!* I'd say it was the least he could do after keeping you up half the night. All the spirits living in this house together never made as much ruckus as the two of you did."

Thoroughly modern Felicity blushed to the roots of her hair.

Aunt Louise walked over and gave her a motherly hug. "Now, now, there's nothing to be embarrassed about. It was meant to be. And now everyone can stop fretting." Without asking Felicity's preference again, she broke two eggs in a frying pan. "Of course, it will be another month or so before you'll have any official results, but most people will take my word for the fact that it's already a done thing."

Felicity wrinkled her forehead as she tried to interpret what Louise was telling her.

"Oh my. You didn't realize it did you? I suppose your being a skeptic keeps you from believing it without a doctor's report."

Frustration caused Felicity to raise her voice. "What *are* you talking about?"

Aunt Louise patted Felicity's stomach. "Why the baby, dear. Wesley Haversham the Thirteenth. And don't worry yourself about what people will think about you having your honeymoon before the marriage. They'll all be too happy to hear that the Haversham tradition won't be ending with Wesley." She popped two slices of bread in the toaster then got out a plate and flatware.

Felicity's head was spinning. The baby? Wesley Haversham XIII? The Haversham tradition?

Whether or not Aunt Louise was truly psychic was

irrelevant. She could be pregnant and it sounded as though the whole town was waiting to hear the good news. Yesterday morning's *spontaneous* breakfast get-together came to mind. Everyone was so very happy to have her there and so very interested in her and Wes's date.

Could it possibly be that saving Haversham involved more than building up the economic base? Did their superstitions go so far as to imagine that the town would die if Wes didn't have a son to carry on the tradition? A chill trickled down her spine and settled like a cold lump in her stomach.

"...to have children underfoot again, seeing them play hide and seek in the secret passageways, making noise...oh my, I can hardly wait." Aunt Louise placed a cup of coffee and a plate of sunny-side-up eggs and toast on a tray. As she carried it out to the dining room, she turned around and smiled at Felicity. "Come along, little mother. You're feeding two now, you know."

Like a sleepwalker, Felicity obediently went into the dining room and sat down. For some reason, she had been royally set up. But why her? Surely there were other women that would have been pleased to act as a breeder for a handsome, wealthy man. Instantly she knew the answer. Other women might not have been able to help promote the town!

If the nefarious scheme didn't directly involve her, she might have admired Wes's ingenuity. With her, he could handle two problems at once. No wonder he never took any precautions with her and was so very anxious to tie the knot.

Love! Bah humbug.

Her brain busily sorted out the previous two days' events. As she swallowed her breakfast without tasting it, Aunt Louise continued chattering away happily across the table from her.

If he lied about loving her, he could have lied about

everything else—her bags being unpacked, the ectoplasmic message, the ridiculous explanation about the magazine article. And of course, if the whole town was in on the plan, they would have all lied about their experiences.

Suddenly an image of the ghostly Lord Wesley flashed in her mind. Examining it critically, she saw what she had missed when she was half asleep. The eerie glow was the same as she had seen created by the kerosene lamp the first night and the *spirit* had kept one arm behind his back, as if he was hiding something. A ghost wouldn't have need of a lamp, but a real man playing a ghost might use one to create a spooky appearance.

Yet if her visitor had been Wes after all, and he hadn't walked out the door, where had he gone from her bedroom?

She tried to sound innocently curious, so as not to alarm the older woman. "Aunt Louise, did you just say something about children playing in secret passageways?"

"Oh my, yes. This old house is full of hidden passages. There's a whole maze behind the walls. Children always love to play hide and seek in them. Don't worry though, they really can't get lost since they all lead back to one place eventually."

Still maintaining a calm front, she asked, "And that one place?"

"The front room—Wes's bedroom. You'll have to ask him to give you the behind the scenes tour when he comes back."

"Yes. I'll certainly have to do that." Felicity couldn't remain seated another second. "Please excuse me. I think I'll go back up and lay down since I don't have an appointment to rush off to."

She didn't wait to hear Aunt Louise's parting comments. The moment she reached her room, she began a thorough examination of the parlor walls. Knocking every few inches, it didn't take long to find a panel that sounded hollow. A few seconds later she discovered that pushing on the right side caused the wall section to pivot like a revolving door. And it was completely silent.

Immediately inside the tunnel, she found a light switch, then two narrow, winding flights of stairs, one going up and one going down. Through trial and error, she eventually found herself in Wes's bedroom. Following her intuition, she inspected the contents of his closet, armoire and chest of drawers. She discovered the secret to his silent walking—a layer of felt over rubber-soled shoes. To spare the wooden floors perhaps? Or to frighten visitors with unexpected appearances?

It wasn't until she lifted the heavy lid on an old cedar chest, however, that she found the final piece of damning evidence. Right on top of a pile of old clothing was the outfit Wes had worn in her room last night. The smell she had detected was a mixture of burning kerosene and cedar.

She considered going back upstairs and clearing out before Wes returned, but that would strip her of the opportunity to curse his black soul to hell with the rest of his ancestors. So she sat down in the chair beside the open trunk where she could see Main Street out the window.

Less than a half hour later, she saw his car pull into the driveway. The minutes ticked by as she imagined him greeting Aunt Louise and learning his patsy had gone back to bed. She was beginning to wonder if she had miscalculated about him going to her room to awaken her, when he stepped through the passageway. His worried gaze darted from her to the open trunk and back. "I can explain everything."

"I don't doubt that," Felicity said in a voice laced with

as much hurt as anger. "You're very good at explaining things...as long as you don't have to be honest."

He strode across the room and knelt before her. He tried to take her hands but she bolted out of the chair and away from him.

"Cut the theatrics, Patron Haversham. I'm not buying them anymore. I only stayed here to let you know that if you did manage to get me pregnant, you will *never* see this child."

Wes rose and walked toward her looking utterly baffled. "What on earth are you talking about? I thought you might be upset if you guessed what I had done last night, but I was desperate to convince you to marry me. I would have confessed...eventually. But what's all this about a child?"

In crisp, concise language, she informed him of her conversation with Aunt Louise and the conclusions she had drawn.

By the time she was finished, he was pacing the floor and scraping his fingers through his hair. "I can't believe this. Yes, I can. I've lived my entire life in a town full of busybodies who mean well. These are good, honest people, who wouldn't know how to pull the kind of scam you're talking about. They're just superstitious and believe in spirits and the mysterious workings of fate. Aunt Louise probably thought that you'd be happy to know that everyone wanted you to stay and be the mother of the next patron. *They* consider it an honor."

He strode to her and grasped her shoulders before she could evade him again. "Think about what you just said, Felicity. Every single person in this town lied to you? *Every one*? All those friendly, uncomplicated people you met yesterday are all expert liars whose greed could provoke them to encourage me to seduce a woman for the sake of the town? Do you honestly believe that?"

He was breathless as he stood there waiting for her response.

She felt herself weakening and willed herself to walk away. Before she reached the door of his suite, however, he blocked her exit.

"Where are you going?" he demanded.

"I'm leaving."

"You can't leave until tomorrow. You have to be here at midnight tonight."

She stared at him, steeling herself against the desperate need she saw in his eyes. "Please let me by." When he didn't move out of her path, she tried to step around him, but he moved as well. Making an about-face, she headed for the passageway. He rushed in front of her and closed the panel.

"At least hear me out first. The only supernatural occurrence that I or any other living person is responsible for was the visit last night. Everything else was absolutely legitimate. I realize what a mistake I made, but I can't undo it now, and I did it for a wholly selfish reason. It was strictly meant to benefit me, not the town, because I sincerely believe we were fated to be together. I have no doubt about my feelings for you. I love you! And I was willing to do anything to keep you here with me. I was just so afraid that if you went away after Christmas the way you planned, I'd never get you back. And if you'll recall, I didn't lie to you about being in your suite. I only changed the subject. Everything I've ever said to you has been the truth."

"Is that it?"

He rubbed the tension out of his forehead. "No. I'm sorry Aunt Louise was indelicate. And I'm sorry if you truly believe I seduced you with nothing in mind but perpetuating the Haversham tradition. I'll admit it occurred to me, but only after it was too late to go back and take preventive measures.

"I don't know what else to say. There is nothing I would enjoy more than to see a child of our making growing inside your body, but not because of any tradition. I loved Joanne and respected her memory enough to let the Haversham line come to an end rather than replace her in my life with someone I had lukewarm feelings about. But then you came along, and it was as if I'd been hit by a bolt of lightning. What I felt for Joanne was good, but entirely different from how you made me feel the instant I set eyes on you. You aren't just a convenient means to an end. You're a dream come true for me."

She was doing her best not to listen to the words coming out of his mouth, but he was making it more difficult by the minute.

Taking a deep breath, she said, "I was married to a man who played me for a fool for five years. I can't let that happen to me again."

"Tell me what to do," he pleaded. "What can I say to convince you that I want you in my life?"

"I don't know, Wes. How do you earn back someone's trust after you've ripped their heart to shreds?" His look of dejection almost swayed her, but she turned and walked out of his suite.

She packed as quickly as possible, holding back the tears for a time when she was far away from Haversham, Vermont. With some effort, she managed to haul her suitcase down the stairs, but Aunt Louise caught her before she made it out the door.

"Felicity, dear. Whatever do you think you're doing with that heavy thing? Consider the poor babe."

"Spare me, Louise. I've had enough nonsense for one week." She ignored the stunned look on the woman's face, but she couldn't ignore the man leaning against the archway of the sitting room.

"Felicity has obviously decided to leave us, Aunt Louise. She is of the opinion that we have all been part of an enormous hoax to take advantage of her talents and her virtue."

Louise's mouth dropped open with an expression of

quite believable shock. "A hoax? I don't understand."

"Your nephew can fill you in," Felicity said as she got her old suede jacket out of the closet. Her hand brushed against the mink coat and the memory of Wes wrapping her in the magnificent fur made her heart clench, but she pushed it out of her mind.

"Please don't go," Wes said quietly.

"You were meant to be part of our family," Aunt Louise added.

Felicity simply shook her head and opened the door. She didn't make it out, however, for half the town seemed to be standing on the porch and in the parking lot between her and her car.

"We heard you were planning to leave," May stated incredulously. "You mustn't do that. If you and Wes had a little tiff over something, I'm sure it can be worked out."

Felicity turned around and frowned at Wes.

"Don't be upset with him, dear," Bernice said, pushing her way forward. She was holding a dress box with a pretty red bow on it. "Wes called to ask me to bring this over immediately, so naturally, I wanted to know why the rush. I mean, it was his gift to you for tonight's party. So he *had* to tell me why, you see. Then I told May, and—"

"Enough. I get it," Felicity said, holding up a hand to stop the explanation. "Please. I have to leave. I'm sorry."

They made a path for her despite the fact that they all looked as though she were taking away their last hope. And maybe she was but that wasn't her problem.

Without looking back, she forced the big suitcase into the back of her Bug. She then got behind the wheel and turned the key in the ignition. If she didn't get out of there soon, she was going to burst into tears.

Click. Click. Click. Click

This can't be happening, she thought. Not a dead battery. Please don't let it be a dead battery.

"Sounds like a dead battery," Chuck shouted beside her door.

She rolled down the window to talk to him. There was no way she was getting out of that car again. "Can you fix it?"

"Of course. Soon as I get a battery to fit this model. I'll be able to make a run up to the parts store in Waitsfield first thing Monday morning."

"Monday morning?" she cried. "But this is only Friday. Why can't you get it today?"

"Sorry," Chuck said, shaking his head. "No can do. They're closed today. For the holiday."

She groaned and closed her eyes. The thought occurred that Chuck probably sabotaged the battery himself, but since she couldn't prove that, or physically force him to repair her car, it was hardly worth the effort to accuse him.

"Best come back inside," he said gently. "It's starting to snow."

That did it! A white Christmas in a fairy tale village was exactly what was needed to round out her make-believe week. With no enthusiasm whatsoever, she climbed out of the car and wended her way back through the crowd. "You win, Wes," she told him as she passed. "I'll be staying a few more days." Climbing the stairs, she spoke in an imperious tone, "Please notify the cook that I'll be taking my meals in my room. I would appreciate not being disturbed otherwise." She heard the anxious murmurs of the crowd begin as she ascended the stairs and did her best not to listen.

Her last order was almost immediately disobeyed by a knock on her door, which she had no intention of answering.

"Miss Flowers? It's Chuck. I have your suitcase."

"Just leave it outside the door," she called back. After she was certain he was gone, she brought it in herself then relocked the door. Next, she tried to think of a way to block the passageway, but any furniture heavy enough to prevent the door from opening was too heavy for her to move. She supposed it would have been futile anyway. If Wes really wanted in, he probably had a key to her door.

Slumping down on the sofa, she was suddenly overwhelmed by fatigue. Was it depression or an early sign of pregnancy? *Damn!* She didn't want to think about that yet. Unable to fight the urge to escape into sleep, she stretched out and closed her eyes. She didn't even realize she had dozed off, until another knock at the door awakened her. Glancing at her watch, she was surprised to note that it was four o'clock.

"Felicity? It's tea time. I brought you a tray." Aunt Louise paused for a response that didn't come. "You hardly ate a thing this morning. I have tea, some cheese and crackers, and some pretty little cakes that May baked."

Felicity's stomach demanded she accept the offering. "Please leave it outside. I'll get it shortly." Again she waited a short time before opening the door, but this time, her visitor hadn't departed.

"It appears that I'm the cause of the problem here," Aunt Louise said, nudging Felicity aside so she could carry the tray into the parlor. She set it down on the table in front of the sofa then perched on the edge of a chair. "I'm not leaving you alone until I have my say, so you may as well join me."

Felicity took a deep, exasperated breath, but she sat down on the sofa and poured herself some tea. Just because she was upset didn't mean she had to go hungry.

"Good girl," Aunt Louise declared with a nod of her head. "Now, it seems to me that you're in a snit for reasons that make no sense whatsoever."

"Hah! You have no idea—"

"Wes told me everything. It was very foolish of him

to try such a silly trick to convince you to marry him, but it was done for love. *You're* the one who has no idea of what's happened here. Wes was a lost soul when Joanne passed on. We thought we would never see him smile again. And if you haven't figured anything else out, you must realize that we're one big family in Haversham. If our most important member is sad, we're all sad.

"Your arrival changed everything. People had hope. Wes came back to life. The town felt happy again. No one lied or made up stories to deceive you, least of all Wes." She paused a moment to be sure she had Felicity's attention. "When I first met you, I sensed the anger inside of you. You've let it rule you for so long, you've forgotten how to be happy. If you'll just quit being angry and let yourself feel the goodness around you, you'll know the truth. Wes loves you. The townspeople respect you and want you to stay. Look deep inside your heart, Felicity, and you'll find a woman who could be extremely happy here."

Felicity felt the tears about to flow and bit her lip to hold them back.

"I'll go now," Aunt Louise said. "You just give what I said some thought."

For some time, Felicity sat there as the tears trickled down her cheeks. She knew Aunt Louise was right about the anger. When Wes offered her a fresh start, she couldn't accept it for fear of being hurt all over again. And when she discovered his deceit, all the anger resurfaced.

Perhaps more than was justified.

Wes and Aunt Louise had said the same things in different ways. Did she *really* believe every person in Haversham had lied? That May and Chuck and Bernice were actually wicked, greedy, con artists hiding behind masks of friendliness? She pictured them as she had seen them earlier that day. If they were faking sincerity, they should all win Academy Awards for superior acting ability.

And what about Wes? Did she honestly believe he had tricked her into having unprotected sex? She knew she could have stopped him at any time. She recalled the look on his face and the sound of his words when he told her she was the only woman he had been with besides Joanne. Had that been a lie? Had his lovemaking been only pretense? The mere thought of his kiss made her shiver.

And yet, the fact remained, that he had brought her here to promote the town, and he did resort to a low trick to convince her to marry him. Besides that, she had no proof that any of the other stories were true.

Dear Lord, what was she to believe?

CHAPTER 6

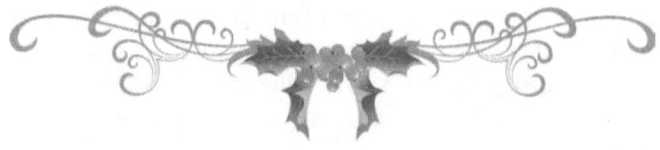

Snow continued to fall for several hours, turning Haversham into a winter paradise. Felicity sat by the window most of the time, thinking and rethinking. She was watching the street when all the twinkle lights came on and the snowflakes stopped falling. Aunt Louise brought her dinner, but there was nothing more the woman could say to help settle her mind.

The nap she had taken prevented her from going to sleep, so she was still gazing out the window when Wes came through the passageway at eleven thirty.

"You've pouted long enough," he said firmly. "It's time to come downstairs. The party begins in thirty minutes."

He didn't come close and that disturbed her. If he had, she might have given in, just to feel his arms around her one more time. "I don't feel like partying."

"Neither does anyone else at the moment. They're all too upset about you. This is the most wonderful night of the year in Haversham and I will not permit you to ruin it for everyone. If you don't have it in your heart to be cooperative for their sakes, consider it research. I'm sure you've never seen anything like what's about to happen."

The guilt had her rising from her chair. Curiosity took her the rest of the way. When Wes offered her the mink coat, she didn't have the willpower to turn it down.

Before they went outside though, she had to tell him the results of all her introspection. "I apologize. I've thought about it all day and I decided that I overreacted. You were right. These aren't bad people. I'm not saying I believe everything I've been told, but I know there was nothing mean behind anything that happened."

The stern expression on his face softened a bit more with each of her admissions.

"You hurt me. But I suppose I understand. If I thought dressing up as Lady Dierdre would make everything turn out the way I wanted, maybe I'd have done the same."

He smiled then and put his arms around her. "I have Dierdre's dress packed away in the attic if you want to try it on later, but I'd rather have Felicity Flowers tonight."

"Am I forgiven for being a bitch?" she asked unnecessarily.

"Watch your language." He gave her a light kiss. "Forgiven. On one condition."

She raised her eyebrows. "Oh?"

"First, do you believe I love you with all my heart and never meant to hurt you?"

She looked into his eyes and saw the truth that her anger had concealed. The last of her anger left her body with a heavy sigh. "It's completely illogical. But I seem to believe you anyway. And you wouldn't have been able to hurt me at all if I hadn't fallen in love with you too."

His answering kiss was quick and hard. "Thank you.

Now the condition. Accept my proposal. Say you'll share the rest of your life with me. Hurry. It's almost midnight." Her slight hesitation caused him to add, "We can leave Haversham and live elsewhere if you wish." Her shocked expression prompted him to make a final concession. "And we don't need to name a single one of our children Wesley."

Shedding the last of her doubts, Felicity gaped at him. "You'd give up three hundred years of tradition for me? You must be crazy."

He pulled her close and murmured in her ear. "I'm not crazy. I'm in love…and waiting for an answer."

"I must be suffering from the same craziness as you," she said softly. "Because the answer is yes. I would very much like to be Mrs. Wesley Haversham the Twelfth. And if Aunt Louise's psychic powers are accurate, number thirteen will be arriving in nine months. Damn, oops, I mean *darned* if I'm going to rile any of your dearly departed by breaking even one tradition. We'll name him…*or her*…Wesley, and he or she will grow up right here in Haversham, just like all the rest of the little Wesleys did."

His head bent to hers and, as their lips touched, she distinctly heard the sound of glass wind chimes. His smile against her mouth told her he'd heard the magical confirmation as well.

He reluctantly ended the kiss. "Time to go."

Before they even reached the street, she felt the anticipation in the air. Lined up on both sides of Main Street were hundreds of people. Every single resident, from the elderly to the babies was there, waiting for the special event Wes had spoken of.

She was a bit embarrassed when Wes tugged her out into the middle of the street and faced the crowd.

"Ladies and gentlemen of Haversham," he shouted. "I have an announcement to make. Felicity Flowers has graciously agreed to be my bride."

A cheer rose up at their end of the street and traveled as people spread the word along. She thought she would never again see or hear anything as incredible as that, but she was wrong.

A chorus of angelic voices suddenly burst into song behind her.

"*Joy to the world...*" the lyrics began, and she turned to see the carolers.

It couldn't be! Her eyes had to be playing tricks on her. Standing before her another throng of people had suddenly appeared from nowhere, but these were somewhat translucent and dressed in old-fashioned clothes. Most of the men in the front of the line looked very much like Wes and she had seen the faces of the women next to them in the portraits on the inn's walls. The man and woman in the center could be none other than the spirits of Lord and Lady Haversham. As she gaped at the lord, he looked directly at her...and winked!

When the ethereal gathering finished the first carol, they went on to another and began promenading down the street. Wes held Felicity close while the spirits of his ancestors walked by, smiling their approval.

One woman, dressed in a contemporary fashion stopped and turned toward them as the procession continued. Felicity felt Wes's body tense and she realized the woman was Joanne. His late wife smiled at the both of them, blew Wes a kiss then mouthed the words, "*Be happy.*" Felicity felt Wes relax and understood they had been given a blessing he had needed very badly.

By the time the last of them had passed, Felicity estimated that thousands of spirits had participated in Haversham's Christmas Eve miracle.

And there wasn't a single footprint left behind to mar the blanket of snow on the street.

The rest of the night passed by in a blur of congratulations and good wishes as everyone in town stopped by the inn for a cup of hot spiced rum…from an antique urn that seemed to be self-replenishing. This, too, Felicity learned, was a tradition in Haversham.

The sun was peeking over the horizon when Felicity and Wes retired to her room, tired, but happy.

"Tell me something," she said snuggling against him under the quilt. "Why do we always end up in this room instead of yours?"

Smiling, he said, "Because I swore to myself, I would only share my bed with my wife. I know I'm being superstitious, but until we make it official..."

"You make it sound like sharing your bed is something worth waiting for," she taunted.

"Aren't all good things?" he teased back.

"Speaking of good things, there's something else I want to discuss."

"You sound serious. What is it?"

She screwed up her courage. "I don't want to write the article about Haversham's spirits."

His smile faded but he said, "If that's your decision, I won't try to change your mind."

"But I have another idea," she said quickly to erase the disappointed look on his face. "The reason I don't want to help with your idea to save the town is that it would be a travesty. Commercializing Haversham might save it in one way, but in the short time I've been here, I've fallen under the spell of this town, just the way it is, and I don't want to see it change. Nor would I want your Christmas Eve miracle to be turned into a circus event, or worse, never see it happen again.

"My thinking is that Haversham would make a marvelous retreat for artist and writers. You could offer scholarships at first, to attract guests. But a more sedate group of guests than what you had planned. Now *that* I'd be willing to write about and help you make it happen."

He propped himself up on his elbow and looked down at her, his eyes bright with enthusiasm. "Just like Lady Dierdre helped the first Wesley establish the town." He kissed her on the forehead. "I love it. But what about our miracle?"

"No reservations over Christmas."

He nodded his agreement. "You really think artists and writers would like it here?"

She laughed. "Like it? It'd be like heaven for creative people. Can you imagine all the spiritual help they'd be getting? Word would get out about how inspirational it is here and in no time we'd be turning people away.

"At any rate..." She traced a pattern in his chest hair. "I know one writer who's looking forward to having her creativity sparked..." Her fingertips trailed down his abdomen. "...happily ever after."

And the tinkling sound of glass wind chimes echoed through the room.

ALSO BY

MARILYN CAMPBELL

The Innerworld Affairs
Romulus
Falcon
Gallant
Gabriel
Logan
Roman
Blaze

Lust and Lies Series
Carnal Vengeance
Twisted Hunger
Unnatural Relations
Wicked Obsessions

Turn the page for an

excerpt from

ROMULUS

Innerworld Affairs Series

Book One

Marilyn Campbell

In the hectic receiving area, Romulus doled out orders in a tone of voice that permitted no questions. His attention was abruptly diverted as the new caretaker, Oona, hurried toward him. He hoped nothing had gone wrong with her assignment.

"Chief Romulus, please excuse the interruption. The woman in room five awoke and became very upset. She fell. It happened so quickly. There was nothing I could do. I was looking for the doctor when I saw you."

"All right, Oona. I'll check on her now." He strode away, annoyed that Oona had not been able to handle the woman. With all the paperwork required to integrate the new arrivals, he did not have time to calm one frightened female.

But the sight of that female crumpled on the floor halted Romulus's unkind thoughts. He knelt down and gathered her into his arms. When he tried to lift her, however, he misjudged his burden. Attempting to shift her weight, he lost his balance and ended up sitting on the floor with her cozily on his lap.

The sudden jolt interrupted Aster's dark oblivion. She

opened her eyes and tried to focus on his face. Groggily, she murmured, "Much better. I know you. You've been in my dreams before." Closing her eyes, she nestled her head against his chest. From the contented look on her face, Romulus concluded it must be a very pleasant dream.

Romulus tried to pull his eyes away from the soft smile and dreamy expression on the woman's face. For a moment he wished he was the man she imagined him to be. His hand disobeyed his disciplined mind and brushed the hair away from her brow. The woman turned her cheek into his palm, and her mass of silver hair spilled over his arm. It was a very appealing feature but nothing like her eyes. When she looked up at him a moment ago, he was shaken by their blue-black color. It reminded him of the midnight sky on his home planet. That thought seemed to bear analyzing but now was not the time.

Just then a deep sigh caused her breasts to rise and lower and the peaks noticeably puckered, betraying the direction her dream had taken. It was enough to jar him back to the situation at hand. Remembering Oona standing expectantly behind him, he realized how unofficial he must look sitting on the floor holding this female. With effort, he stood up and placed the female gently on the bed, feeling oddly reluctant to release her.

"Oona, what's the medical on this one?" There, he was all business again.

"Cerebral hemorrhage, multiple bruises, fractures and contusions. She did not remain under the beam long enough for a complete recovery and may have reinjured herself from that fall. Sir, I am afraid I provoked her unintentionally. I understood I was not to offer explanations, but she was very agitated and when she detected the difference between my voice and lip movement, I told her about the universal translator."

Chief Romulus considered the extraordinary

pronouncement that the new arrival had been able to discern the translator's miniscule lapse. Apparently, besides her striking exterior, a definite possibility of higher intelligence existed as well.

"What is her name?"

"Aster Mackenzie. She prefers to be called Miss Mackenzie."

"Go find the doctor. I'll stay with her until you return." His motives for remaining with the patient were unclear. A backlog of work beckoned to him but he ignored its plaintive call. Something stronger held him back.

It seemed to him that this woman possessed some invisible characteristic that lured him to her. After Oona exited, he tried to appease his curiosity with a visual examination.

Her physical beauty did not stop with her face. Every inch of her was impressive. Her breasts were full but firm, her abdomen muscles taut, her waist narrow compared to her hips. Her limbs revealed additional proof of attentive conditioning.

Whatever was he doing? Here he was, in the midst of turmoil, ogling a nude woman like some adolescent boy. She was only a female, and a new arrival at that. What was taking that caretaker so long?

By the time Oona returned with the doctor, Rom had exiled himself to the hall outside the patient's room. "Good, you're back. I must return to my office. I've spent too much time here already. Orientation is scheduled for eighteen hundred hours in Conference Room B." Before he finished his last sentence, he was already heading back to a more rational domain.

"Rom? Is something out of order?" Tarla's voice filled with concern as the chief administrator stalked past her to his office.

"What? Oh, no. A new caretaker waylaid me. She had a problem with one of the arrivals and now I'm behind schedule. This is the third time this month. The more polluted Outerworld becomes, the harder it is to prevent these accidents. Something is going to have to be done about it soon, whether the Tribunal is ready or not." He planted himself behind his desk, intending to immerse himself in his work and forget the interruption.

Romulus stared at the large vidcom monitor on the wall next to his desk, but he could not read the report displayed there. Instead, he saw those blue-black eyes seducing him. What madness was this? He assured himself that his imagination running amok must be an aftereffect from trying to analyze his strange dream.

He concentrated on preparing for the upcoming orientation. From his earliest days in Administration, he had taken on the responsibility of the new arrivals and had always enjoyed it. It would go smoothly, as usual…if he could just stop his hands from shaking.

ROMULUS
available in print and ebook

MARILYN CAMPBELL has been published in the genres of suspense, erotic thrillers, futuristic, time-travel, paranormal, erotic and lighthearted contemporary romances, non-fiction metaphysical works and has had a screenplay produced. A true thrill-junkie, she has jumped out of an airplane, raced around the Indy 500 track, driven solo throughout the United States and believes a great roller coaster ride can cure whatever ails her. She currently resides in Massachusetts with her daughter and their four-legged companions, Milk-Dud and Sweetie.

www.ingramcontent.com/pod-product-compliance
Lightning Source LLC
Chambersburg PA
CBHW020614260626
47157CB00003B/1009